# You know that gnawing in the pit of your stomach...

The kind that warns you that you are about to do the absolute stupidest thing you could do? Something that will ruin life as you know it?

I've got that feeling now, standing at the butcher counter in King Kullen. I realize being in the wrong supermarket probably doesn't sound exactly dire to you, but you aren't the one buying your father brisket at a store your mother will somehow know isn't Waldbaum's.

The woman behind the counter has agreed to go into the freezer to find a brisket, since there aren't any in the case.

Warning Number Two, right? I should be so out of here.

But no, I'm still in the same spot when she comes back out, *brisketless*, her face ashen. "He's deeeeeeeaad! Joey's deeeeeead!"

My first thought is *You should always trust your gut.*

# Stevi Mittman

Stevi Mittman has always been a decorator at heart. When she was little she cut the butterflies from her wallpaper and let them fly off the walls onto her ceiling and across her window shades. She remembers doing an entire bathroom in black-and-white houndstooth patent leather contact paper and putting strips of trim on her cupboards.

The Teddi Bayer murder mysteries have allowed her to combine her love of writing and her passion for decorating, and she couldn't be happier. As a fictional decorator she doles out advice on Teddi's Web site, TipsFromTeddi.com, and receives and responds to e-mails on behalf of Teddi.

Decorating is a third career for the prolific Mittman, who is also a stained-glass artist with work in the Museum of the City of New York and private commissions around the country and, of course, an award-winning author.

In her spare time (you must be kidding) she also makes jewelry and indulges in gourmet cooking. Visit her at www.stevimittman.com.

For those of you who are putting any TipsFromTeddi.com advice to use, please e-mail her your successes and failures at Teddi@TipsFromTeddi.com, and be sure to visit Teddi's Web site, www.TipsFromTeddi.com, for more murder, mayhem and sage advice on decorating!

# Whose NUMBER IS UP,
## *Anyway?*

## STEVI MITTMAN

WHOSE NUMBER IS UP, ANYWAY?

copyright © 2007 by Stephanie Mittman

isbn-13: 978-0-373-88139-0

isbn-10:      0-373-88139-8

TheNextNovel.com

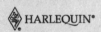 HARLEQUIN®

PRINTED IN U.S.A.

---

# From the Author

Dear Reader,

Writing Teddi's stories has been such a joy for me. For one thing, I get to play decorator, which gives me a great excuse for all those subscriptions to *Domino*, *House Beautiful*, etc. For another, through Teddi I get to do wild, wacky, brave things I'd never do in my real life. And then there's all that passionate romance...oh, wait...thanks to a wonderful husband, I've got that in my life! What I don't have, and never did, is a mother like June Bayer. Seems as though everyone else has one somewhere in their family. I wish I could remember all the stories people tell me about their own Grandma Junes. It would keep the series going forever!

I'm posting some of the Grandma June stories to my Web site, www.stevimittman.com. Come and see them and send me one of your own!

Love,

Stevi

I usually dedicate my books to the wonderful friends who read my drafts, laugh in all the right places and applaud when I ask them to, but lately I've had so many wonderful e-mails from readers telling me how much they are enjoying this series that I think this book should be dedicated to them. It's those e-mails that keep my bottom glued to the chair and send my fingers flying over the keyboard even when the sun is shining and there are sales at the mall. Thanks for the praise, the encouragement, the loyalty, and for taking the time to write and tell me I'm doing something right!

## CHAPTER 1

Before redecorating a room, I always advise my clients to empty it of everything but one chair. Then I suggest they move that chair from place to place, sitting in it, until the placement feels right. Trust your instincts when deciding on furniture placement. Your room should "feel right."

—TipsFromTeddi.com

**Gut** feelings. You know, that gnawing in the pit of your stomach that warns you that you are about to do the absolute stupidest thing you could do. Something that will ruin life as you know it.

I've got one now, standing at the butcher counter in King Kullen, the grocery store in the same strip mall as L.I. Lanes, the bowling alley *cum* billiard parlor I'm in the process of redecorating for its "Grand Opening."

I realize being in the wrong supermarket probably doesn't sound exactly dire to you, but you aren't the one buying your father a brisket at a store your mother will somehow know isn't Waldbaum's.

But then, June Bayer isn't your mother.

The woman behind the counter has agreed to go into the freezer to find a brisket for me since there aren't any in the case. There are packages of pork tenderloins, piles of spare-ribs and rolls of sausage, but no briskets.

Warning number two, right? I should so be out of here.

But no, I'm still in the same spot when she comes back out, *brisketless*, her face ashen. She opens her mouth like she is going to scream, but only a gurgle comes out.

And then she pinballs out from behind the counter, knocking bottles of Peter Luger Steak Sauce to the floor on her way, hitting the tower of cans at the end of the prepared-foods aisle and sending them sprawling, making her way down the aisle, careening from side to side as she goes.

Finally, from the distance, I hear her shout. "He's deeeeeeaaaad! Joey's deeeeeaaaad."

My first thought is, *you should always trust your gut*.

My second thought is that now my mother will know I was in King Kullen. For weeks I will have to hear "What did you expect?" as though whenever you go to King Kullen someone turns up dead. And if the detective investigating the case turns out to be Detective Drew Scoones…well, I'll never hear the end of that from her, either.

Several people head for the butcher's freezer and I position myself to block them. If there's one thing I've learned from finding people dead—and this guy is not my first—it's that the police get very testy when you mess with their murder scenes.

"You can't go in there until the police get here," I say, stationing myself at the end of the butcher's counter and in front of the Employees Only door, acting like I'm some sort of authority. "You'll contaminate the evidence if it turns out to be murder."

Shouts and chaos. You'd think I'd know better than to throw the word *murder* around. Cell phones are flipping open and tongues are wagging.

I amend my statement quickly. "Which, of course, it probably isn't. Murder, I mean. People die all the time and it's not always in hospitals or their own beds, or…" I babble when I'm nervous and the idea of someone dead on the other side of the freezer door makes me very nervous.

So does the idea of seeing Drew Scoones again. Drew and I have this on-again, off-again sort of thing…that I kind of turned off.

Who knew he'd take it so personally when he tried to get serious and I responded by saying we could talk about *us* tomorrow—and then caught a plane to my parents condo in Boca the next day? In July. In the middle of a job.

For some crazy reason, he took that to mean that I was avoiding him and the subject of *us*.

That was three months ago. I haven't seen him since.

The manager, who identifies himself and points to his name tag in case I don't believe him, says he has to go into *his cooler*. "Maybe Joey's not dead," he says. "Maybe he can be saved, and you're letting him die in there. Did you ever think of that?"

In fact, I hadn't. But I had thought that the murderer might try to go back in to make sure his tracks were covered, so I say that I will go in and check.

Which means that the manager and I couple up and go in together while everyone pushes against the doorway to peer in, erasing any chance of finding clean prints on that Employee Only door.

I expect to find carcasses of dead animals hanging from hooks and maybe Joey hanging from one, too. I think it's going to be very creepy and I steel myself, only to find a rather benign series of shelves with large slabs of meat laid out carefully on them, along with boxes and boxes marked simply "chicken."

Nothing scary here, unless you count the body of a middle-aged man with graying hair sprawled faceup on the floor. His eyes are wide open and unblinking. His shirt is stiff. His pants are stiff. His body is stiff. And his expression, you should forgive the pun—is frozen. Bill-the-manager crosses himself and stands mute while I pronounce the guy dead in a sort of *happy-now?* tone.

"We should not be in here," I say, and he nods his head emphatically and helps me push people out of the doorway just in time to hear the police sirens and see the cop cars pull up outside the big store windows.

Bobbie Lyons, my partner in *Teddi Bayer Interior Designs* (and also my neighbor, best friend and private fashion police), and Mark, our carpenter (and my dog-sitter, confidant and ego-booster), rush in from next door. They beat the cops by a half step and shout out my name. People point in my direction.

After all the publicity that followed the unfortunate incident during which I shot my ex-husband, Rio Gallo, and then the subsequent murder of my first client—which I solved, I might add—it seems like the whole world, or at least all of Long Island, knows who I am.

Mark asks if I'm all right. (Did I remember to mention that the man is drop-dead-gorgeous-but-a-decade-too-young-for-me-yet-too-old-for-my-daughter-thank-God?) I don't get a chance to answer him because the police are quickly closing in on the store manager and me.

"The woman—" I begin telling the police. Then I have to pause for the manager to fill in her name, which he does: *Fran*.

I continue. "Right. Fran. Fran went into the freezer to get a brisket. A moment later she came out and screamed that Joey was dead. So, I'd say she was the one who discovered the body."

"And you are…?" the cop asks me. It comes out a bit like who do I *think* I am, rather than who am I really?

"An innocent bystander," Bobbie, hair perfect, makeup just right, says, carefully placing her body between the cop and me.

"And she was just leaving," Mark adds. They each take one of my arms.

Fran comes into the inner circle surrounding the cops. In case it isn't obvious from the hairnet and blood-stained white apron with "Fran" embroidered on it, I explain that she was the butcher who was going for the brisket. Mark and Bobbie take that as a signal that I've done my job and they can now get me out of here. They twist around, with me in the middle, like we're a Rockettes line, until we are facing away from the butcher counter. They've managed to propel me a few steps toward the exit when disaster—in the form of a Mazda RX-7 pulling up at the loading curb—strikes.

Mark's grip on my arm tightens like a vise. "Too late," he says.

Bobbie's expletive is unprintable. "Maybe there's a back door," she suggests, but Mark is right. It's too late.

I've laid my eyes on Detective Scoones. And while my gut is trying to warn me that my heart shouldn't go there, regions farther south are melting at just the sight of him.

"Walk," Bobbie orders me.

And I try to. Really.

*Walk*, I tell myself. *Just put one foot in front of the other.*

I can do this because I know, in my heart of hearts, that if Drew Scoones were still interested in me, he'd have gotten in touch with me after I returned from Boca. And he didn't.

Since he's a detective, Drew doesn't have to wear one of those dark blue Nassau County Police Department uniforms. Instead, he's got on jeans, a tight-fitting T-shirt and a tweedy sports jacket. If you think that sounds good, you should see him. Chiseled features, cleft chin, brown hair that's naturally a little sandy in the front, a smile that…well, that doesn't matter. He isn't smiling now.

He walks up to me, tucks his sunglasses into his breast pocket and looks me over from head to toe.

"Well, if it isn't Miss Cut and Run," he says. "Aren't you supposed to be somewhere in Florida or something?" He looks at Mark accusingly, as if he were covering for me when he told Drew I was gone.

"Detective Scoones?" one of the uniforms says. "The stiff's in the cooler and the woman who found him is over there." He jerks his head in Fran's direction.

Drew continues to stare at me.

You know how when you were young, your mother always told you to wear clean underwear in case you were in an accident? And how, a little farther on, she told you not to go out in hair rollers because you never knew who you might see—or who might see you? And how now your best friend says she wouldn't be caught dead without makeup and suggests you shouldn't either?

Okay, today, *finally*, in my overalls and Converse sneakers, I get it.

I brush my hair out of my eyes. "Well, I'm back," I say. Like he hasn't known my exact whereabouts. The man is a detective, for heaven's sake. "Been back a while."

Bobbie has watched the exchange and apparently decided she's given Drew all the time he deserves. "And we've got work to do, so…" she says, grabbing my arm and giving Drew a little two-fingered wave goodbye.

As I back up a foot or two, the store manager sees his chance and places himself in front of Drew, trying to get his attention. Maybe what makes Drew such a good detective is his ability to focus.

Only what he's focusing on is me.

"Phone broken? Carrier pigeon died?" he asks me, taking in Fran, the manager, the meat counter and that Employees Only door, all without taking his eyes off me.

Mark tries to break the spell. "We've got work to do

there, you've got work to do here, Scoones," Mark says to him, gesturing toward next door. "So it's back to the alley for us."

Drew's lip twitches. "You working the alley now?" he says.

"If you'd like to follow me," Bill-the-manager, clearly exasperated, says to Drew—who doesn't respond. It's as if waiting for my answer is all he has to do.

So, fine. "You knew I was back," I say.

The man has known my whereabouts every hour of the day for as long as I've known him. And my mother's not the only one who won't buy that he "just happened" to answer this particular call. In fact, I'm willing to bet my children's lunch money that he's taken every call within ten miles of my home since the day I got back.

And now he's gotten lucky.

"*You* could have called *me*," I say.

"You're the one who set *tomorrow* for our talk and then flew the coop, chickie," he says. "I figured the ball was in your court."

"Detective?" the uniform says. "There's something you ought to see in here."

Drew gives me a look that amounts to *in or out?*

He could be talking about the investigation, or about our relationship.

Bobbie tries to steer me away. Mark's fists are balled. Drew waits me out, knowing I won't be able to resist what might be a murder investigation.

Finally he turns and heads for the cooler.

And, like a puppy dog, I follow.

Bobbie grabs the back of my shirt and pulls me to a halt.

"I'm just going to show him something," I say, yanking away.

"Yeah," Bobbie says, pointedly looking at the buttons on my blouse. The two at breast level have popped. "That's what I'm afraid of."

THE GUY IN THE FREEZER looks very familiar, but I can't quite place him. I mean the dead one. The other guy I know so well that it's hard not to just pick up where we left off.

If where we left off hadn't been a precipice I wasn't ready to fall from.

"You wanna tell me what happened?" Drew asks.

I tell him about how I should have gone to Waldbaum's for the brisket, but that since I'm working next door... And here I segue into how the original decorator quit and I am finishing up her work and how I don't get paid if I don't get it done in time for their grand opening in just over a month—though they aren't closed during the renovations so "Grand Opening" is really a misnomer—

He gives me the get-to-the-point look. It's one of those benefits of knowing someone well: they don't really have to use words.

"So I came here because it would save time. I thought I could pick up the meat first thing this morning, put it in the fridge at the alley and then take it home with me tonight. This month is all about saving time, because of the grand-opening thing—"

He knows I babble when I'm nervous, so he's being patient. He only sighs rather than signaling me to hurry up.

"And there was no brisket in the case, so I asked the woman who was putting out the chicken breasts—the cutlet kind, sliced thin—if she had any in the back and she went to get some and, well—" I point at the guy on the floor.

Drew looks as though, when he asked what happened, he really meant it in the larger sense—the *us* sense.

I tell him that I've seen the guy before. He isn't impressed. I tell him, no, really recently, only I can't place him.

"Picture him upright," Drew says. "Blinking. Maybe behind the meat counter?" he suggests sarcastically.

Gently two cops turn the body over. Across the back of the man's shirt, through the ice that coats it, I see some bowling pins and a ball. Above the flying pins are the words The Spare Slices.

I gasp.

"Bad taste? Your mother wouldn't approve?" Drew asks testily as he crouches over the body. Not surprisingly, there's no love lost between Drew and my mother.

"Last night," I say, remembering seeing the team at the bowling alley. They stood out because Max, the deli guy I know from Waldbaum's, the one who always gives my youngest daughter, Alyssa, extra slices of Sweet Muenster while I order cold cuts, was one of them. "I saw him last night."

"Really?" Drew asks, like this would be the sort of thing a person might make up. "When was that, exactly?"

"All night," I say, then realize how that sounds. "All *evening*. Until about eleven-thirty." I'm about to explain that I was working on the grand opening and this guy was bowling, but Drew doesn't ask and I decide to let him make his own assumptions. I think, alive, Joey wasn't bad-looking. A little old for me, but hey, I'm getting older every day myself.

"I'd like you to come down to the station," he says, and I think he's having too much fun busting my chops. I say something that sounds a lot like *in your dreams*—if you happen to be listening carefully.

Seems the two uniforms are. Their jaws drop.

Drew lets it roll off his back. He comes to his feet and takes my chin in his hand. "You, my dear, are a material witness. You may have been the last person to see your date alive."

AFTER EXPLAINING that the man was not with me, but with an entire bowling league, I'm released. I'm back at the bowling alley when my cell phone, announcing a call from my mother, plays the theme from *Looney Tunes*.

"How do you do it?" I ask her while Mark gestures for me to show him how high I want the new dark green Formica-that-looks-like-granite paneling to go.

"I have spies," she says matter-of-factly, as I place my hand about hip high on the wall. We're going ultra modern for the billiards area, with brushed steel above faux-marble wainscoting. Wouldn't have been my choice, but all the materials were already ordered when Percy Michaels decided she was too good to decorate bowling alleys and took a powder.

That's when Teddi *the scavenger* Bayer, the hungriest (and some say most dangerous) decorator on Long Island, swooped in. I get a premium if I finish the job on time and nothing for my end of the work if I don't. And as of today, *nothing* seems only too real.

"They're everywhere, so don't think you can get away with seeing that Detective Spoonbreath again. I didn't lend you my condo for two weeks so that you could come home and pick up where you left off with him."

"You didn't, but I did," my father says into the extension. "If that's what she wants. Leave her be, for God's sake, June."

I love my father.

Not that I don't love my mother—I just don't *like* her very much.

My mother continues as if my father hasn't said anything at all. "Mildred Waynick said you barricaded the freezer door and were in there alone with him for twenty minutes. And you weren't cold when you came out."

"Leave her be, June," my father says without enthusiasm—probably because he knows, after all these years, that his words are falling on deaf ears.

"Did Mildred mention there was a dead body in there?" I ask, checking on angles to make sure that the light won't reflect into a player's eyes when he's taking a pool shot. "Not what you'd call romantic, exactly."

"It must have been very upsetting," my father says. I hear him tsking. Or he could be cleaning between his teeth with a matchbook cover.

"Teddi's used to it by now," my mother snaps back. "And it gave her an excuse to see Detective Dreamboat."

"My, my. He's moving up in the world," I say, putting my hand just under my breasts to show Mark how high the bar should be. He gestures for me to stand still while he measures. Yeah, fat chance. "What happened to *Spoonbreath?*"

"Nothing bad enough, it seems," my mother counters.

I remind her that she's caught me at work and tell her that I've got to go. Not that this stops her.

"Who were you on the phone with before I called?" she asks. "I got voice mail."

I tell her it was a wrong number, which, although true, doesn't satisfy her. So I admit it was Mel Gibson, out of rehab and looking for a nice Jewish girl.

She makes an ugly noise and moves on. "You joke, but my reputation gets dragged through the mud along with yours," she says dramatically. "I have a daughter who decorates bowling alleys, shops in *goyish* food stores and lusts after cops. And she lies to me. Can you just tell me what it was I did to you that was so awful, so terrible, that you need to punish me like this?"

"I'm earning an honest living here, Mother. There's no cross over King Kullen's doors and I'm not lusting after anyone." Okay, so that part's a lie. "What did *I* do to deserve this?"

"Be that way, Teddi." I hear her exhale her cigarette smoke. "Go ahead. I won't even tell you about the lottery ticket I bought for you. The mega-millions one they drew last night."

My heart stops. "What about it?" I ask her, having heard this morning on the radio that it wasn't claimed yet. Though they also said the winning ticket—for thirty-seven million dollars—was purchased in Plainview and I know that there is no way my mother would shop in Plainview, just a stone's throw (and a step down, according to her) from where I live in Syosset. Not even for a lottery ticket.

"You didn't win," she tells me while I look at the phone with utter amazement. "But you could have, so don't blame me. At least I tried to fix your life. Imagine the man you could get if you'd won that lottery."

I tell her to keep trying, and until she wins me either a fortune or a man, I better keep working. And that includes doing bowling alleys and any other places that will pay me.

"Will brothels be next, Teddi? Or funeral homes? Do you get some sort of perverse pleasure embarrassing me like this? Are you getting back at me?" my mother asks. "Is that it?"

She probably says a few other nasty things, but I don't know, because I've already pressed End.

Bobbie opens her mouth to weigh in on Drew Scoones's place in my life, but I tell her we have work to do. Between Bobbie's I-don't-smoke-anymore-but-I-still-deserve-a-break breaks, her shopping, her trips to her husband, Mike's, chiropractic office in the middle of the day to find this patient's file or that one's X-rays, it's no wonder she occasionally forgets we're actually working.

She was not the one who was here until nearly midnight last night, measuring and leaving notes for Mark so that he could get the Formica cut at the lumber yard and ready to install before L.I. Lanes opened today. She didn't have to fend off two drunk guys who didn't understand any part of *no* even after the jukebox played Lorrie Morgan's song twice.

She wasn't the one who locked up the place and had to walk to her car alone in the dark, her heels clicking on the asphalt so loudly in her ears that it nearly drowned out the sound of the men arguing in front of the bagel shop.

I close my eyes and try to picture them because, if my mind isn't playing tricks on me, they were The Spare Slices and they were pretty angry.

"You okay?" Mark asks, taking my elbow. "You look like you've just seen a ghost."

"I may have," I say, trying to remember what they were arguing about.

Whatever it was, Drew needs to know.

"I've got to call him," I say, and neither Mark nor Bobbie needs to ask who.

"What a surprise," Bobbie says, rolling her eyes and holding out her hand, palm up, to Mark.

"Thanks," Mark tells me sarcastically, taking out a five and putting it in Bobbie's hand as I dial Drew's number from memory.

"I just remembered something," I say when he answers the phone.

"What's that?" Drew asks.

"Okay, we need to talk…"

There's a beat before he answers me. "Sure," he says. "Tomorrow."

CHAPTER 2

Anyone who has ever repainted a wall or replaced a carpet or even gotten a new set of kitchen pots knows one thing just leads inexorably to another. The bright walls make the ceiling look dull. The new light to make the ceiling brighter reveals the wear spots in the carpet. The carpet installation wrecks the molding. As long as the base molding is being replaced…

—TipsFromTeddi.com

I may not love decorating a bowling alley, but I have to admit there are certain perks to it. Like that the owner has agreed to let my kids and their friends bowl free whenever I'm on the job. This makes my eleven-year-old son, Jesse, very happy. It ought to make all the moms in the neighborhood happy, too, since I'm making sure the place is really kid-friendly so they'll all have a viable alternative to the usual weekend mall-ratting.

L.I. Lanes isn't just a cheaper way for the kids to spend a Saturday afternoon, it's also only a good, hearty walk from our house. Not that Dana, my thirteen-going-on-thirty daughter will admit it's walkable. She's the original princess, requiring chauffeuring everywhere. If she'd been born a century or two ago in China, she'd be demanding her feet be bound so that no one could expect her to go as far as the refrigerator to get her own ice cream.

Anyway, my kids have found that if they stay on the school bus past our stop, they get dropped only a few blocks from the bowling alley and Carvel. And in they walk now, separately so that, *God forbid!*, no one thinks they came in together.

"Is it true?" Dana asks me. She's connected to my mother by more than simple DNA. They've both read the elusive *Secret Handbook of Long Island*—the one everyone tries to tell me doesn't exist—and I'm sure their spy networks overlap.

I feign ignorance. "Is what true?" Of course, I know what she knows. I just don't know how she could already know it.

"You found another dead guy and the cops want to question you."

Note there is no question mark at the end of that sentence.

"It *is* getting to be a habit," Jesse adds as he checks out where the new pool tables are slated to be, making fake shots with an imaginary pool cue and checking behind him to see if I've left enough room.

I have my doubts myself, but I'm pretty sure I can get in the four tables I'm planning. And I've finally found someone who can get them for me within my rapidly shrinking time frame.

Anyway, I assure my children that while a man was found dead, it in no way means—

And then a cop walks in the door. We watch him stop at the desk and talk to Steve, the owner of L.I. Lanes. Steve points me out and, with a nod, the cop heads in my direction.

"Detective Scoones wants you down at the precinct to-morrow at nine a.m.," he says, handing me one of Drew's cards.

"Sure," I say, trying to be offhanded about it as I shove the card in the back pocket of my jeans.

"Guess it's not just *in his dreams*," he says. He snickers and heads for the door.

"This is so embarrassing," Dana announces loudly, in case anyone has missed the entire episode, which, judging from the stares, no one has. "Why do I have to have a mother who is a murder magnet?" She storms out the back door to the alley, headed, I suppose, for someplace where she can actually spend money.

Not too long after I've embarrassed my children, my mother calls, because life was just a bowl of cherries until now. It's like that foul they're always calling in football—*piling on*.

"I forgot to tell you that I got you a new job," she says when I answer my cell. I remind her that I have a job and that I'm actually doing it at the moment.

"That?" she asks. "The bowling alley? That's not a job, it's penance. This is a real job. And I'm still in shock, so listen carefully. You remember Rita and Jerry Kroll from around the corner?"

How could I forget the Krolls? They had a son, Robert, who, despite being at least a decade older than we were, used to ride around the neighborhood on his bicycle every day, all day, in any kind of weather, speeding up behind little kids and honking his horn, scaring the wits out of us. He was Cedarhurst's answer to *To Kill a Mockingbird*. Our very own

Boo Radley. And it wasn't until we'd grown up that we learned he wasn't scary at all, just mentally disabled. Robby, as his parents called him, was simply never going to grow up.

"They bought a house in Woodbury last month and she wants you to decorate it. Can you believe this? What can she be thinking?"

"Excuse me, but I'm a good decorator, Mom," I remind her. "Of course people are going to want to hire me." That is, if my mother doesn't convince them otherwise.

"Sure, sure," my mother says dismissively. It comes out like we can discuss the possibility that I might have talent some other time. "But moving from the South Shore to Woodbury? From Cedarhurst yet? I mean, leaving Mel the butcher? Dominick at Tresses? The World's Best dry cleaners. For Woodbury?"

I assure her that we actually have overpriced hairdressers and butchers and dry cleaners on the North Shore, too. Especially in Woodbury, which borders Syosset on "the good side"—which is to say the side that isn't Plainview or Hicksville. Up, up, up the social ladder you go as you get closer to the Long Island Sound.

My mother reminds me that you get what you pay for.

"Which is why you have to double your prices for Rita. She's used to being overcharged. It's how she knows what something's worth."

Sometimes I believe that Cedarhurst is just north of Bizarro Land and just south of Topsy Turvy.

"I made an appointment for you last week. Maybe it was

the week before. Anyway, it's a good thing I remembered because it's for nine o'clock tomorrow morning." She recites the address and starts giving me directions as if I have a pen and paper at the ready.

I tell her I can't make it at nine and she somehow worms out of me the fact that I am wanted down at the police station.

"He called you?" she asks. "That's why I got voice mail? For Spoonbreath?"

"No, that was the pool table salesman," I say, accepting the fact that she all but monitors my phone and always knows when I've gotten a call. "A policeman dropped by the bowling alley to tell me I'm wanted at the precinct in the morning."

"Of course he wants you," my mother says. "Tell him too bad. Tell him you've got a job to do. Tell him to sniff at someone else's skirts…"

I, OF COURSE, tell him none of those things.

Sitting across the desk from him at the station the next morning, I tell him that I saw Joey arguing with several other men outside the bowling alley the night before he died. And they all had The Spare Slices shirts on.

"You hear what they were arguing about?" he asks me. He's all business, but I notice his leg is going up and down a mile a minute, which he only does when he's nervous.

I shake my head. "Was it murder?" I ask.

"Doesn't really look like it," he says. "But there are a few loose ends I want to tie up."

He waits for me to respond. And he waits. The air in

the room gets stuffy. Finally I say, "Okay, fine. Because I was scared."

"Was that an answer to an old question or to one I didn't ask yet?" he asks me.

I nod.

"Come on, Teddi," he says. He's almost whining. "Help me out here, okay? Just a clue what we're talking about."

"I ran because I was alone, which is scary," I say.

"Is that you-leave-me-before-I-leave-you?" Drew asks.

I take a moment to figure out where that came from. He means running to Boca. I meant running to my car. I explain that because I was running, I couldn't hear what the men were shouting about.

"Right," he says.

*Leave him before he left me?* Is that what he thinks? Is that what *he* was going to do? "*Were* you going to leave me?" I ask.

He has the file open on his desk. A picture of Joey— frozen—is on top and he fingers it and pulls out a report sheet from behind it. "Where?" he says.

I figure we're back to the investigation, so I say, "In front of the bagel place—you know, between L.I. Lanes and King Kullen. The one with the mini-everything bagels. Not too many places do the everythings in mini-size."

He grimaces. "Leave you where?" he asks.

Is your head spinning yet? Because mine is. And while it's been three months, I'm still not ready to talk about *us*. "What did he die of?" I ask instead of answering him.

"Heart attack," he says. "Guy had a history of heart disease. He was living on borrowed time."

I pick Dana's old purse up off the floor and throw the strap over my shoulder. Bobbie would kill me if she saw the depths to which I've sunk, but Alyssa, my seven-year-old, painted my purse with magic marker. A new purse is not exactly in the budget at the moment, not even one from T.J.Maxx, which would pain Bobbie almost as much as Dana's old one, I think. Nowadays you need to take out a second mortgage to buy a nice handbag. I can't imagine what you're left with to put inside it. You certainly don't need a wallet cause there'd be nothing to keep in it.

"So that's it then," I say, coming to my feet.

"Looks like," he says. "Only…"

He's baiting me, but I refuse to get hooked. Still, asking "Only *what?*" doesn't seem like much of a risk.

"Only the guy works in the deli, not the meat department. It's after hours and he's just had an argument with his buddies."

"So why was he in the freezer?" I ask.

"And why was his shirt frozen?" he adds.

"He was locked in?" I ask. "Like you see in old movies?"

Drew shakes his head at me and smiles like it amuses him that I'm once again relating the world to some movie I've seen. "They don't use that kind anymore. There are always latches on the inside to prevent accidental lock-ins."

"And so he goes into the freezer, maybe to steal some filets, and the door closes behind him—" I start.

"One, they call it a *cooler*. The freezer's where they keep the real frozen stuff—ice cream and the like. And two, there's no reason he can't just let himself out."

"But he doesn't." I sit back down. "He has a sudden pain in his chest." I clutch my chest. "He knows it's the big one. He gropes for the door in the dark—" I flail my arms with my eyes closed.

"Light goes on automatically when you open the door."

I open my eyes and remind him that the door is closed behind him.

"Stays on for thirty minutes," Drew says. "And there's an emergency button to push."

"His shirt was wet?" I ask. "From sweat?"

Drew shakes his head. "Coroner says tap water."

"And you say?" I ask.

Drew looks at the file. He leafs through a paper or two, studies the photograph of Joey. "Suspicious," he says.

He doesn't have to ask what I'd say.

*Murder.*

## CHAPTER 3

Just like you can't judge a book by its cover, you can't judge a house by its appearance from the street. But you can provide a hint of what's to be found inside so that the result doesn't jar the senses. A Chinese umbrella stand on the porch, an arts and crafts mailbox, Victorian cornices—these all signal your style.

—TipsFromTeddi.com

I am not investigating anything, I tell myself. I am merely picking up some deli at Waldbaum's for the kids' lunches. Or just in case my father should happen to drop by. I mean, really, how can you not have some corned beef around, just in case?

"And maybe some potato salad," I tell Max, who seems a bit more flushed than usual.

He hands me one of those white deli bags with some chocolate-covered raspberry Jell Rings for Alyssa. "No charge," he says with a wink.

I thank him and remark how funny it was to see him a few nights ago. He doesn't seem to think there was anything odd about it.

"I'm really sorry about your friend," I say, lowering my voice as though at work he isn't allowed to have friends.

"Joey?" he asks, surprised that I know. "Damn shame. Just when things were looking up."

"Looking up?" I ask. Someone nudges my arm while reaching for the Turn-O-Matic machine.

"We're not taking numbers," someone else informs her, which I take to mean that she was here first and didn't take one.

"Could have been looking up," he hedges. "Who knows?"

*Why is he backtracking?* I can't help but wonder. Only it doesn't seem like a line I can pursue, so I go back to how odd it was to see him at the alley. *With the dead guy.*

"I mean seeing you there out of context," I say. "At first I didn't even recognize you."

"You think this is my whole life?" he asks, fanning his hands out to encompass his domain. The counters are full of twenty kinds of turkey, every manner of pastrami, salami, bologna and corned beef. There's herring salad, white-fish salad, crab salad… He slaps his hand on the top of the counter. "God, no. I got a life outside of here."

"I know," I say with a big smile, like bowling once a week is a whole life—and don't I know it? "I saw last night."

He shakes his head.

"I got a lot more in mind than bowling once a week with those losers," he says. "A new car, a boat. Maybe even a house on some island. Hawaii, maybe. You think the houses are cheaper in Hawaii or Florida?"

"I don't know," I tell him, putting a bag of onion rolls in

my cart so that the women around me know I'm shopping and not just shooting the breeze. "But I do know you can live pretty cheaply in the Bahamas. I've got a brother who's lived down there ever since college." I don't go into how the trip was a graduation present from my parents and David simply decided not to come back, even though my father's store, Bayer Furniture (the home of headache-free buying and hassle-free finance), was waiting for him.

Max asks if maybe I could give him David's name and he might get in touch one day.

Okay, by now, people around me are getting testy. I tell Max just a half pound of the potato salad and maybe a pound of coleslaw. He nods, but he doesn't make a move to fill my order.

"He like it in the Bahamas? Your brother?" he asks me.

I nod and smile and gesture toward the potato salad without trying to appear rude. There are sounds of disgruntlement growing behind me.

Bernie, another counter guy, comes over from the cheese portion of the counter and clicks the Turn-O-Matic, calls out the number after mine, and helps the woman beside me.

"Finally," someone says.

"He have a Web site?" Max asks.

I picture my brother in cutoffs, no shoes, chasing after a naked little boy named Cody while Izzy, his pregnant wife, laughs at him. "I don't think so."

"E-mail?" Max asks. "I got a new computer last week. First one. Gotta keep up, you know?"

"I do." I look at my watch and gesture toward the

wrapped package of corned beef that is still on his side of the glass. "You know what? I think I'll just take the corned beef," I say.

"No, no. I'll get your salads." He waves his hand like filling my order isn't important, like it's not why he's here, never mind why *I'm* here. "So are you working over there? At the alley, I mean?"

I explain how I've taken over the job of decorating the place while a woman pushes me out of the way on the pretense of reaching for a package of rugelach.

"Remind me nevah to go thayh," the woman behind me says in a loud gravelly voice thick with Long Island.

I tell Max that I'm in kind of a rush and that maybe I'll see him next week at the bowling alley.

"Isn't it next week already?" the same woman asks in an even louder voice.

"You don't like my service?" Max asks her. He squints his eyes at her like he could burn her with them. "Go to King Kullen."

I want to warn her that King Kullen's a bad idea, but she's off looking for a manager.

"I won't miss her," Max says, handing me my corned beef, my potato salad, my coleslaw and a loose piece of halvah. "You, I'm gonna miss."

"When you buy your island?" I ask, happy to feed the fantasy now that I'm backing away from the counter.

"Exactly," he says as he listens to someone else's order and nods. "A pound of pastrami. Got it. You want it should be lean? Sliced thin?"

"MO-OM!" Dana whines in response to my innocently mentioning at dinner in Pastaeria (the local pizza joint no one is sure how to pronounce), that Max was acting strangely and that I think I should tell Drew about his pie-in-the-sky plans. "You don't know what kind of money he has stashed away. He could be a millionaire. He could be Donald Trump's long-lost father and—"

I remind her that Max is around my age, which makes him way too young to be The Donald's father. Dana seems skeptical, like maybe I don't know just how old I really am. Remember when everyone who'd graduated from high school more than two years before you did was old? That's what my kids think.

They may be right.

Jesse thinks it's a great idea and I should pull out my cell phone and call Drew immediately. This, of course, has nothing to do with his fondness for Drew and his fervent wish that I marry the handsome detective.

Dana, picking all the cheese off her pizza and giving me a look which implies I should be doing the same, tells Jesse that he—and I—are just using Max as an excuse to call Drew. But, unlike her usual carping tone that implies I'm leading Drew on and ruining her life, she sounds like she's actually teasing me. Could she be growing up? Adjusting to the fact that her father and I will not get back together in this lifetime?

"If it was murder, then maybe you and he would, you know, *get together* again," she says. "At least, you hope."

Unfortunately, she may have me dead to rights.

In the meantime, little Alyssa ate so many garlic knots before the pizza showed up that she can't even pretend to eat her slice. That doesn't mean she isn't interested in dessert and she asks whether Max sent her anything.

I avoid answering because then I'd have to admit that on my way home I ate the Jell Rings meant for her.

I've got to go back to work if I've any hope of getting done before the grand opening, so I beg them to pass on dessert, remind everyone there is ice cream in the freezer, prevail and head for home. I arrive in my driveway at the same time my father pulls up at the curb. He's there to watch the Mets game with Jesse, who doesn't have the heart to tell him that he's gone over to the dark side. He's now a Yankees fan.

"Once a week I can root for the Mets for Grandpa," he tells me, reminding me why it is I still like the kid. "Sometimes you have to bend the truth a little for someone you love."

It's taken me years to learn what he already knows at eleven.

I kiss the kids and Dad goodbye and I'm back at the alley, knee-deep in lighting wires when Drew and his partner, Hal Nelson, saunter in.

Saying that Hal and I don't care for each other is like saying there may be a little traffic on the Long Island Expressway at rush hour. I don't know what I ever did to him—except maybe show up the police department once or twice.

And I didn't really do that, even.

*Newsday* just made it sound that way.

There are only about a half-dozen patrons left in the place, only a couple still bowling. The others are taking off their shoes, packing up their bags, reliving a frame or two and sharing a joke. I see Drew take note of each and every one as he makes his way over to where I'm waiting for the glue to cure on a section of wall.

"You wanted to tell me something?" Drew asks. I stare at him blankly for a minute, unable to believe he'd bring Hal with him to talk about *us*. I guess he sees my confusion, because he offers a hint. "About the guy in the cooler? You called the precinct?"

"Oh, right," I say, looking like the dolt Hal has me pegged for. Maybe I can blame it on the glue fumes. "I just wanted to tell you about a conversation I had with Max. He's one of The Spare Slices—"

"Oh hell," Hal says, blowing a balloon of air out toward his thinning hairline and addressing Drew. "She's not suggesting this was a murder or that we need her help, is she? That's not why we came all the way over here, is it, Scoones?"

It's his way of daring me to say I think I'm smarter than the police. I tell him that first of all, he can talk to me directly. He doesn't have to do it through Drew, who's leaning back against the wall looking thoroughly amused.

In fact, he appears so amused that I decide not to tell him about the adhesive for the brushed steel sheets.

The police don't screw up investigations, Hal tells me, snicker, snicker, snicker. "At least, *I* don't."

I'm hoping he leans up against the same wall Drew is going to find himself stuck to.

"Not that I'm implying Detective Scoones over here

screws up, either," he says, gesturing at Drew with his thumb and adding a few more gratuitous snickers. "He just screws. Right, honey?" He looks at me to drive the point home. When Drew says nothing, any guilt I was harboring about his ruined jacket dissolves.

So, fine. I get to the point. "One of the other Spare Slices is talking about buying an island," I say. "Could be wishful thinking, could be a pipe dream. On the other hand, it could mean something."

"An island?" Hal says. Actually, he sneers. Hal always sneers. In my presence, anyway. Drew maintains he's really a nice guy. I've seen no evidence. Not that the police seem to rely on little things like evidence all that much, in my experience. "What was he smoking at the time?"

"Salmon," I say.

Drew licks his pointer finger and draws an imaginary one in my air column.

"Been determined to be an accident," Hal says, and he leans right up against the wall beside Drew. "Familiar territory for you."

I run the scenario, perhaps a tad contemptuously. "So he goes into the cooler, for whatever reason, and he brings in a pitcher of water, because, hey, he might get thirsty in there, right? And he pours it all over himself because—I don't know—he was warm? No accounting for someone's body temperature, I suppose. And then he feels the pain of a heart attack in his chest, but he doesn't reach for the emergency button or anything and—"

"Light was out," Hal says. "Burned out bulb, probably."

"And you're not investigating any further?" I ask.

"Oh, *we're* investigating," he says, his face contorted with an even more intense sneer than usual. "*You're* not. It was an accident, we'll tie up a couple of loose ends and that will be that. Got it?"

He goes to look at his watch, only he has trouble raising his hand. He tries to jerk it away from the wall, but it's not going anywhere. "What the—?" he says, trying to pull away from the wall.

Drew pushes himself off the wall easily. Behind him are two squares of brushed steel which I pretend I knew were there all along.

"You wanna get some coffee?" he asks me, ignoring Hal, who is fighting with his jacket and cursing a blue streak, causing every head left in the place to look our way. Drew ignores the stares. "Maybe a little something to eat?"

I tell him I've got to stay. Otherwise, someone might accidentally touch the wall—though the fact that Hal's jacket is now hanging there and he's swearing down the house and turning red in the face would probably provide a strong enough deterrent. Besides, it seems pretty clear that in a minute or two there will be no one left around.

"Right," he says, only it sounds more like he gets my unintended message and he won't ask twice.

"I'll be out of here in about an hour," I say. It might actually take a little longer now that I've got to scrape off Hal's jacket and reapply the adhesive. "Maybe we could—"

"Fuck!" Hal says, ripping most of his jacket from the wall, leaving a good portion of the back panel there.

Drew says something to the effect that *that* wasn't exactly what he had in mind, but hey, if I'm game…

It gives me pause, because Drew and I have made love a number of times. We've fooled around, we've brought each other satisfaction, we've even screwed, but we have never done the F word. Not as far as I'm concerned, because for me, if the F word has any emotion attached to it, it's anger.

And I've been there and done that and banished the anger from my bed and my heart and it's not coming back.

Not ever.

"You!" Hal shouts at me, pointing his finger and being struck dumb for words.

"It's going to turn out to be a murder," I tell him.

He sputters something about murder all right—he'd be happy to kill me on the spot.

And I'm thinking that I'd so love to prove it was murder and shove a warrant right up his…uniform.

## CHAPTER 4

Accommodating everyone's needs can be a challenge in the family room. Essentials include a good reading light beside a comfortable chair; a stain-resistant couch facing the TV with a coffee table in front of it for the sports fan and the kids; music for the rare moment the TV is not on; carpeting or a rug to absorb the noise; and a healthy dose of good cheer. A large bottle of Prozac is not a bad idea, as well.

—TipsFromTeddi.com

I spend all day working with Bobbie on the walls in the "billiard parlor" at L.I. Lanes. And I totally get why Percy Michaels, who originally had this job, gets the big bucks. This place is coming out unbelievably gorgeous. I bet even the high-roller executive types from Woodbury would come down here for a few racks and a cup of cappuccino.

Did I mention I convinced Steve to put in an espresso bar? He's so sure I won't get finished in time that he's spending my forfeited fee in advance.

At any rate, I posted new TipsFromTeddi on my Web site and the kids and I have had dinner at home—Dana is on her vegetarian kick again, so she had cheese quesadillas with no cheese and Jesse had a hot dog and I had some leftover chicken. Alyssa picked at some French toast. Just a typical dinner at the Bayers, all of us sitting down to a nice meal together—except for Dana who was in her bedroom doing a chat with the school drama club. And Alyssa who wanted to see the end of *SpongeBob*. Oh, and Jesse, who was reading the new Harry Potter.

So Maggie May, the bichon frise I stole from my first client after she was murdered, kept me company while I ate.

Now I could take the night off, but it's clear the kids don't need me, don't want me, wouldn't miss me if I were gone. If I pay Dana her usual babysitting fee—five downloads from iTunes—I can go back to the bowling alley and get a jump on tomorrow's work.

I'm not even sure they'll notice I'm gone.

And it is league night at the Lanes, so I yell to the children that I'm off to work and out I go, hoping to run into The Spare Slices again.

Which I do.

I find them huddled together just outside the door as I am walking in, and I go up to them to offer my condolences.

You know how in old movies there'll be a bunch of guys shooting craps and when the police show up they all jump about six feet? Well, I come up to the group and that's just what they do.

Maybe it's the money that several of them are holding that brings that image to mind. They stare at me until Max introduces me as a customer from the store who's redecorating the alley.

Then they look at me expectantly, waiting for me to go on into L.I. Lanes, and frankly, there really is nothing stopping me.

"I just wanted to say how sorry I was to hear about your friend," I say, flashing them all a tentative smile and not mentioning how I was there when they found Joey.

They mumble a bit and act contrite, making noises about how bad they feel about bowling just a week after their teammate was found dead.

"He'd have wanted you to carry on the game," I say, like they are being brave despite their heartbreak, and a couple of them nod. One, Milt according to the embroidery on his shirt pocket, says that he told them all they shouldn't play.

"Outta respect for the dead," he says.

"Is that what you're doing?" I ask, gesturing toward the money in his teammate's hand. "Collecting for flowers or something, because I'd like to—"

"We *should* do that," Dave says.

Note to myself—never let my kids wear their names on anything. It's too easy to pretend familiarity.

"Well, Dave," I start to say, but Max jumps in before I can finish.

"We're *gonna*," Max says like he's reminding Dave, who I take it might be a little dim-witted. "If we win, we're gonna use Joey's share for a big headstone or something, remember?"

"No, we gotta give his share to his kids," Dave says. "If

he's got some, I mean." He looks confused, but on him it looks like a familiar state.

"Win?" I ask.

"The lottery," Max explains, while Milt says, "Ya gotta be in it to win it," in a sing-songy voice. "We've been going in on twenty tickets every week for years. We never win, but we figure we're due. Right, guys?"

They all agree and I do, too, saying that you always hear about winners who've been playing as a group for years. There were those workers who changed the lightbulbs in Rockefeller Center, I think...

"And this week ain't any different than any other," Milt says.

"Except for Joey's being dead," Dave adds. "Maybe he could bring us luck." He shrugs like *hey, you never know.*

Russ—I know from his shirt pocket—scoffs. "Yeah, Joey was real lucky, wasn't he?" He sighs a heavy sigh and adds, "Poor dumb jerk."

WHEN I GET HOME, Drew's car is in the circular driveway in front of my split-level and every light in the house is on. I rush up the front steps and Dana lets me in. Maggie does her best to tell me what's happened, circling my legs and woofing.

At least someone is trying to tell me.

"I told him to call Daddy," Dana says over her shoulder as she heads down the freshly wallpapered hallway toward my beautiful salmon-colored kitchen which looks alternately like an early sunrise or a deep sunset depending on where the real sun is at the moment. Of course, there is no sun now. "But no, your son had to call *Drew*." She says his name like it's covered in bird droppings.

"Call for what?" I ask, hurrying into the living room where I find Drew and Jesse playing cards and Alyssa in her pajamas all but asleep in Drew's lap. My living room is a beautiful deep hunter-green. Drew looks like he belongs there. And he looks good with my little girl in his lap, too. Damn good.

"Turned out to be nothing," Jesse says, while Drew points at Alyssa and smiles apologetically to indicate that if he moves Alyssa will wake up. She's got her thumb in her mouth and her face is tear-stained.

"*What* turned out to be nothing?" I ask while Jesse picks a card from the deck like I'm not even there.

"Your idiot son thought someone was shooting at us," Dana says. She's got her arms crossed over her chest, where I know her sleep shirt says Bite Me.

"Shooting—" I start to say, but Drew interrupts me.

"Everything is fine," he says in a voice that insists *don't lose it now*, while he casts a warning glance at Dana. "Jesse had the presence of mind to call me, I happened to be in the neighborhood. There were no gunshots."

"And no one called me because…?" I ask.

"Because I thought someone was shooting at us. When there are gunshots, you call the police," Jesse says.

Alyssa stirs in Drew's arms and I take her and head for the stairway, carrying her up to bed while Dana reminds Jesse he didn't call *the police*. He called *Drew*.

"I thought you were never coming home," Lys says against my neck.

I want to tell her that she could have called me. That my cell phone is on the kitchen phone's automatic dial, which she certainly knows how to use—heck, she does it often enough—but I figure we can have that talk tomorrow. This is just the animated feature and I've got the best-picture-of-the-year award waiting downstairs. So I just kiss her forehead, slip her under the covers and go back to the living room.

"From the beginning," I order Jesse. He discards a seven of clubs before I take his cards away. "Now."

"I heard a series of cracks," Jesse says. Dana says she heard nothing and he's crazy.

"Well, not entirely crazy," Drew says, and I feel my heart skip a beat—and not the romantic, he-walks-in-the-room-and-you-see-him-for-the-first-time kind of beat-skipping. More like the-masked-men-arrive-at-your-door-and-it's-not-Halloween kind of beat-skipping.

Two years ago my ex-husband, Rio, tried to drive me crazy—literally. He moved things, made me think I'd done things I hadn't and hadn't done things I had. And all because he wanted to start his own business and I wouldn't let him put up the house as collateral.

At any rate, he didn't quite succeed. But I'm well acquainted with mind games and what I call the Chinese insanity torture, and tonight I realize that if Rio had had the help of the three people lounging in my living room, I'd be a permanent resident of my mother's home-away-from-home, the South Winds Psychiatric Center.

"Tell me what happened," I order from between gritted teeth.

"I'm trying to," Jesse says. "So I heard a noise and then the window in Dana's room broke."

Before I can say, "It what?" Dana corrects him and says it's just a little cracked.

"And there's a little hole in it," Jesse says. He leaves off the so *there*, but we all hear it just the same. "So I thought it was a bullet hole and I called Drew."

"And not me," I say, just making sure I'm clear on this.

"I told him to call Daddy," Dana says again. "But no, he had to make a federal case out of it."

"And nobody, not you, not your brother and not *you*," I say, looking pointedly at Drew, "thought you should call me."

"We knew you'd have to come home eventually," Drew says. Maggie jumps up on the couch she's forbidden to sit on, makes two circles and then snuggles down next to Drew. "And I think I'm better equipped to handle this sort of thing, don't you?"

I ignore the dig. "What broke the window?" I ask, snapping my fingers for Maggie to get down. She ignores me and closes her eyes.

"It was a tiny pebble," Dana says. I could swear she's almost proud of it. "Probably got kicked up by a car, you know, like when our windshield got broken? *He* found it by my bed."

It's a long way from the street to her window on the second floor, not to mention that her bedroom is on the side of the house.

Drew says that it could have happened the way Dana surmises.

"Right," I say—like on the other hand it could have been a small asteroid from the planet Moron. "So really, someone threw a rock at Dana's window."

"That's possible, too," he says, hiding a smile.

I ask him if he thinks we should sleep at my mother's, thinking that my children's safety has to come before my own desires, which include never, ever, throwing myself on my mother's mercy. But he tells me he doesn't think it's necessary.

As a precaution, he offers to hang around for a while.

The idea doesn't sound half bad to me, so I try sending the kids to bed. After the protests that it's too early, that they are too shaken to sleep (this from Jesse, the card shark), that Dana shouldn't have to go to bed as early as Jesse since she's older, and blah, blah, blah, they finally go upstairs.

Making coffee in the kitchen, I ask Drew what he thinks really happened.

"Best guess? Someone with the hots for your daughter was trying to get her attention. Wouldn't hurt for her to pull down her shades when she's undressing, Ted."

I feel my cheeks go red. After watching me do a striptease through the window of a cottage I was doing in the Hamptons over the summer, is he thinking *like mother, like daughter?*

"And I think that Jesse saw it as the perfect excuse to get me over here," he adds, rubbing my back while I get the coffee going.

Better he think Jesse's plotting to get him here than me.

"And no one called me because…?" I ask.

"Maybe Hal isn't the only one tired of you playing cop, Teddi." He reaches over my shoulder and pulls out the mugs and the sugar bowl from the cabinets like the house is his. "Maybe your kids have had all they can take, too. And maybe they'd like a mom who's home at night, watching TV with them, watching over them."

It's so easy for people without kids to know what's right for parents. "Maybe they like eating, too, and having a roof over their heads," I say in my own defense. Of course, I say this despite the fact that I'm feeling like a negligent parent, like something could have happened tonight and I wouldn't have been here to protect them. "Maybe it's not fair that they have to live with my mistakes—but they do," I say. And with that I manage to spill the coffee I'm pouring and burn my hand.

Drew grabs the pot and my hand and in one motion manages to put the carafe back in the Mr. Coffee unit and my hand under the faucet. "They're fine," he tells me. "Nothing happened. Nothing's gonna happen."

I should have been here, and I say as much.

"You had work to do," he says, examining my hand and pronouncing with a look that it's fine. "Right?"

When I don't answer, he knows it was more than that.

"You saw the slice and dice boys," he says with a sigh.

I admit that I ran into Max and his teammates. Drew waits. Finally I tell him about how the team goes in on lottery tickets together every week.

He makes a production of reaching around behind him to make sure his handcuffs are in his back pocket. "Ooh! I better run 'em in," he says sarcastically. "Think I should call for backup?"

"Mock me," I say, "but there could be millions involved and—"

"*Mega* millions," he corrects.

"I'm not kidding. Let's say that Joey had the winning ticket and one of the others knew it and pushed him into the freezer—"

"The cooler. And this Slicer counted on the light being burned out?" Drew says. "And then what? He's still got to kill off an entire team's worth of players so that he can claim all the winnings himself. You don't think that would be a little obvious?"

"Still," I say. After all, a couple of The Spare Slices are a slice short of a sandwich.

He orders me to sit down, but I refuse. One thing I've become adamant about in my single life is that no one can order me around.

"Fine," he says. "Stand there."

Now, if I stand, I'm listening to him and if I sit I'm listening to him.

"Try pacing," he offers, like he's read my mind.

"No one's claimed last week's lottery," I remind him.

"Look," he says, watching me go back and forth. "Could you please sit? I'll sit first."

And he does.

"So happens we knew about the lottery tickets. That woman—Fran—over at King Kullen told the detectives on the case all about it. Said that Joey was always planning what he'd do if he won. Like your friend at Waldbaum's."

"Max."

"Right," he says. "Max. Only I checked with the detectives assigned to the case and they assured me that the five remaining Spare Slices all say they saw the twenty losing tickets, same as every week for the last three years."

"But—" I start to say.

He waits. The truth is, I've got nothing.

"Has it occurred to you that maybe you've got murder on the brain? That you're seeing conspiracies where there aren't any? And that your imagination is running away with your common sense?"

I suppose my body language says *No, that hasn't occurred to me. And furthermore, I do not think that is the case here.*

I mean, a man is dead under very suspicious circumstances.

"The man's death has been ruled an accident, Teddi. Why he brought that water in with him, I don't know, but I do know what happened after that. Some spilled, he slipped on it, hit his head, got disoriented, panicked, heart attack, done. Or, he gets the pain in his chest, clutches it, spills the water, takes a nose dive, done. Whichever, it was the heart attack that killed him. Live with it."

"How do you know he banged his head?" I ask. "And how do you know someone didn't bang it for him?"

"And if the man went to sleep in his bed and died there, you'd figure it was murder because his pajamas were buttoned wrong." He doesn't say this like that would be a clue. Which, of course, I think it would. I remember a *Columbo* where the woman's panties were on backward and that was how he knew that she hadn't dressed herself.

"Let it go," he says, like he can see the wheels turning in my head.

"Okay, but what if," I hypothesize, "I'm on to something and that rock through Dana's window was a warning?"

He agrees it was a warning. "That your daughter is growing up and boys are interested in her."

I ask what makes him so sure.

"Been there, done that." He plays with a lock of my hair and I jerk my head away. "And there are times I'd like to throw a rock at her mother's window."

## CHAPTER 5

Service men (or women) can make or break your project. Always investigate their qualifications, check their references, and let reputation guide you. Remember that when they *finish* a job is more important than when they *start* it, and you'll have to live with the results for a long time.

—TipsFromTeddi.com

**"This** is a joke, right?"

My ex-husband, the bane of my existence, the pain in my butt, the rain on the parade of my life, the—well, you get the general idea—is standing with Steve when I get to L.I. Lanes in the morning.

Now, this morning has been bad enough already. Dana's window will cost me almost two hundred dollars to fix. I want to have the boy's parents pay for the repair, only Dana insists there is no boy. And no boy's parents. She's beyond adamant and she has no trouble looking me in the eye about it.

Jesse, who has probably never ratted on anyone, appears unwilling to start now and all I can get out of him is a shrug.

And I learned from Alyssa that Drew isn't *Daddy* and that Daddy should live with us.

Which brings me back to Daddy, otherwise known as Rio *the rat* Gallo, standing in my place of business, chatting up the owner.

"Hey Teddi," he says. "You see my new truck?" He points with his chin toward the bowling alley doors through which I've just come without noticing anything except that I have a message on my cell phone from Rita Kroll, that friend of my mother's who is moving up to Woodbury.

Or *down* to Woodbury, in my mother's eyes.

I bother looking—against my better instincts—and outside is a big white truck with the words Rio Grande Security written on the side. The O in Rio is a camera and a wire snakes its way through the words. It's actually a nice logo. Not that I'd tell him so if my life depended on it.

I put two and two—and two—together and hope I'm not getting the right sum. There's Rio's name on the truck, the truck is here at L.I. Lanes and I think Steve casually mentioned something to me the other day about putting in some security cameras.

Steve asks if Rio and I know each other. I pray that Rio doesn't answer "in the Biblical sense."

Do I have to tell you?

I didn't think so.

Before Steve gets ideas, I tell him that we were once married, a long, long time ago.

Rio corrects me and tells him we've only been divorced a couple of years.

"Rio's putting in a system for me," Steve says.

I bite my tongue so that "well then, I'm out of here," can't slip out. "Great," I say instead, drawing out the word like I'm drowning.

"It'll be like old times," Rio says, throwing an arm around me and hugging me against his side. "Remember when we did Lys's room? You doing all the painting and me wiring up her lights?"

"How could I forget?" I say with a weak smile. I doubt the fire department has forgotten either. And in the damp weather you can still faintly smell the smoke in her room.

He's still hugging me against him when the phone on the counter rings and Steve turns to answer it.

"Please don't blow this for me," Rio whispers. "I gotta pay Carmine back for the truck and I've got—"

Carmine? He borrowed money from my mother's old boyfriend to start his business? The old boyfriend who is so blatantly mafioso that he could give James Gandolfini lessons?

"Problem?" Steve asks, hanging up the phone.

I consider my options. I can either tell Steve how inept Rio is, how, when he tried to get naked pictures of me to sell to a girly magazine, billing me as Long Island's Most Dangerous Decorator after poor Elise Meyers, my first client, got murdered, he didn't know the camera had to be attached to anything. I could tell him that Rio and wires in the same vicinity can only lead to disaster, thereby lousing up his new business and any chance I might have to be free of his constant requests for financial assistance so that he can fulfill the ridiculous promises he makes to our children. And in the process come off like a bitchy, vindictive ex-wife—not unlike the one Steve is always complaining about.

Not so good. And that's not even considering what my mother's old boyfriend, Carmine De'Guisseppe, would have his goons do to Rio if he couldn't make his payments.

Since I really don't want to see my children's father castrated...

Oh, wait.

Let me think.

No. Despite some sort of poetic justice for his misdeeds, I can see clearly that my only viable option is to oversee his job myself and simply check on his work after hours when no one else is around. Maybe with a little help from Drew, even. He knows surveillance inside and out, so to speak. And the idea of testing it with ourselves—in a pool hall, no less—just might appeal to him, too.

I GET MARK SET doing the steel squares, which I've tested to my satisfaction, and then attempt to convince Bobbie to spend a couple of hours helping me win Rita Kroll as a client before my appointment with the pool-table salesman.

Rita no doubt remembers me as the dumpy little girl around the corner who had no sense of style. The girl who wore black for six years running and even went goth before it had its moment in the sun.

Which is why it's so important that Bobbie come with me. She exudes a certain air of confidence which, to be honest, I lack. It's not that I don't know I'm talented, professional and competent. It's just that, from her perfectly-styled-and-colored hair (red with gold highlights this week) to her freshly-pedicured toes (with French tips, of course), Bobbie's whole persona seems to shout that she knows what she's doing. And if you have any desire to appear the same way, she's who you'd hire.

Not that Bobbie knows a thing about decorating or anything beyond the right person to hire to acquire "the look."

I'm the one with the degree.

Bobbie's the one with panache.

We're a good team.

While it takes me a good half hour and the promise that we can stop at DSW (Designer Shoe Warehouse) to look for Jimmy Choos—which I can guarantee won't be there—on the way back, she does agree to go with me. At which point I remember that there is a message from Rita waiting for me on my cell phone.

Punching up the message, I listen to a tearful voice canceling our appointment. Great. I really can't afford to lose clients, especially ones I don't even have yet. Even if they are referrals from my mother and sure to be disasters.

I reach Rita to tell her that I've gotten her message. Okay, I admit that I thought about pretending I didn't receive it and just showing up because it would be really hard for her to send me from her doorstep. But I don't.

"It's a bad time, Teddi dear," she tells me.

I offer to rearrange my schedule and see her later in the week, if that would help.

It won't. "It's not that I'm avoiding you," she says. "You know I'd do anything for your mother. It's just…" She sniffs and I hear her blowing her nose before she continues. "I lost my brother last week. We just finished sitting shivah the day before yesterday. I really can't think about decorating now."

I make all the requisite noises, tell her I'm so sorry for her loss, that of course I understand, that whenever she's ready to reschedule, just let me know.

"Call me next week," she says, taking me by surprise. My mother must have really put the screws to her.

As for me, I'm relieved to have the extra time to put in at the alley without losing a potential customer.

And no, that does not mean I'm glad the woman's brother died, for heaven's sake. She's a sweet old lady. Her brother was probably a hundred and two.

"Good," Bobbie says when I tell her. "Then I'm off to get gorgeous shoes while the sale is still on."

Mark clucks as Bobbie leaves. He's up on a ladder and he asks me to hand him a few squares.

"A man is dead," I say as I hold up the pieces of steel and he leans down to take them. "Doesn't anybody care?"

"I don't know, Teddi. Maybe they're used to it. With you, there's usually a body, beautiful."

His eyes stray down my cleavage and because I'm reaching up and my hands are full there isn't much I can do about it.

"Or maybe I should say, 'With you, there's usually a beautiful body.'"

Before I can tell him that teasing an old lady isn't nice,

someone sidles up from behind and reaches around me. "Want me to help you hold those?" a deep voice asks and I realize it's Rio.

Ordinarily, Mark would think the remark was funny…it's the kind he'd make. But he dislikes my ex-husband almost as much as I do, and almost as much as he dislikes Drew.

I take a hard step back, right on Rio's instep, and get him in the ribs with my elbow, apologizing profusely as I do, claiming I didn't realize he was there.

"Do give these to Mark," I say, trying to hand him the steel sheets, but he's busy looking for a chair or maybe a sympathetic witness.

THIS AFTERNOON, my little one, Alyssa, is going home with Jill Roseman. My big ones are meeting me at L.I. Lanes. Dana will be thrilled to see her dad. Jesse will be morose.

They will both be watching for signs that I might be softening toward their father—Dana hoping, Jesse dreading.

Before I head for the alley, I stop by Bobbie's to pick up some carpet samples I left there. Under the pretext of not knowing where she's put them, she drags me up to her bedroom, where she's got several outfits laid out on her bed.

"Try this," she says, holding her shortest skirt up in front of my jeans. "It's stretch and it'll go perfectly with my little strippy strappy Manolos."

Looking down, I notice that—ta da—I'm already dressed. And I point this out to Bobbie, who looks me over and simply says, "Not."

"Try the skirt," she insists.

I remind her that I am going to work, and not as a streetwalker.

"Part of your work is *attitude*," she tells me. I swear she and my mother have read and reread the same chapter of that *Secret Handbook of Long Island Rules* a hundred times. "And to exude attitude you've got to feel it—feel in charge. More than in charge. You've got to feel and project superiority. In this skirt and a pair of stilettos, you're too good for the likes of your ex-husband and for decorating bowling alleys and for everything—except me, of course."

She isn't kidding.

"Try it on. See if it doesn't make you feel like an authority."

"On what?" I ask, slipping out of my jeans and holding the skirt up in front of my ratty underwear—which I really ought to replace if Drew Scoones is back in my life.

I can barely make myself put the skirt on, but I know that Bobbie won't let me refuse it until I do. Meanwhile she roots around in the closet, no doubt looking for shoes I could break an ankle in.

"Perfect!" she shouts when she reemerges from the closet and takes a look at me. I look in the mirror, trying to see what she sees, while she straightens my shoulders before taking a step back. "What do you think?"

I stare at the woman in the mirror. "I think I'd never again be able to tell Dana any of her clothes were out of the question."

"Maybe, but Rio will eat his two-timing, scum-sucking heart out. Here, you need these, too," she says, throwing a pair of fishnet pantyhose at me. I don't make any effort to catch them. "Don't you want—"

No, I don't. It's been a long time since I cared what Rio Gallo thought about me. And while Bobbie fusses around, picking up piles of discarded clothes, I tell her as much. I have a job, I have kids, I have more important things to worry about.

"My, my," Bobbie says, tsking when she looks at her watch. "Don't you have to meet some salesman over at the Lanes? Where does the time go?"

I look at my watch. It's a half hour later than the clock on her nightstand—the one I've been carefully watching—reads.

"I wonder where your jeans are," she says. I look down and the carpet is completely devoid of any clothing—including mine. "I know they were here earlier."

I tell her that this isn't funny, that I'm late and that I can't go to the alley looking like I want to have a tryst in one.

She offers to loan me a pair of her jeans, knowing that I couldn't get them up higher than my knees, and I order her into her closet to get mine.

Instead, she comes out with high boots and a white shirt to wear with the little skirt.

"Couldn't find them," she says.

I look in the mirror. *Another job well done by Bobbie Lyons,* I think to myself. *Not.*

SO THIS IS HOW I come to be standing in L.I. Lanes in very high-heeled boots, a very short skirt, a blouse with very few buttons and a pair of very red cheeks.

"Wow," Steve, standing behind the counter counting cash, says, and adds a whistle. Mark leans over on his ladder to see what has Rio's tongue hanging out and nearly topples over.

"Is the pool-table salesman here yet?" I ask, feigning that superior attitude the skirt was supposed to give me.

"Back here," Mark says, only his voice breaks and it sounds like he's croaking. "With your kids," he adds, like it's a warning.

I walk carefully, because if I don't, I'll wind up showing even more leg, not to mention my underwear, when I fall flat on my face.

The pool-table salesman is facing me, leaning over the table, intent on his shot. His fingers make a bridge through which the cue goes back and forth, back and forth.

"Oh, God!" Dana, just coming in from the back door of the alley, says when she sees me. She looks quickly around the joint. Her eyes are wide, her jaw drops and out comes a very plaintive "Mo-om! What if my friends or someone who knows me, saw you in that?"

Which causes Jesse to look up and gasp, which makes the pool-table salesman glance away from his shot and wind up seeing me. That causes him to nearly rip the table with the cue, sending the cue ball over the rail, which hits me in the chest and nearly knocks me over.

All in the house that Jack built.

Mark hurries down his ladder, Rio comes running, no doubt to massage my wound, and the pool-table salesman rushes toward me telling me he can't say he's sorry enough.

Only, with everyone coming at me so fast, I lose my balance on Bobbie's idiotic shoes and stumble backward.

Steve, reaching out to catch me before I go down, winds up providing a soft landing as the two of us slip down the two steps and slide past a bunch of kids trying to figure out how to score a second spare in the settee area. We don't stop until we're halfway down the alley where, with Bobbie's skirt around my waist, the heel of her left boot wedges in the gutter.

Dana dies on the spot. I wish I could, but everyone is making a fuss over me so I can't just cry and run out of the bowling alley the way she does.

Jesse is staring and trying not to stare at the same time.

Rio's holding up his new camera phone and I just know he's snapping pictures.

And Mark is laughing his head off as he heads toward me, taking off his overshirt as he comes.

"You might wanna..." he says as he drops it in my lap.

"Wanna what?" I ask him. "Die?"

He helps me up, despite Steve's offer to let me stay where I am as long as I'd like.

The pool-table salesman slicks back his hair and smiles at me. His eyes go up and down any parts of my body he hasn't gotten a good enough look at. I can't imagine what parts those could be.

"Don Pardol," he says, offering me his hand.

Ignoring his outstretched hand I scoot past him to the ladies' room, cursing Bobbie Lyons and her stupid shoes the entire way.

In the restroom, another area that needs redoing before the grand opening, I tug at my belt until it's a skirt again, put Mark's shirt on, grateful it comes down to my knees, and take a look at myself in the mirror.

I am a wreck, but things could be worse.

Oh, wait. They are.

Someone sticks her head into the ladies' room. "Are you Teddi Bayer?"

I try pleading the fifth.

She tells me there's a policeman outside who wants to talk to me.

Have you ever heard God laughing? I mean, yeah, it's possible what I'm hearing is just thunder, but under the circumstances...

Drew is leaning up against a pole when I emerge. His hair is slightly wet, the shoulders on his jacket are sprinkled with rain. He looks like a commercial for a Jeep or Irish Spring.

He pushes himself off the post and tells me he caught Dana walking in the rain and gave her a lift home. Okay, it's more like "that kid doesn't have the sense to come in outta the rain. And stubborn? Had to nearly drag her ass into the car. Don't know where she gets *that* from."

And all the while he's talking, he's taking in my outfit.

"I can't imagine what you did to piss her off," he says and he's measuring the height of my heels with his eyes while he talks. "Noticed your ex is here, too," he adds.

"Everyone's here but my mother and the press," I tell him. And the way my luck is going, one or the other will be next.

Unlike the usually cocky Drew, he almost seems self-conscious, standing there—like he's trying to be casual, but knows he isn't pulling it off. "So, you want to maybe grab something to eat when you're done here?" he asks me.

Actually, he asks my legs.

I tell him what I really need is for him to help me check over Rio's work after hours. He tells my legs that sounds okay and then his cell rings.

"Gotta run," he says, and he tilts his head slightly at the hem of my skirt. "She's probably just jealous," he says over his shoulder as he leaves.

That was a compliment, I think. I'm not flattered and the last thing I want is for my thirteen year-old to feel in competition with me.

But at least I know she's home and safe, even if she is pissed.

Not something I can worry about now, I figure, so I go back to the billiards area, where Don is anxious to show me how to play pool.

"Your son's got a natural aptitude," he tells me, being careful to keep his eyes averted when he thinks I'm looking. Rio, who is supposed to be working on the wiring for the security system, puffs out his chest, as though hanging around in a pool hall and being a pool shark is the avocation he had in mind for our son.

It might be.

"Dad's getting me my own stick," Jesse says as he sinks three balls in a row. Gently, Don corrects him and calls it a cue. I call it a bribe and can see the writing on the wall— Rio earning some money means that he'll be buying the kids' favors before his paycheck even makes it into his pocket.

While Jesse impresses his father and a bunch of boys who have gathered around to watch, I explain to Don that I need the new tables, four of them, in two weeks. He promises that he can deliver.

Two of the boys whistle as Jesse hits the white ball into the red one, causing it to hit the yellow one into the pocket.

"Combination shot," Don says. "Boy's good. How long has he been playing?"

Jesse looks at his watch.

"No," Don says. "Really."

Jesse looks guiltily at me. "Dad and I have played a few times," he says.

This, of course, is news to me. All I've heard is how much he hates his father.

"How much would a pool table for the house cost?" I ask Don. If Jesse is going to play pool, I figure it's better if I know where and with whom. Jesse's eyes light up like it's Christmas and immediately I regret asking in front of him.

Don tells me that I can get "junk" for under a thousand, or a good one for a little over that.

"Just sold a gorgeous antique one for seventeen big ones," he tells me. "But the guy froze to death before the deal was done. How's that for rotten luck? Almost sixty degrees out and a guy freezes to death."

"Seventeen thousand?" Rio asks, and his voice cracks. He's standing on a ladder with a bunch of wires in his hands and I'm hoping he knows what to do with half of them. "You can get that much for a pool table?"

"Nope," Don says, "for a *billiards* table."

"What's the difference?" Jesse asks him.

"About ten grand," Don says with a laugh.

"The man who froze to death," I say, wondering out loud. "His name didn't happen to be Joey, did it?"

Don looks at me and nods. "It sure did."

## CHAPTER 6

It only takes one piece to upgrade the look of an entire room if that piece is the focal point. Rather than evenly allotting a strained budget, concentrate the bulk of your spending on the area that is going to have the greatest impact—a fabulous rug, a fireplace mantel, an impressive painting. Make sure, though, that you love it, since it's what your eye will be drawn to.

—TipsFromTeddi.com

**"You** tell me how a deli-counter man could buy a pool table for seventeen thousand dollars," I ask Drew when I finally reach him by phone after I've gone home to change.

"You tell me how you wiggled into that skirt," he says. "There are still some mysteries left in the universe, I guess."

Does the word *irritating* mean anything to you? I hold a biscuit up for Maggie and tell her she's got to promise to bite Drew the next time she sees him if she wants her treat.

I swear she nods, but she's a slut for biscuits and I've found that sometimes she'll lie.

"All I'm saying," I tell Drew, "is that you need to check

into what else Joey Ingraham was buying and where the money was coming from."

"And all *I'm* saying," he parrots back, "is that even if this case wasn't closed, it wasn't my case to begin with. I can't just go investigate some other cop's case."

When I ask why not, he tells me it would imply that the cop wasn't doing his job.

"Exactly my point," I say and I hear him sigh.

"Let it go, Teddi," he says. "Even if I was interested, which I'm not, and even if it was my case, which it isn't, it'd be strictly back burner. The whole department has its nuts in the wringer right now."

In the background, I can hear his name being called in that staccato way that means business.

"Can't talk now," he tells me. "And tonight's off. Sorry, kiddo."

"Drew?" I say before he hangs up. "What's going on?"

"Turn on the news," he says. And then he's gone.

As soon as I hang up the phone, it rings. When I answer it, the caller hangs up.

"Overactive imagination," I mumble to myself, refusing to let my mind go where it naturally wants to.

"Dana," I yell upstairs. "You get any breaking news on that computer of yours?"

She's still not talking to me, like I purposely embarrassed her. I didn't think she'd answer, but I don't mind talking to the wall. It's just one more part of being a parent, I think.

"Jess?"

"No," he says sharply. He can't believe I told his father

not to buy him a pool table. I know how Rio's mind works and seeing how good Jesse shot today, he's figuring Jesse could earn back the cost of a table in no time.

Lys wanders into the kitchen looking for a cookie and a hug. Bobbie knocks on the back door and lets herself in.

"Isn't it terrible about that dead woman doctor?" she asks, helping herself to a couple of Oreos as long as I have them out. Bobbie is the only person I know who is never hungry unless she sees food. She could go all day without eating, never even think of it, until she sees one potato chip.

Then look out.

I send Lys into the TV room so that she doesn't hear whatever it is that's terrible and ask Bobbie to fill me in.

We go up to my room and turn on the TV while she talks.

"They didn't know anything half an hour ago except that she was a surgeon and someone knocked a hole in her scull with a hammer or something," she tells me. "Only then I had to find a file for Mike and have another heart-to-heart with the skinnier daughter."

"It would be nice if Mike's secretary could find a few of the files she files," I say.

Bobbie shrugs because she likes being indispensable. I think that's why she convinced Mike to hire Marguerite in the first place. That and the fact that the woman is at least a hundred and seven and looks like an escapee from Munchkinland. Not that Bobbie doesn't trust Mike implicitly, but after his affair a few years ago with the hypnotherapist he claimed he knew in another life, she just feels she can't be too careful.

"Something new with Kristen?" I ask as we settle on my bed and the TV comes to life.

"She just wants to stop therapy. She claims she's cured and doesn't have any more eating issues. I'll believe it when the scale tells me so."

I ask what the therapist thinks. I know she's making progress because they haven't mentioned hospitalizing her for her anorexia in months.

"Like being thirteen isn't hard enough," Bobbie says.

"Tell me about it," I agree, and my heart melts a little for Dana. I know what it's like to have a mother who makes you crazy.

"That's her," Bobbie says, pointing toward the blond woman whose picture fills the TV screen. "Vascular surgeon."

"Really? She looks too young to be a vascular surgeon," I say.

"Don't you watch *Grey's Anatomy*? They're all young and gorgeous."

"Dreamy," I say.

"McDreamy," she corrects.

We turn our attention back to the screen. According to the reporter, Dr. Doris Peterson, who worked at Plainview Hospital, was found in the far end of the parking lot of her office building on Jericho Turnpike this morning at seven forty-five by a fellow doctor who was on his way in.

"Who names their daughter Doris these days?" Bobbie asks.

"There must be twenty cops there," I say, pointing at the screen as they go to a long shot of the parking lot. "Look at that!"

"So?" Bobbie asks me.

"So did you see that many cops in King Kullen? It's just like when that girl vanished in Aruba. You tell me how much news that would have made if she'd been some old guy instead of some young, pretty blonde."

"You're jealous," Bobbie says. "Your boy toy is investigating this pretty blond lady's murder instead of your old guy's."

"It's not jealousy," I insist. "It's a sense of justice. It doesn't bother you that poor Joey is on a slab at the morgue while—"

"His funeral was over a week ago, Ted. He's not on some slab."

"He had a funeral?" I ask. "How come I didn't know that?"

WHEN THE PHONE RINGS at 11:30 p.m., I'm livid. *Private caller* has called and hung up three times tonight and my patience is now nonexistent. It's enough to make me want to cave and get Dana a cell phone of her own.

I pick up the phone and don't say anything.

"Teddi?"

"Drew?"

"Who were you expecting at this time of night?" he asks. He almost sounds jealous.

"How's the case coming?" I ask instead of going into the whole thing.

"It's not," he says. "Dead ends all over the place. Everybody's got alibis. We're checking out patients she lost for grudges."

"Did you check into Joey Ingraham's spending, because—"

"Don't start," he tells me. "I'm tired and I've got to get up in four hours and start in at square one again."

"On the blonde," I say.

"On the doctor with a hole in her skull. Yeah."

"And Joey?" I ask. "Are you planning to just sweep his death under the rug in favor of some dead blonde you're more interested in?"

Drew tells me that no one is sweeping anything under any rug. The man had a heart attack and died. Happens every day. Maybe not in a cooler, but a man's got to die somewhere and that doesn't make it murder.

I say something juvenile, like that all he cares about is this dead blond woman.

Which turns out to be quite a mistake when he assures me that I've got it wrong. "I'm interested in live blondes, too, Teddi. Plenty of them."

And I'm twirling my dark brown hair nervously when I hear him hang up.

He doesn't even bother to say good night.

IT'S NOT THAT I consider myself an unlucky woman—despite having the mother from hell who I can't even be mad at, the ex-husband from hell who I can't get rid of, the mortgage from hell because we borrowed against it, etc. Still, it does take me by surprise when things go right.

Which is why, when I woke up this morning and looked out my window to see Bobbie's sister Diane's car in her driveway, I almost couldn't believe my eyes. Diane's only been a cop a couple of years, and if there's one thing she loves more than the *Police Academy* movies (all of them) it's showing off the newest way she's learned to find things out about people.

Ever since she helped me prove that Rio was trying to drive me crazy before I divorced him, thanks to her honed-by-the-department skills, she's been regaling Bobbie and me with tales of her emerging detective skills. Anyway, she's at her sister's now. I hurry to get dressed in something Bobbie won't make me change out of and run across our backyards to Bobbie's kitchen door.

"Love it!" Bobbie says of my layers, the lace from the camisole sticking out under the U-necked cotton T-shirt like the mannequin in Express was wearing it. She pulls me into her kitchen and before I can even say hello to Diane I've got a cup of coffee in my hand and a muffin on a plate in front of me.

"Some people don't like their wardrobes critiqued," Diane tells Bobbie as she rolls her eyes at me. "You do look good," she adds.

"She's got a glow," Bobbie says, eyeing my face critically. "A sort of…oh, shit. You're investigating that murder, aren't you?"

"The doctor?" Diane asks, coming down off the kitchen stool to brush the crumbs from her uniform. "You know something about that?"

When I tell her it's Joey Ingraham I have on my mind, she quickly loses interest.

"Why does nobody care about this case?" I ask. It comes out a little whiny, which doesn't escape unnoticed.

"Because, Teddi," Bobbie says in the tone you use to

address a small, unreasonable child, "there *isn't* any case. Drew told you, his partner told you. The man just died. Heart attack. End of story. Why don't you investigate the doctor's murder? That's much juicier."

Diane suggests a cogent reason. "Uh…because she's not a police officer? Jeesh!"

I tell them about the seventeen-thousand dollar pool table. Bobbie says we should try to sell it to our next client, since the commission would be huge.

"So you don't know anything about the doctor, then?" Diane asks, clearly disappointed. "What about Detective Scoones? Does he?" Cracking a high-profile case like this would be good for her career and we all know it. And looking into Joey Ingraham's finances would be just the opposite.

If anyone found out.

"You couldn't find out what else Joey was planning to buy without leaving even one little track, could you?" I ask her, knowing how Diane loves a challenge. "And maybe even a teammate or two?"

"Of course I can," she says.

Bobbie pours us each another cup of coffee. "Nobody's fooling anybody here, right?" she asks.

Diane grabs a notepad from Bobbie's counter and pulls a pen from her breast pocket. "No promises," she tells me, and I nod.

And then I tell her everything I know so far.

A COUPLE OF DAYS LATER I find out who the rest of The Spare Slices are by simply opening up the League Register that Steve keeps behind the counter and finding the application they had to submit to the alley to join the league. I carefully write down the names, addresses and telephone numbers for Milt Sherman, Max Koppel, Dave Blumstein, Miles Weissman and Russ Oberman. I figure while Diane's doing her snooping, I can do some of my own. My first job is to be sure that all the men go in on the lottery tickets and Dave seems like the easiest mark to pry information from, so I give his home number a ring.

"Who is this?" a woman wants to know.

"I'm calling from L.I. Lanes," I say. Absolutely true. Here I stand at the counter of the bowling alley. "I'm just checking some information on his league application." I am so much better with the truth than I am with fibbing. I mean, you can always tell I'm fibbing because I babble.

She tells me he's at work.

"Is this his wife?" I ask.

"This isn't about the bowling, is it?" she asks me. "You're trying to find out if he's married. You girls are all alike. Desperate. You see a man who has a few bucks in his pocket and you—"

"This is his mother, isn't it?" I say, though I really don't have to ask. Teamed up with my mother, these two could be Starsky and Hutch, Nick and Nora, McMillan and wife. Aren't there any famous female pairs of detectives? Even on Google? "I just want to ask him a couple of questions."

"Well, you've got his name, you've got his phone number. What more could you need to know for a damn bowling league? He wears a ten and a half."

"Excuse me?" I say.

"His bowling shoes," she tells me. I realize I'm not going to get anything out of this gatekeeper.

"Thank you," I tell her. "That's what I needed to know. We're ordering some new shoes and we want to be sure that we order enough of the popular sizes, but to tell you the truth, I'm new here and I don't know much about men's bowling shoes, so—"

"Recently divorced?" she asks me.

I don't answer her at first. Then I ask how she could possibly know that.

"New job. What grown woman takes a job in a bowling alley at your stage in life, honey, except one who's been home taking care of kids and suddenly is forced back out into the workforce. Been there, done that, as the kids say."

I sigh heavily for effect. I feel a bit of luck coming my way.

"My Davey's a rare one," she says.

"I've seen him around," I admit. "He looks nice. I mean, like a nice guy."

By the time I'm done, I've wangled an invitation to dinner tomorrow night.

Score one for the designing dick.

## CHAPTER 7

When shopping for accessories, think outside the box.
You don't have to go to a home goods shop to find
something good for your home. Rope tie-backs from
the hardware store add to a nautical theme. Garden
shops can bring the outdoors into a country theme.
Office supply places are full of ultra modern for every
room in the house. And even the supermarket has accessories to use throughout the house—how about
putting your bubble bath into a fancy olive oil de-
canter with a spout?

—TipsFromTeddi.com

**It** takes some deep breathing to get myself to walk back into
King Kullen again. I know what they say about the murderer
always returning to the scene of the crime, but it's different
for witnesses.

Not that I am one. Technically, I mean. Can you be a
witness-after-the-fact like you can be an accessory-after-
the-fact? Somehow I think I'd make a lousy accessory. None
of my shoes match Dana's old purse.

Anyway, I've gone back to murder scenes before. There

was that trip back to Elise Meyer's house after I found her murdered. That was great—I found her newly widowed husband in bed with his sister-in-law and wound up stealing the dog.

So maybe their motives are different, but it seems to me that when something awful happens you can't help but be drawn back to the place it happened so that you can make sense of it.

My point is, I'm not in King Kullen for another brisket.

I feel incredibly conspicuous. Maybe those two cashiers aren't whispering about me and how bossy I was when they wanted to see Joey's body in the cooler and I wouldn't let them. Maybe they are just trying to decide if the coupon one of them is holding is still good.

But I don't think so.

And it's not like I'm the millionth customer and the manager is rushing my way to give me a shopping cart's worth of free groceries.

I mean, I don't think so.

I have the feeling I should have come incognito. Maybe if I were wearing Bobbie's hooker outfit again no one would even bother looking at my face.

"Have you heard anything?" Bill-the-manager asks me.

I explain that I'm not with the police, that I just came for a pound of ground beef and then it occurs to me that maybe he's heard something I haven't.

"I thought—" he says, looking confused.

Finding dead people makes you a liar. At least it makes me one and I put my finger to my lips like the fact that I'm investigating the crime is supposed to be a secret. Hey, it's a secret from the police, isn't it?

He nods at me. Now it's *our* secret. He takes me by the arm, announcing loudly that they are out of stock on that item, but he thinks he has something else I'd like.

In an empty aisle he asks "Is there anything you can tell me?" in a whisper.

I explain—patiently, of course—that it really doesn't work that way. I'm here to *be told*, not *to tell*. "Have you noticed any odd behavior on the part of the other employees?" I ask. Hey, years of *Law & Order* haven't been wasted on me.

Bill-the-manager suggests I talk with Fran. He thinks, though he isn't sure, that she and Joey might have had "something going," he says with a wink. "Strictly against store policy," he adds.

This is because he's afraid they'll sneak off into the stockroom and…? *Or sneak into the cooler.* I think to myself.

"Yes," I say. "Fran might be a good place to start." And besides, now that I think about it, I actually could use a pound of lean ground beef.

Fran is behind the counter at the butcher department. She's wearing a slightly bloody white apron, a hairnet and a worried expression. She perks up when she sees me.

"Have you found Joey's killer?" she asks me.

Now, I could tell her that I'm not the police. I could tell her that the police wouldn't be less interested if Joey had been a homeless man living under a bridge in another county. Or I could tell her the truth. My version of the truth.

"I'm working on it."

She seems to take heart at the news.

"Hasn't anyone else been in to take your statement?" I ask, and her look says I must be kidding.

"Not since the day it happened," she says. "When you were here."

I'm really not a great liar, but as you can see, I'm a whiz at slightly bending the truth. So I put it to her this way: "What do you want the police to know?"

She tells me that she and Joey weren't exactly a couple or anything, though he'd parked his boots under her bed once or twice, if I knew what she meant. Thanks to country music, I do.

"And we talked, Joey and me," she says. "About what we wanted out of life, you know?"

My nod encourages her.

"Joey, he had all these dreams...." She stops and wipes at her eye with her apron—the dirty, bloody apron. And I try not to cringe.

"So he wanted expensive things?"

She asks me who doesn't. She's got a point.

The pool table comes to mind and I ask her about it.

"He bought it?" she asks. "Really? I mean, he was always talking about stuff like that. And he had a whole list of the things he was gonna get when he won the lottery—"

"He planned on winning the lottery?"

Again, she asks me who doesn't. "Ya gotta dream, don'tcha? I mean, is this all there is?" she waves her hands over the piles of raw meat. "'Cause if it is, you can just lock me in the cooler, too."

I don't have a good comeback for that. But it does raise a question. "Technically, you can't get locked in the cooler, can you?" I ask.

"Nah," she says. "'Course, with the light out in there, and not knowing your way around…"

The fact that Joey would be unfamiliar with the setup and safety features of the cooler hadn't occurred to me. I wonder if it has to the police.

"Funny thing is," she says, and I know I'm not going to find this funny, "the light wasn't out. Damn bulb was just loose. Imagine that."

I'm imagining. Of course, with my imagination, I'm imagining that someone purposely loosened it.

"All the opening and slamming of the door, it sometimes happens," she says.

"Do you think that Joey knew he couldn't get locked in?" I ask.

Fran considers my question for a minute. She gestures for me to follow her and heads for the deli counter. "Nancy," she says to the woman slicing cheese, "you ever go in my meat locker?"

Nancy shudders. "No way," she says. "You think I want to get locked in there like Joey?"

Fran puts up her hands and gives me a there-you-have-it look.

I thank her and stop by the case to pick up my ground beef. On the way out of the store I notice the stacks of newspapers, *Newsday*, *Daily News*, *New York Post*.

On each is a picture of Dr. Doris and various headlines that all mirror the one on the *Post*: Police Baffled.

And all I can think is on this one, at least they're trying.

I CALL MY DAD to ask if he might drop by this evening to check on the kids. With Dana too old for a sitter and Alyssa too young to be without one but too used to Dana to obey her, and on top of this the recent window incident, I'm just a little uncomfortable leaving them to their own devices. Unfortunately, I reach my mother, who wants to know who has invited me to dinner. Because I am a rotten daughter and a nasty person with a twisted sense of humor, I tell her the truth.

"And he lives at home?" she asks me. I hear her unwrapping the cellophane on a new pack of Newport Menthols. I've asked her a million times to give up smoking, the kids have begged her, quoting statistics and showing her pictures of blackened lungs. She claims cigarettes are her one vice.

Which means that badgering her daughter to death isn't considered a vice in her *Secret Handbook*.

I assure her he lives at home. Closing in on fifty, I'd guess, and still home with mama.

"Don't be so quick to judge. He sounds like a good son to me," she says, proving she's even more desperate for me to get married than I thought. "An angel to put up with a mother like that. Imagine giving someone the third degree on the phone. So what does he do for a living, this bowler of yours?"

I could tell her that he works in a deli or that he plays the lottery every week. Instead I go for the gusto. "He gambles."

"Like on TV? Texas hold'em? Or like at the tables in Vegas?"

"Like scratching off silver circles on cardboard cards," I tell her. I think of him behind a deli counter. "He's into numbers."

"The numbers racket?" she asks me. "Maybe Carmine knows him."

I GO LOOKING FOR my father and my mother shows up to watch the kids. Best laid plans and all that. And she's not alone. She's got Carmine De'Guisseppe in tow. Carmine's been very good to me, saving Dana's bat mitzvah from becoming a total disaster, and his men actually saved my life when a crazed restaurateur went after me. He hired me to refurbish his beach house and forgave me when I walked (or ran) away from the project for a few weeks to avoid Drew Scoones.

Uh, I mean, to clear my head.

Anyway, here are my mother and Carmine, I've got this date with Dave and his mother, and the kids and I all want to know where Grandpa is but we can't exactly ask with Carmine standing in the front hall, can we?

Well, Alyssa can, and she does. My mother claims she doesn't know and doesn't care. Carmine pats her hand and says he was just giving her a lift, a statement that I doubt could be true, since Mom seems to be floating above her orthopedic pumps with the high toe box I had to drive her into Manhattan to get.

"You don't know where Dad is?" I say. The last time one of my parents went missing it was my mother's faux kidnapping, which almost ended in both of them being lost at sea.

My mother shrugs off my question, but Carmine gives me a reassuring nod, a sort of all-is-well.

Yeah, but for whom?

"Go ahead, dear," my mother says, all but shoving me out the door.

"ABD?" I ask her as I fight with my coat sleeve and my sharp green pashmina scarf.

"Yes, darling," she says and she does this magical thing that makes the scarf fall exactly as it should. "Anyone but Drew."

"SO YOU WORK AT THE ALLEY," Dave's mother asks me. I've been sitting in her straight-out-of-the-discount-furniture-showroom living room for twenty minutes, hearing Dave puttering upstairs while his mother interrogates me. I will never, never do this to one of Dana's dates.

Should I ever let her date.

I tell Mrs. Blumstein that I'm actually an interior designer and that I'm working on the grand opening.

"Oh," she says, and I can hear the disapproval in her voice. Before I can defend my profession she looks at my legs—thankfully ensconced in navy blue wool pants, and says, "you're *that* woman."

And I think I might as well get up and leave now.

Only another thought strikes me. Just as my mother is trying to get me interested in someone else to prevent a match, so might Mrs. Blumstein.

"The other men Dave bowls with," I say somewhat vaguely. "They seem very nice."

She jumps on this like a misprint from Macy's omitting a zero or two from their sale price. "The salt of the earth," she says. Then she turns toward the stairs and yells up to Dave. "Come on and get down here, David. You got company."

Dave comes down the steps. He's wearing a white shirt with a brown stripe, a red tie and a brown crew neck sweater over both. They look new and like they came together as a set in one box; I think Mrs. Blumstein probably bought the outfit special for tonight. I feel terrible about what I'm doing here.

"Dave, hi," I say, jumping up like I'm here to take him to the prom. All I'm missing is his corsage. "How handsome you look."

Mama doesn't want me setting my cap for him, but she can't help but preen.

We sit and chat, drinking surprisingly nice Chablis and munching on Tam Tam crackers and gefilte fish. I talk about my work. He had no idea there were so many different white wall paints. He talks about his work. I had no idea there were so many different kinds of ham.

"And none of it kosher," Mrs. Blumstein adds.

Eventually, we mosey to the dining room, after I've been asked my opinion of the living room and I've told her that gray and brown is just about my favorite color combination. And I say it with a smile, too. "Restful," I offer, while deadly, deadly dull rattles around in my head trying to sneak out my lips if I'm not careful.

In the green and yellow dining room, where Mrs. B explains she wanted a livelier look, we take our seats and I finally get down to work, asking about the lottery tickets and whether all The Spare Slices went in on them.

I am assured by Mrs. B. that Davey doesn't waste his money on such things. Of course, I know better, but I'm thrilled that Dave will owe me one, somewhere down the line, because, as they say about the lottery, *hey, you never know.*

During the course of dinner I learn that with the *wink, wink,* exception of Dave, all The Slices have gone in on the tickets together for more than three years. That all of them have plans for what they'd buy if they won and that all the men are either single, divorced or widowed.

I can see I have my work cut out for me.

## CHAPTER 8

A great way to choose a color palette for your room is to pull the colors from a favorite painting, oriental screen, needlepoint pillow, etc. Pull out three colors—a dominant color, a secondary color and an accent color. The dominant color should be the easiest on the eye, the secondary color should complement it, set it off, make it seem special, and the accent color should pop out at you. Use the accent sparingly, as a...

—TipsFromTeddi.com

A couple of days later, I'm entering something new on TipsFromTeddi when the phone rings. Dana doesn't answer the house phone anymore, since Rio's gotten her a brand-new cell phone. I've made her agree to pay the monthly fees herself which apparently exempts her from answering the house phone. Half an hour after she got it, all her friends were trained to call her private line.

Jesse is out walking Maggie and Lys has been forbidden to answer since she told someone I was having trouble with my Tampax and I'd have to call them back.

Because I think it may be Diane with some news on The

Slices, I unwind myself and get up from the floor where I'm working out a furniture arrangement for a spec room. I check the caller ID before answering because I'm getting sick of *private caller* hanging up. *Gerald Kroll* appears on my screen.

"Yes, hello Teddi, dear," he says after I professionally answer the phone with "Teddi Bayer Interior Designs, Teddi Bayer speaking."

"You remember me? Mr. Kroll? I used to live around the corner from your mother and father. My wife, Rita, used to be so fond of you. Remember that? She talked to you about doing our place," he says.

I assure him I'm acquainted with the project and again express my sympathy for their loss.

"You're a sweet girl," he says, bringing me back twenty-five years to a Halloween where I'm standing on their porch wearing chains and studs and this dreadful dagger hanging from my ear and hearing him ask me why a sweet girl would want to look like that. He'd forgotten it was Halloween, I think. "So, dahlink, we're ready to go ahead now."

"So soon?" I say, not able to keep the surprise out of my voice. Maybe a little disapproval slips out, too, but a cough breaks the silence and I add some stuff about how throwing yourself into a project can be so therapeutic.

"Ritzala's a mess," Jerry says, using his pet name for her. "You shouldn't know from it. Her baby brother. But a good project is just what she needs, don't you think? You and I can get the ball rolling and soon enough she'll be rolling right along with us."

*Of course,* I say. *Not a problem,* I say. *Blah, blah, blah.*

But I'm not as happy as I pretend. For one thing, men are rarely up to the task. For a second, whatever he picks she's likely to hate. Now you could guess the reverse would be true as well, but, in general, men don't really care all that much about their surroundings. As long as the bottom line doesn't change, I come in under budget and I deliver on a plasma TV, they're usually satisfied.

I make an appointment and as soon as I'm off the phone, I dial up my mother to get the real skinny on old Gerald Kroll.

"A marshmallow," my mother says. "She wants it, he gives it to her."

"So then he's like Dad."

I don't know what makes me say that. Maybe, in the time of Carmine, I want to remind my mother that it's my father who loves her and wants her to be happy. Or maybe I just like poking the dragon with a sharp stick. I know it's going to breathe fire and I'll be the one to get scorched, but I can't seem to help myself.

There is silence on the other end of the line.

"Mom?"

"Your father and Jerry Kroll couldn't be more different," she finally says.

"Dad doesn't give you everything you want?"

"Of course he does," my mother says. I can hear the exasperation in her voice. "But it's because he loves me and wants me to be happy. He sees that as his job in life and he wants to do his job well. He takes pride in it."

I ask why Jerry gives Rita whatever she wants. Doesn't he love her?

"He gives her what she wants in the hope that she'll stop asking, that she'll finally be satisfied."

I shouldn't. I know I shouldn't. But I say, "And since Dad knows you'll never be satisfied…"

I hear her exhale her cigarette smoke. Slowly. We may not have television phones, but believe me, I can see her face and those lifted eyes are blazing.

She tells me maybe if her life had turned out differently, if she hadn't lost a child, if her oldest son didn't live thousands of miles away, if her husband didn't keep going AWOL. If her daughter…

"If your daughter *what?*" I ask, daring her to bring up my lousy marriage, my fledgling career, the fact that I haven't remarried. I'm ready.

"If my daughter loved me even a little, she wouldn't wound me this way."

She's good, isn't she? I say what I have to: "I love you Mom. I really do. Now tell me about Jerry and Rita Kroll."

She spends some time on how it is I could say I love her and still hurt her the way I do, and I have to twice remind her that I need to know about the Krolls.

"Don't get me wrong," she says. "I like them. I mean, poor Rita is one of my best friends, after all. But she's a little…I don't know…delicate? Jerry's got to do everything for her. Run her errands, do the grocery shopping, pick up her pills. She'd give him her head to take to the salon if she could.

"If she'd had to live through what I've lived through, she wouldn't just visit South Winds occasionally, if you know what I mean."

I wonder what constitutes *occasionally*. Once a year? Twice? Must be more than that, since there have been years that my mother divided her time pretty equally between South Winds and our house in Cedarhurst. "She does have Robert," I say. "That's got to be a cross to bear."

"Is *he* dead?" my mother demands, playing my brother like a trump card.

"You didn't get to see Markie grown up," I say. "And Rita will never see Robert grow up, will she? Not really. He's always going to be…what did they say? Eight? Nine?"

My mother assures me that it's not the same. I suppose not, but you'd think there'd be some sympathy for a fellow traveler on the misery train.

"That Jerry. You know he's an accountant, right? You remember he used to do our taxes. He did everyone's in the neighborhood. He probably moved poor Rita up to Woodbury to get some new clients. I can't imagine why else he would have moved them there. I mean, really, what's Woodbury got that we don't have better on the South Shore?"

Well, it doesn't have my mother, for one thing. But whether that's a plus or a minus depends on who's filling in the columns.

Of course, I don't say that aloud. I don't remind her that Woodbury is snug up against Syosset and the two share a fabulous school system, nice shops, good roads…and that while the kids from Woodbury expect BMWs and Jeeps when they get their licenses whereas the kids from Syosset expect Toyotas, in my eyes we're all lucky to be here and I could have done—could be doing—a whole lot worse, because I don't want to hear her tell me how being in walking distance of Woodbury doesn't qualify me for anything except an inferiority complex.

Instead I ask about the Kroll's taste, which my mother describes as strictly Fortunoff. For those of you who don't live on Long Island, Fortunoff is a store known for its fabulous jewelry department, but it also carries bedding, some furniture and lots of gold-tone accessories for the bath. What my mother means is that Rita's house has ornate chandeliers and custom plastic slipcovers over the couches—implying you aren't the company worth taking them off for.

"You'll like working with them, Teddi dear," my mother says. "They like cheap things."

"I do love you, Mom," I repeat like a mantra. "I do."

"Of course you do," my mother says. "What's not to love?"

BACK AT THE ALLEY, where things are moving along faster than I'd hoped and I've praised Mark until he's put up his hands to stop me, I'm happy to see The Slices there for league night.

The only problem is that I honestly think Dave told his buddies that I put out. I mean, what else would explain their sudden interest in me? Mark thinks it's hilarious and keeps sending me across the alley for one thing or another—just to watch their heads follow me as though they were watching a tennis match.

One pushes the other toward me until, after five or six

trips, Milt collides with me and goes all red in the face. "I was wondering," he says after he apologizes, "if you might consider having a drink with me sometime. I mean like coffee or something."

"Sure," I say. "That would be nice." I wonder if it's this easy for Drew. And then I think about how good-looking he is and his easy manner, and I think that if the suspect is a woman, then yeah, it's this easy.

Hell, I was this easy.

"I just bought a new boat," Milt says, and man does that make my ears perk up. "Maybe you'd like to see it."

"Would I!" I say, since there's no reason to hide my enthusiasm. "When?"

We make a date for Saturday and I go back to the billiards area like I've won a Grammy, which is only slightly less self-satisfied than Milt, who seems to think he's Stud of the Year.

Back at the billiards section, Rio shows Mark and me how his security system works.

"And see," he says. "Motion activated. Anybody walks by and—"

We all stare at the blank screen.

Okay, back at the billiards section, Rio shows Mark and me how his security system *doesn't* work.

"Must be a loose wire," he says, looking at me like I went around last night undoing the work he did.

Had I thought of it, it would have been tempting. Of course, had the idea of bollixing up his job occurred to me, the next thing that would have occurred to me is that Rio would somehow do that on his own.

And voila!

"Maybe the batteries are dead," he says, slapping at the remote that controls the playback.

I put out my hand for the remote and he turns it over to me. Noticing how light it is, I flip open the battery case and, of course, there are no batteries in it.

"How was I supposed to know it didn't come with 'em," he asks me, carefully avoiding any eye contact with Mark.

"Aren't you supposed to be the expert?" I ask, handing back the remote and shaking my head sadly. "And shouldn't this system be digital? I mean, isn't that what they're using these days?"

Rio gives me *the stare*. "Some people are using them," he says, "but I prefer the VCR style. They're much more reliable."

"They fall off someone's truck?" I ask. I'm wondering how in the world he got Steve to go for a system that's been outmoded for several years before I remember that Rio was the best salesman my father ever had.

"Computer systems crash all the time," he tells me. "Tapes are reliable. Been around long enough to prove themselves. They're what you call tangible. You can hold 'em in your hand and play them at home or at the police station, if need be. You got a broken DVR, you got nothing. No way to take the information out and run it someplace else."

"I bet you got a great deal on them, too," I say. Rio thinks I'm praising him and tells me that he got the systems for a song.

He leans in and talks in a voice so quiet even I can barely hear him. "Charging six times what they cost me," he says.

Loudly, he says how he's passed on the savings to Steve and how these systems aren't easy to come by anymore.

"I'm sure they're not," is all I can manage to say before shifting my attention to the work Mark got done before I got to the alley.

All the brushed-steel tiles are up and the carpets have been laid. How he managed to get all that done by himself is a mystery, but I just tell him that should I manage to get paid, it'll be thanks to him. He's so cute about it, going all red in the face.

He tries to be all business as we discuss the faux-marble Formica that is going on the lower half of the walls and what kind of molding we will use, and I can see that all the praise made him uncomfortable.

And finally, one of the new tables is set up and it is stunning. Mark and I admire our handiwork while Rio rummages behind the counter, looking, I suppose, for spare batteries. Unless there are electronic bowling shoes back there, it's not likely he'll find any.

Meanwhile, wires are everywhere. Mark picks up the end of a cable that runs under the molding. It's not connected to anything on his end.

Over the summer, when Rio was working at the job Carmine got him, he did a pretty fair imitation of someone who knew what he was doing. My guess is that someone back at the shop handed him the parts and told him where they went.

Now that he is on his own, I get the sense that he's not exactly up to the task. Dana tells me that the alarm in Rio's apartment goes off every hour. Something about how it's wired into the clock, she tells me.

She seems to think it's adorable, but then, she thinks her dad is adorable, and that I'm the Wicked Witch of the West. She's said, "You don't understand, Mom," so many times that even I'm beginning to believe it's true.

IT WOULD BE NICE if once in a while someone in the family didn't storm from the dinner table. Especially when that table is in a restaurant. When I casually mention that, Bobbie laughs.

"Dream on," she says as Dana exits loudly stage left. Teenage girls can be so theatrical.

"Something wrong?" Sammy, the waiter at Szechuan Gourmet, asks me as he lowers his tray onto the stand beside the table.

"Too many hormones at one table," I tell him, taking in the tears welling in Kristen's eyes as she faces her little plate of food, the set of Kimmie's jaw as she glares at Dana's empty seat, the strumming of Bobbie's fingernails against her glass and my desire to just get up and move to another table.

Preferably one in Hong Kong.

Sammy puts the spareribs in front of Lys, who he knows will eat only them, despite what else she insisted we order. He ceremoniously takes the lid off the dim sum and places it between Jesse and me. The green, vegetarian dumplings he puts between Kimmie and the empty seat once occupied by Dana, who we trust will be lured back into the restaurant by the incredible smells. Kristen and Bobbie share a bowl of wonton soup.

I don't want to ask, I really don't, but I drew the Mom card and the rules of the game require it. "Anyone know what's bothering Dana this time?" I ask.

Kristen, straight as an arrow, starts to open her mouth, but Kimmie coughs loudly and she closes it. I don't know what Kimmie is holding over Kristen's head, but something is stopping her from telling me what Dana is up to.

*How did this get to be my life?* I can't help wondering. Sometimes I wish I had a scorecard to know just who's playing on whose team, especially when Jesse starts humming—a sure sign that he knows.

Lys, my usually reliable source (though interpreting just what she knows is always a challenge) shouts, "Ow!" and adds that she wasn't going to tell.

"Tell what?" I ask, trying to keep my voice from sounding shrill and only half succeeding.

"She's just pissed at Dad," Jesse offers and gets death threats from all the eyes around the table except Bobbie's.

"Because?" I ask.

"Because nothing," Dana says, coming back and glaring at Lys while she takes her seat. Through gritted teeth she says that, "No one's telling because there's nothing to tell."

*Shoot me now*, I think. *Just shoot me now.*

I make nice, soothing noises, implying that something must be bothering her and pretending that I'm a good listener.

"Can't I just be mad at Daddy? I'd think that would make you happy. You're always mad at him, aren't you?"

I try to discern why she's mad at him, but get nowhere. Except that now I'm the heavy, unwilling to drop the subject.

There is only one thing worse than being a thirteen-year-old girl—being the mother of a thirteen-year-old girl.

"You wouldn't understand," she says with finality.

She may be right.

Usually, I remember to turn my cell phone off when we are dining out because it's incredibly rude to take a call during dinner. Okay, this is what I tell the kids and if I insist Dana's new phone be off, then do I have a choice?

Only I've forgotten and the theme from *NYPD Blue* is emanating from my handbag.

"I thought we couldn't take calls at the table," Dana says in that voice that makes a parent want to send a child to boarding school until she's thirty. "Or does that only apply to me?"

"Take it, Mom," Jesse says, like Bono is calling and if I don't answer in three rings he'll hang up. "It's Drew."

"I had it on to get an important call from Aunt Diane," I lie, though it would be nice if my rookie cop had even the slightest bit of information for me. That is, beyond the fact that so far two of The Slices have bought nothing unusual—blowing my lottery theory right out of the water.

People in the restaurant are giving me dirty looks as I fish frantically for the phone in my purse, the theme getting louder and more insistent.

I tell the kids I'll be right back and run from the restaurant clutching my handbag and apologizing to people along the way.

When I finally get to answer it, Drew is gone.

Now, I could just turn the phone off, go back into the restaurant, call him back later. But since Jews don't get to become saints in this day and age, I don't see much point to this. I call him back.

"Too much crap in your purse to find your phone?" he asks.

A *hello* would have done.

"I'm out to dinner with the kids and Bobbie," I say. "I'm not allowed to take calls."

Drew has two laughs. One is cynical and annoying, the other is genuine. I expect the cynical laugh, but the one I get is genuine. And one little piece of my heart melts just a little.

"Who's not *allowing* you?" he asks. "Alyssa?"

I explain how I made a rule when Dana got her new phone from Rio. And how it's supposed to apply to all of us.

"Do you think you might be *allowed* to go out after dinner? I mean, if your homework is all done?"

I'm smiling. Two people coming into the restaurant smile back at me in the vestibule. Their children don't and I hear the older one saying, "*She* can be on the phone," as they make their way into the place.

"I could check out the security system," Drew says, and his voice holds the promise of more...a lot more.

I tell him to meet me at L.I. Lanes at eleven.

And I scoot back to the table and announce that the call was business.

*Monkey business*, my mother would say.

## CHAPTER 9

Back in the day, lots of furniture was made of metal. There were medicine cabinets, kitchen tables and chairs, Hoosier cabinets. Most of the finishes on them, especially the ones you can find at salvage places and flea markets, haven't fared well. To the rescue—car paint! Just take that bargain to an auto shop and have them paint it better than new. Maybe you can't afford the Jaguar…British racing green, anyone?

—TipsFromTeddi.com

**Drew's** car is parked in front of the alley and when I pull up he gets out and walks over to mine.

"It's eleven o'clock," he says in an announcer's sotto voce. "Do your children know where you are?"

"Very funny," I say, alighting from my car and heading with him toward the alley. Leaving the house wasn't easy, with Dana still so tied up in knots. But with Lys already asleep, Jesse nearly so and Dana getting the solace she needs over the phone, there didn't seem much point in my hanging around. The last thing I heard her tell whoever it was she was talking to was that I'd just take her father's side.

Now there's a hard scenario to imagine.

Anyway, Steve is just closing up and I tell him that Drew is a cop and that he and I will lock up after he checks out the security system for me.

"What's the matter with the system? Your ex have some kind of problem with it?" he asks, eyeing Drew suspiciously.

"I'm just making sure it's working perfectly," I say. He doesn't seem convinced, so I add, "And that it's legal."

"Legal?" Steve says, his voice a couple of octaves higher than normal. "It cost me three grand. It better be legal."

Drew explains that what I meant was that what it captured would be admissible in court, "Should you ever need to go that route."

Steve wants to know what it will cost him.

Drew says a few games on that new table I told him about ought to cover it. Suddenly Steve is thrilled to have Drew's expertise. And he pulls out three beers from behind the bar like we're all going to stay and do the work together.

"This is tedious work," Drew says. "So I'm real glad you can stay. No more than four hours. Five, tops. We've got to trace the wires, go over the connections—"

Steve's eyes glaze over.

"Tricky business," Drew says. "Gotta see that the light is right, do some testing—"

At which point Steve conveniently remembers that he has an appointment in Hicksville. He glances at his watch and says he's late already.

"Help yourself to beers, try out the new cappuccino

maker, whatever," he says as he shrugs into his jacket and hurries out the door.

We stand there awkwardly for a minute or two. I offer to make us some coffee, saying that the machine is supposed to make it impossible for even me to mess up a good cup. Drew shrugs and agrees to try it out.

For several minutes the only sounds come from the machine. When our cappuccinos are ready we sit at the bar and sip, adding murmurs of appreciation to the whooshing of the machine.

Finally Drew puts his hand over mine. He's got that serious look on his face that sends chills down my spine. "Teddi, I—" he starts.

"Did I tell you that my mother got me a new client?" I ask, pulling my hand back and using it to put a lock of hair behind my ear. He waits patiently while I drone on about Rita Kroll and paying bills and the intricacies of working for a friend of my mother's. Eventually, I run out of chitchat.

"Done?" he asks me, not even pretending that what I had to say interested him in the least. He's playing with the empty third finger on my right hand, circling it over and over with his fingers. "Because—"

I jump up and go behind the counter for some sugar, though Steve had thrown some packets on the table already. "How's the case going?" I ask. "Dr. Doris?"

I can see his mood shift as he accepts the fact that I am still not ready to talk about *us*.

"You find your killer yet?"

He takes a deep breath and then dives in. "No. It's been

one blind alley after another. I might as well be in some maze or something."

I tell him that doesn't sound like him.

He says it's the story of his life. He's tracing my fingers with his. "I think I know just where I'm headed, but the facts seem to say otherwise."

"Sometimes it just takes time," I tell him, reaching across the bar to refill our cups.

"Sometimes time's the real enemy," he says. "Suspects slip away, evidence gets mislaid, people forget the really important details."

I don't answer him.

"Found a coincidence that might amuse you," he says, lightening. "Our Dr. Doris, as the papers are fond of calling her, operated on your friend Joey Ingraham a few months back."

I nearly fall off my seat. He steadies me against him.

"My dead doc and your dead guy. It must be kismet, huh?" he says. He's breathing in my hair and raising goose bumps down my arms.

"And you think it's just a coincidence?" I ask him. My voice says *NOT* in capital letters.

"Well, it'd be hard for Joey to have killed Doris after he was already dead. Even you have to agree with that, right?" he asks. He's grown an extra hand and he's playing with my belt, unhooking my bra and brushing the hair away from my eyes all at the same time.

"Maybe Doris killed Joey," I say, only that doesn't make any sense. It's hard to make sense when there are so many hands distracting you. "Or maybe the same person killed them both."

That's a theory. I like it.

Drew doesn't. "Motive? You got a motive to tie these murders together, Teddi?"

"Not yet," I admit. Of course, I have a couple of theories, though they may be a little far-fetched. Life insurance? But if she was the beneficiary and she killed him, who killed her? And why? Back to the lottery? Joey went in with the bowling boys—what could Dr. Doris have to do with that?

The fact that none of my theories make sense doesn't stop me from proposing them as motives. I don't mention the fact that he's referred to both cases as *murders*.

To his credit, Drew doesn't laugh at me. He says he admires my tenacity. "You don't give up easy, do you?"

Okay, there are things that I am more than willing to give up without a fight. And what I'm thinking he has in mind right now is one of them. I'm sure I could be easily persuaded....

Is he willing to test Rio's security system? After all, that's what I asked him here for.

"What's the camera trained on?" he asks, throwing an eye toward the first of the new pool tables across the alley from us.

I explain that there are several cameras. One is on the area outside the back door, one is behind the counter, one is on the bar, and one sweeps the pool tables.

"Bingo," he says, pulling me with him toward the table. We look up as a red light begins to flash below the ceiling cam. "The best way to test these things is to do something to document the time and then, after some space of time, to check the tapes."

"So, like wave?" I ask coyly, wiggling my fingers at the camera.

Without a word he picks me up and sets me on the pool table.

"It always this bright in here?" he asks me. I tell him where the light switches are and he makes some excuses about testing the camera in low lights.

I stay where I am while he turns down the lights.

"Kiss me," he says when he comes back and stands between my dangling legs.

I do.

"No. Kiss me like there's nothing else on your mind."

I try again. He shakes his head.

"Kiss me like I've just told you that I've been investigating the other Slices in my spare time—such as it is."

I wrap my legs around him and kiss him like, well, like he's just told me he's been investigating the other Spare Slices.

He leans me back on the pool table and lifts my sweater. "You really are gorgeous," he says, like maybe he'd remembered wrong.

"What did you find out?" I ask, unbuttoning his shirt so hurriedly I pop one of the buttons clear off it.

"Whole team, all six of 'em, went in on the lottery tickets," he says, like I haven't already gotten that information myself. He looks at the camera and then goes around to the other side of the table, trying to take me with him as he goes. "Swing around this way," he says.

"And?" I ask.

"And get your jeans off," he says, pulling his shirt off and yanking his T-shirt over his head.

"No," I say, though I'm working on my zipper. "The Spare Slices. They all went in on the tickets and…?"

He's pulling my cowboy boots off, but they are fighting him every inch of the way. "And nothing," he says.

I stop struggling with my jeans.

"Every one of them swears they saw the losing tickets," he says, succeeding with one boot and starting in on the other. He turns and takes my foot between his legs. "Put your other foot on my ass and push," he tells me.

I do as I'm told. I think he's surprised because he goes flying with the boot in his hand.

"Lean back," he says. I lie down on the table, my legs dangling over the rail.

He positions himself between them and leans over me. After enough kissing for us both to forget where we are—okay, for me to *overlook* where we are, anyway—he manages to rid me of my jeans.

"So gorgeous," he says again and holds my hands above my head when I try to cover myself.

"But not blond," I tell him.

He looks at my hair and he looks at my sweet spot and says he can see that.

I shiver slightly from the cool air on my naked skin and he presses himself against me, offering to warm me up.

And warm me he does, from the tips of my toes to the top of my head and back again.

"Teddi Bayer in the corner pocket," he says, positioning me on the edge of the table while saying something about sliding his cue stick into my pocket.

Let's just say the man has very good aim.

And every now and then he turns his head to check on the blinking red light below the camera.

In another minute, we're loving on a brand-new pool table in a deserted billiard parlor on a school night. And it's every bit as exciting as it would have been twenty years ago.

"What if Steve comes back?" I ask when we're catching our breath.

"He'll have to get his own girl," Drew says, and, having caught his breath, he goes about catching mine.

Finally, when it's over, when we're done and done in and I've been done over, he hoists himself up on the table next to me.

The camera is blinking down on both our bodies.

"You know this is every man's fantasy," he says. "A beautiful woman, a pool table and a camera catching it all. I don't suppose you'd make a copy..."

"As soon as I make sure it worked, I am erasing everything," I assure him.

He says it's a damn shame. And then he shifts uncomfortably. "Man this thing is hard as a rock."

"Well, it's slate," I say, grateful when he helps me down off the table and I'm feeling every vertebra, every muscle. Even the cellulite on my butt hurts. You'd think with all the padding I've got there...

We're still kind of dazed when we hear the keys jangling in the door.

"Oh my God!" I say, grabbing up my clothes and running for the darkest corner of the alley while Drew calmly pulls on his jeans and unhurriedly buttons his shirt.

"What are you doing here?" an all-too-familiar voice says. I'm relieved it isn't Steve, but only my mother or my kids would be worse than my ex.

"Checking out your security system," Drew says. "What are you doing here?"

"Same thing as you," Rio says, but something in his voice seems to imply otherwise.

Drew asks what he's "got there," while I stay hidden in the shadows because I can't find several articles of clothing, and besides, I'm a coward who abhors confrontation and even if Rio is my ex and has no say regarding how I conduct myself, there are still things I don't want him to know.

Though seeing him eat his heart out to know I did it on a pool table is very tempting.

Rio says it's "just a tape."

The lights snap on, and from Drew's tone, I'm figuring he's responsible. "You planning on replacing a tape in the machine with one of your own, Mr. Gallo?"

Rio says "huh?" but I know where Drew's going.

"You got a tape there that shows no one here? Is that it? You come in here, empty the cash register and then put your tape in the machine so no one knows you were here?"

Rio repeats how he came to check the system.

"At two a.m.?" Drew asks.

"You're here, aren't you?" I reach out and pull my belt back toward me with my foot.

"Good thing I am, huh? What were you gonna do, huh, Rio?"

There's no answer.

"What happened to your hand?" Drew asks. "You been in some kind of fight, Rio? That it?"

"I hurt it, is all," Rio mumbles. "Working."

"Right," Drew says in a tone that implies whatever Rio's selling, he ain't buying.

"Where do you think you're going?" Drew asks. And I plaster myself against the wall.

"Okay, look," Rio says. "I forgot to put a tape in the machine, okay? I got the whole thing set up just like I was supposed to, but then Teddi started—"

Drew asks him if he's blaming his ex-wife for his own mistakes.

"It's just she—" Rio tries again.

"So it's her fault there's no tape in the machine?" Drew asks.

Now, there's an interesting question.

"Did she know there was no tape in there?"

"Yeah," Rio says. "She told me I didn't have to put one in, but I got to thinking about it at home and—"

"Liar," I say, tucking my turtleneck into my jeans and fastening the belt as I come out from behind the pile of Formica slabs.

Rio's jaw drops. Drew tries to hide his amusement. I don't know what he thinks is funnier, my indignation or Rio's reaction.

"Holy Christ!" Rio says. "Teddi!"

"Tell him," I insist, "that I didn't know there was no tape in there."

Rio can't find his voice.

Drew begins to laugh.

"I need all the tapes," I say, stomping in one boot to the multiplexer where I'm ready to just start pulling wires.

"You didn't…?" Rio starts to say, but Drew interrupts him.

"Steve know you have a key to this place? Because he told me—"

Okay, we all know that Steve didn't tell Drew anything, but I'm not about to tell Rio that.

"I'm the security company," Rio tells him. Drew says it seems like Steve needs to be secured from the likes of Rio, showing up in the middle of the night with some half-assed excuse….

"That's it. I'm outta here," Rio says, slamming a tape down on the counter. "Find the damn tapes yourself."

"Or what, Rio?" I shout after him. "You'll sell them on the Internet?"

"Would serve you right," he says, standing in the doorway, the light silhouetting him. He may have been stupid, he may have been cruel. Those, of course, are matters of opinion. Gorgeous? There's no doubt.

"Why? Why would it serve me right, Rio? What did I ever do to you?"

"Besides leave me?" he asks. "And turn my kids against me?"

"Yeah, besides that," I say, thinking that whatever went down between him and Dana, he'd done the deed himself.

He stares at me and at Drew. He looks at my naked right foot, which I try to hide behind my left boot. "It's not what you did, Teddi. It's what you'd never have done." He gestures with his head towards the pool table.

He leaves me with my mouth open and Drew chuckling behind me.

## CHAPTER 10

Every house has an underlying theme, though some houses don't know it. Neither do some owners. Even eclectic is a theme. If your house is neither Asian nor antique, not modern or macho, what is it? What do you want your house to say? *I'm a lover of the arts? I'm a bibliophile? I'm a sailor?*

—TipsFromTeddi.com

**Just** two days later, Bobbie sends me off for my "date" with Milt amid great reservations. She's not worried that anything will happen to me or that this guy will find his way into my panties or anything like that. She just couldn't figure out how to dress me for a boating date in late October, since it's too late for white and too cold for anything nautical either of us have in our closets.

Needless to say, this is not my biggest worry when I meet Milt at the marina in Northport. *He has nothing to gain by killing me*, I keep telling myself as I grip the little spray can of Mace in my pocket. I'll just make nice noises about his new boat, ask how much it cost, whether he was saving long for it, how the hell he paid for a boat and wasn't it a coincidence that Joey was going to buy a pool table at just the same time.

Hey, maybe they both opened those Christmas Club accounts at the bank.

Milt is waiting on the dock with two steaming cups of coffee from Dunkin' Donuts. He's better looking in the daylight, with a ruggedness I hadn't expected. His skin is lined in that sportsman sort of way, and he hands me a foam cup before saying hello.

We stand awkwardly on the dock, me shuffling from the cold, Milt looking anywhere but at me.

"So which one is yours?" I ask, looking at the few boats still floating in the marina this late in the year. Milt gestures toward the biggest one, a cigarette racer with its nose so high out of the water it's amazing it doesn't just take off and fly.

Why am I not surprised?

"Wow," I say appreciatively as I stamp my feet to keep the circulation going.

He asks if I want to check it out.

"Sure," I say enthusiastically, thinking that if he makes a move on me I'll whip out my Mace and run like hell. Of course, I wasn't counting on how hard it is to get into a boat at low tide and how much harder it will be to get back up to the dock.

Milt gets down into the boat first. He's probably in his early forties and pretty limber. Under other circumstances, like if I was the least bit interested in him or if I wanted to hire him to do some work for me or even if I wanted him to slice my bologna, that would be a good thing.

Here, now, it's not.

"Permission to come aboard," I say, exhausting with that one phrase my complete knowledge of boat etiquette.

He holds out his hand to help me and I hand him my foam cup, which he puts on a built-in table before assisting me down into the boat. First he takes my hand, then halfway down the ladder he takes my waist and swings me onto the boat deck. I straighten my jacket and learn quickly that even when you're trying to seduce someone, heels don't cut it on a boat.

Luckily Milt has a hand on me—now there's a thought I never expected to have—and is keeping me upright.

"Milt, it's beautiful," I say, running my gloved hand along what probably isn't called a dashboard in a boat. I say this as though I really, really mean it, because I do. The wood is so highly polished that it gleams like a mirror. It's a finish I have to learn to do so that I can use it on this set of old mahogany end tables that would be so totally perfect next to a winter-white leather couch….

"I said, 'Do you want me to start her up?'" Milt asks. He's standing just a little too close behind me. "Motor purrs like a kitten. A big, jungle kitten."

I tell him I'm really too cold to go for a ride, but I'm just so impressed with his big, sleek, powerful boat… "What does something like this cost?"

He's smelling my hair, inhaling it. I try not to shudder. "Between three and four," he says.

I can't believe it. I thought these babies had to be over a hundred grand. "Really?" I say, wondering if he's just renting this thing and since it's off-season—

"New, half a mil, at least," he says. "But this baby was a bargain since the season's over. Got it for just under four hundred thou."

I don't tell him that I was off by a couple of decimal points since what are a few zeroes worth, anyway? Nothing.

I ask about how he managed to finance this purchase and he gets very cagey. I make a joke about winning the lottery and he jumps on it.

"Yeah," he says and laughs. "That's it. I won the lottery."

Which makes me think that I'm totally offtrack.

And late.

I've got an appointment with the Krolls I've got to get to, and before that I've got to get home, change and pick up Bobbie. I explain and Milt appears genuinely disappointed. I try to appear the same.

He enjoys helping me out of the boat way too much, his hands all over my rear.

I promise myself this is the last time I go fishing on Milt Sherman's boat.

IN THE BIG CIRCULAR DRIVEWAY at the Krolls' house sits an old bicycle with a horn on the handlebars and a little license plate that reads Robby.

"He must be inside," I tell Bobbie, to whom I've explained all about Robby Kroll. It's been almost twenty years since I've seen him, and now I'm a grown-up, old enough to understand his situation. I remind myself that inside Robby's head he is still a little boy and that he probably doesn't understand that the things that seem cute when an eight-year-old does them are scary when done by a grown man.

Jerry answers the door when we ring and shows us into the living room, where a tearful Rita sits on one of two plastic-covered couches.

"Those have to go," Bobbie says authoritatively before she's even been introduced.

I explain who she is and that there are certain things we feel strongly about. And, apologetically, I say that sometimes Bobbie's thoughts slip out from between her lips.

Bobbie's nose goes up in the air, her hands cross her chest, and I'm guessing she won't say another word through this entire interview.

Great. Just great.

Ignoring her, I tell Rita how sorry I am about her brother, how she probably remembers that I actually know from firsthand experience what it's like to lose a brother and she has my sincerest condolences.

Since she's an old neighbor and a friend of my mother's, she knows about Markie and so I don't have to go into the whole story of how my little brother drowned in the family pool when he was a baby. At the moment, she isn't interested in anyone's misery but her own.

"He was so happy," she says three or four times, until Jerry gently tells her that she's repeating herself, which, it seems to me, she's entitled to do. "He talked about getting a new car. On the very day he died, he told me he was going to get a new car. A Corvette or a Maserati, even."

"Wow," I say and smile wistfully. "I owned an old Corvette once upon a time."

"I remember," Rita says, her head bobbing. "Isn't that how you wound up with your first husband?"

"The way my mother tells it, it is," I agree. Which reminds me to convey my mother's regards and her sympathy. Not that she actually sent either, but I'm sure she meant to. And she no doubt sent a tasteful bouquet of flowers to the funeral home, as required by *The Handbook*, though she probably didn't attend the funeral since Rita moved beyond the distance requirements.

I ask after Robby and Rita tells me he's out on his new bicycle. "Jerry bought him one with all the bells and whistles," she says, looking adoringly at her husband of maybe a million years. "Nothing is too good for our Robby. Not according to Jerry, anyway. Like we're made of money, nothing's too good for the people he loves."

Embarrassed, Jerry cuts short the discussion, claiming that Rita needs to move on and put all this sadness behind her. He asks what I think about a fireplace in the living room.

"There isn't one," Bobbie says sullenly, which isn't much better than her just remaining silent.

Jerry is well aware of that, but he is thinking about having one put in. What do I think?

"It's costly," I say, but his shrug indicates that isn't a concern for him. "Eventually though, when you sell, you'll get back close to twice what you'd pay to put it in."

He seems utterly unconcerned with the money and insists on knowing how I think it would *look*.

"Wonderful," I admit. "And it's a great place for all these family photos," I say, noting the shrine to her brother that Rita's got going on the side table.

And then I notice something familiar about the framed pictures that are draped in black. And the breath catches in my throat.

Drew keeps telling me I'm seeing murder everywhere I turn, but now I'm seeing murder victims. I figure I must be wrong, but I have to know.

So I say, "You could put pictures of…?" And I wait for her to fill in a name.

"Joey," she says. I swear I feel my heart stop beating for a second. "Joseph. My baby brother, Joey." And she begins to cry softly yet again.

I go to say something, but no words come out. I pat Rita gently on the shoulder and shake my head sadly. I sniff along with her, but inside my head, bells and whistles are going off like it's jackpot time at Caesars Palace.

"Okay," Jerry says, clapping his hands together like that will snap Rita out of it. "So a fireplace. What else?"

I suggest that maybe Rita could use a little tea about now, and I offer to make it. Without enthusiasm Jerry says he'll do it and he leaves Bobbie and me alone with Rita just long enough to get a conversation about her brother started.

"What did Joey die of?" I ask, and Bobbie elbows me hard in the ribs. I give her an I-know-what-I'm-doing glance, but she isn't buying it.

Instead she looks around the room and proclaims, "A dark rust would look good on the walls in here. Don't you think so, Teddi? Unless they're going to do wood for the fire-place. Rust would be striking with a pale marble."

The two subjects hang out there, waiting for Rita to re-spond to either one.

"He had a heart attack," she says. *Yesss*, I think, despite feeling a little ghoulish at my delight.

"Just suddenly?" I ask. "Or did he have some sort of condition?"

Bobbie looks at me like I've gone too far.

"You know my Dad has a heart condition now and I just, I don't know, want to do everything I can to prevent anything happening to him, you know?" *God will get me for this*, I think. *If I am barking up the wrong tree and pulling my father's illness out for a fishing expedition…*

But, I don't think I am.

She tells me that Joey had coronary artery disease for years before his heart attack. "It runs in the family."

"Would have happened sooner or later. I mean, the man ate like a pig, he should rest in peace," Jerry says, coming back into the living room with a cup of tea for his wife. "You want?" he asks Bobbie and me.

Rita says she should get up and get it for us, but doesn't. We encourage her not to give it a thought.

"He tried to diet," Rita says. "But he was around food all day. Who can resist those Jell Rings? And there was all that medicine after the surgery…"

"He had surgery?" I say, feigning surprise. I really don't think that it would give Rita any comfort to know that (a) the police aren't the least bit interested in her brother's case, which (b) I suspect was murder.

"Not six weeks ago," Rita says. "That doctor who just got killed did it. At Plainview Hospital. Such a nice woman she was. What a pity."

"That's who it was?" Jerry asks. "Small world."

"Small, sad world," Rita agrees. "Six weeks ago she was doing a very tricky procedure on my Joey, saving his life. And now she's dead and so is he. Small, sad world.

"And you were the one who remembered her, Jerry. Not me," she adds.

Jerry gives me the look my father often gives me about my mother. It says that the wheels have come off the cart and she's careening down a steep decline.

"Whatever you say, dear," he says, patting her shoulder. "Though I do remember we were in the bedroom when the news about the doctor came on the television and you asked me how many vascular surgeons named Doris I thought there could be in North Shore. Remember?"

"I said that?" Rita says. "Now, if I remembered the doctor's name, but I don't remember remembering it, does that mean I'm getting Alzheimer's or not?"

It all becomes clear how Rita and my mother could be friends. They share the *It's All About Me* philosophy of life.

Bobbie plunks my portfolio on the coffee table with a resounding thud, reminding us all that the reason we're here is to offer our decorating services.

"Jerry's probably right about trying to put all this behind you," I say, having had all the questions I have about Joey answered. At least, for now. "Tell me about the nicest room you've ever been in. What was it like? What were the colors? How did it make you feel?"

"We like blue," Jerry says.

Of course. Blue is a what I call a safety color. Unless it's deep midnight blue or vibrant turquoise, it says absolutely nothing, which, in its own way, speaks volumes, doesn't it? After white, in all its various shades, pale blue is the most common wall color going.

"Blue," I say, nodding my head and keeping my opinion to myself. "Deep midnight blue with yellow could work in here. Chinese theme, ming vases, oriental rug."

"Light blue," Jerry says.

Bobbie rolls her eyes. I'm praying she won't blurt out, "Boooorrring."

"Light blue with mushroom can be very soothing," I say. "Or we could go with light blue and a parma violet."

They look at me blankly.

"Very dark blue-violet. It would play off the pale—"

"Cream," Jerry says. I'm beginning to hope Rita will weigh in on some of this. "We like light blue and cream. Right, honey?"

Rita smiles weakly at me.

"With peach or something like that."

I'm praying I don't look as sick as Bobbie. I mean, really. What could be worse than a peach, light blue and cream room?

"Actually," Rita says, and I hold my breath, hoping she'll say that she is looking for something with a little more drama, a little more pizzazz…. "I've always liked your mother's house."

I can see Bobbie trying to hold it in, but losing the battle. Her laughter comes out like an explosion.

"Beige," I say. "Just beige."

Jerry and Rita smile at me.

If not for Rita's loss and the fact that the house is new and does need to be decorated, I'd swear my mother put them up to this.

## CHAPTER 11

Here are some helpful guidelines for designing your bedroom: do not place furniture between your bedroom and bathroom or you are guaranteed to stub your toes in the middle of the night. That closet you are planning will not be big enough—no matter how big you make it. You need room-darkening shades on your windows because, after too much merrymaking, the sun shouldn't be able to do what you've warned your children not to. There should be a lock on your door for private moments which could, if interrupted, scar your children for life. And your bed should be placed where you have a view of your door.

—TipsFromTeddi.com

**The** tapes are in the safe I had installed after the last time Rio borrowed Dana's keys to "get something of his out of the basement." The fact that he was looking for old Polaroids of me from back in the day when Polaroids were synonymous with private, which meant porny, which rhymed with horny and meant trouble in River City…

Thinking of Rio and his plan to sell dirty pictures of me obviously scrambles my brains.

At any rate, after the kids are all asleep, I wedge a chair against my bedroom door, take the tapes from the safe and fire up the old VCR. I slide in the tape labeled "billards," and no, I'm not the one who spelled it wrong. He could have just written "pool tables," but he was showing off.

It occurs to me that there shouldn't be a tape labeled "billiards" at all. I mean, according to Rio, there wasn't any "billiards" tape. That's why he was in the bowling alley at 2:00 a.m. Supposedly.

According to my TV screen, there surely is a tape and Rio must be eating his heart out that not only didn't he get to make this particular tape, he didn't even get to watch it.

I see Steve hitting a few shots around on the table. The way the taping works, it only shoots every four seconds, or something like that. At least, that's what Rio says accounts for the herky-jerky quality of the picture. It's almost like watching one of those old movies or a kinescope.

I see Steve set up the balls for a combination shot, then a miss. He glances up toward the camera and then a moment later he is pushing the ball into the pocket.

I fast forward to the "good stuff."

Wow. The camera really does add ten pounds. But only on me. Drew looks as good on the screen as he does in person. There's nothing jerky about him.

I make a solemn vow never to eat again. Tomorrow I start on that starvation diet that's supposed to make you live forever. Though really, without chocolate, do I want to?

Boy, but I look good with my hair spread out against the table. Maybe I should wear green more often. Actually, that would be ever.

Oh! And Drew should never wear anything. Oh… my…God….

"Mommy?" the door I've closed so tightly gives way a little and I jump up, hit every button on the TV until the screen goes dark and run to the door on rubbery legs.

"Alyssa? Honey, what are you doing up?" I ask, struggling to get the chair out of the way and my mind back in gear.

"How come there's a chair in front of your door?" she asks.

A valid question.

I tell her I was trying to kill a bug over the doorway. I'm nothing if not a quick thinker when it comes to my children. Okay, I'm a liar and a quick thinker.

Eventually—it seems like it takes hours—I get the chair out of the way and let Lys in. I ask if she had a bad dream.

"Dana's mad at me," she says. "She said she hates me and that I'm going to hell and everyone else in the family will be in heaven and I'll never see anybody again. Except maybe Daddy."

I tell her that was a terrible, horrible, no-good dream. We should take that dream and flush it down the toilet. And I start to lead her to the bathroom for our occasional ritual when she says that it wasn't a dream.

I assure her it was, but she is adamant. And her feet aren't moving toward the bathroom.

"You want to sleep with me tonight?" I ask, breaking my cardinal rule.

Hey, what are rules for, anyway?

"Am I going to go to hell?"

"There is no such place," I tell her. "And no, little girls don't get sent there anyway." I know it doesn't make sense, but it's nearly 1:00 a.m. and there's a tape in my machine that could get *me* sent to hell if the wrong people got hold of it.

"Even if they do something really, really bad?" she asks.

I ask what she could have done that was so bad, expecting a cookie theft confession or some such thing.

"I told on Dana," she says.

I ask if she means in her dream. When she says no, I tell her that she didn't tell on Dana because I would know, wouldn't I?

I mean, who else would she tell?

"I told Daddy."

I ask again if she's sure this isn't a dream and she shakes her head seriously.

"And what did you tell Daddy about Dana?" I ask her.

"About how when you were at work that boy came over and they were kissing." She climbs up on my bed, pushing Maggie over and then cuddling the dog against her chest like she's a stuffed animal.

"Dana and what boy?" I ask.

"The big one," she says. Her words are getting slurred as she heads back for dreamland. "The one with the black car."

"Dana was kissing a boy with a car?" I ask, my voice a few octaves higher than usual.

Lys's head nods against the pillow.

"And she touched him where you're not supposed to let people touch you."

I DON'T REALLY FEEL MUCH LIKE watching my descent into slutdom captured on tape after I've carried Lys back into her room. I have my proof that the camera works and I erase the tape despite how much I know Drew would have enjoyed watching it. I don't want it around.

Besides, I looked fat.

But I can't sleep. I can hardly breathe. So I decide to check the tapes from the other three cameras because, face it, I'm not going to be sleeping tonight, am I?

The first one I pick up is labeled "back door." I replace the "billards" tape with it and press play. And, sure enough, there is the back door. A man is standing there, biting his nails. As I reach for the eject button, I see the back door open. My daughter steps outside. He holds her at arm's length and indicates that she turn around. She pirouettes and he nods at her and says something which makes the corners of her mouth turn up.

And my stomach turn.

She leans against the door, the man's arms on either side of her head. He leans in to kiss her. I don't know if he does before she ducks under his arm and scoots out of range on the camera.

Nothing. Maybe an arm, a shoulder. A shadow moves. A fist.

I fast forward. I have no idea how much time goes by as the picture of the back door doesn't change.

Forward…

Forward…

And then the man is fully back in the frame. I slow it down to normal speed. The man touches the side of his mouth with the back of his hand. It's bleeding.

*Dana is in her bed*, I tell myself. *Dana is safe, here, in bed.*

I see another man's back, pushing the bleeding man aside and opening the door, ushering Dana in. She is tugging at the hem of her skirt.

She goes in the door and the man turns and raises a warning finger at Dana's lover.

I freeze the frame and nearly press my nose to the screen. I stare at the man holding his hand up in warning. His knuckles are bloody. His expression is deadly.

And his face…I blink twice to make sure I'm seeing what I'm seeing.

It's Rio.

ALL NIGHT I TOSS AND TURN, putting pieces together. So, Rio was coming to the bowling alley with a blank tape, all right, but I'm guessing it wasn't to put into the pool table system. It was for the back door.

How could he not tell me about this?

What is he thinking? Am I any better? What have I been thinking about? A murder that's probably all in my mind?

*Keep calm*, I tell myself. *Keep cool.*

Who am I maddest at? Dana, for hanging out with a grown man instead of some pimply-faced kid? Rio, for not telling me this was going on?

Or me. Me, who is too busy with her own sex life, her business, all the other things in her life, to be keeping a close enough eye on her oldest child.

We all know the answer to that one, so by morning my psyche is deservedly black and blue.

"We need to talk," is all I tell Dana as she gathers up her books and gets ready to walk out the door to catch the school bus. "I'll be here when you get home."

"I have rehearsal," she tells me. Do I even know what she's rehearsing for?

One more lash against my soul. Unless, of course, she's just using that as an excuse to see her not-so-little friend.

*Not trusting your own child.* How many lashes does that earn you?

"Skip it," I say.

"I can't just skip it," she says. There's more panic in her eyes than missing a rehearsal merits. "I have to be there. Everyone is counting on me."

I offer to pick her up at the school auditorium. More panic. I offer to call the teacher in charge of the play—not that I even know it's a play—to tell her that Dana has an appointment she can't miss.

"I'll do it," she says, shooting darts from her eyes. "But I don't see why it can't wait until after."

I think about what Lys told her father—and not me. Another person to be angry at, even if she is only seven. And I think that it can't wait until "after" because "after" could be too late.

It could already be too late.

THERE'S NO SIGN of Rio's truck in the parking lot of L.I. Lanes. Rio probably figures that by now I've seen the tape and so he's laying low.

Inside, I find Mark standing over the pool table, staring at it. Because Rio showed up last night, I don't think Drew and I actually checked the table for…evidence.

"Problem?" I ask, trying to make it sound off-handed as I come up next to him.

"Doesn't the felt look kind of gouged there?" Mark asks, running his hand over just the spot my belt might have been at some point in last night's exploits. What belt was I wearing yesterday?

Sadly, the one with the rivets on it.

I must turn six shades of red. I don't think Mark misses even one of them.

"Well, I guess it could be worse," he says, an understatement if I ever heard one. "I don't know how that screwdriver fell out of my pocket."

"Screwdriver?"

"Yeah," he says. He looks up at the light fixture which hangs above the table. "I was, uh, screwing over the table and somehow I just lost it. You know how that is, right?"

If crawling under the table was a possibility, I'd do it. "Don't worry about it," I say as breezily as I can manage. "It could happen to anyone."

"Yeah. Probably could," he says, and he takes a deep breath and shakes his head. "Although, if someone was actually concerned with getting this job done in time and that someone was actually working when that someone was supposed to…"

"I am very worried about this job getting done in time," I say. Of course, my actions last night say otherwise.

"Yeah. Putting your heart and soul into it, aren't you?" He clenches his jaw like he'd like to say more but doesn't dare.

I don't bother answering.

"Putting anything else into it, are we?" he asks, pulling something out of his back pocket. "I take it you and the good detective patched things up, huh?"

"Sort of," I say, trying to figure out what he's got in his hand.

"Uh-huh," he says, handing it to me. "Whatever. You might want to put this away."

In my hand are Drew's shorts. At least I suspect they're Drew's.

I could claim I don't know what this is about, but frankly, I just don't have the energy.

"Thanks," I say. "It was—"

"Irresistible," he says with a shrug, like there's nothing to be done about it.

"The fantasy?" I say, gesturing toward the table.

"You," he says, picking up his hammer and getting back to work. "I knew our detective would come around. Just a matter of time."

I TRY TO BE OF USE, but I just can't seem to be. I've got ten thumbs, and all of them seem to be full of WD-40. I fight with

Bobbie because she's got to take Kristen to the therapist despite being the one who insisted she get help for Kristen in the first place. I yell at the pool-table salesman because the remaining tables aren't arriving for three more days.

I storm out when Steve reminds me that I've only got another couple of weeks to get the place ready for the grand opening he's been advertising (like that's *my* fault?), or I won't get paid.

I'm home half an hour before the bus. I decide that I will just show Dana the tape and then let her explain herself to me. I go up and open the safe, take out the top tape and put it in the recorder.

Only it turns out to be the front of the bowling alley instead of the back. And there are two men having a heated argument. One turns his back to the camera and I see he's got a Spare Slices shirt on. I'm pretty sure the second one is Max.

He keeps flailing his arms while the other man keeps poking him in the chest. It is clear they are furious, but with no sound it's impossible to tell what they are fighting about.

Max looks to his left, points something out to the second man. Immediately, their demeanor changes. Max takes out his wallet and shows something to the other man, who pats him on the back. A third man joins them and they show the wallet to him. He studies it for a while, smiles and claps Max on the back.

Grandchild's picture? Motorcycle license? I'll have to ask Max, though I certainly can't tell him I was spying on him. The three move out of the camera's range, into the alley, I suppose.

I rewind and watch the argument again, trying to decipher what it could be about. I think if it was a DVD and I could enlarge it on the computer, I could maybe read Max's lips.

I pick up the phone to call Drew and ask if someone in the department can transfer videotapes to DVDs when Dana comes in. I can't believe I'd almost forgotten why I came home.

"Upstairs," I yell when I hear the front door close. "In my room."

A tearful Dana appears at my bedroom door.

Why do I have the feeling I'm going to be consoling her instead of chastising her? Taking her for ice cream instead of taking her to task?

"Come on in," I say, reaching for the "back door" tape as I indicate she should take a seat on my bed.

"So who told you?" She wants to know.

I tell her she did, in part because I don't want her taking it out on Alyssa and because I feel she should know that it was her own actions that are the problem, not someone else's "betrayal."

I slip in the tape and press play. Instead of being furious, Dana dissolves into tears.

"Freeze it!" she screams at me. "Freeze it!"

Stunned, I do, and watch her get up from the bed and lay her hand gently on the TV screen, tracing the image of the man on the screen.

"Dana, who is this creep?" I ask. Okay, yeah, I could have been more diplomatic, since she's clearly taken with the creep. Uh…man.

She naturally tells me he's not a creep, he's wonderful, the most wonderful boy she's ever met, the only one she'll ever love, yadda, yadda, yadda.

"Do you know how old this boy is?" I put quotes in the air around the word *boy.*

"Almost nineteen," she tells me.

"He's almost nineteen and he thinks there's nothing wrong with going out with a thirteen-year-old girl? In my book, honey, that makes him a man, not a boy, and a creepy man at that."

Dana doesn't answer. Lightbulbs go off in my head.

"He's not a creep because he doesn't know you're only thirteen, right?" I wait for her to confirm my suspicions. "Or he didn't know until yesterday."

She sobs, falling at my feet. "You have to let me see him. Daddy scared him away, but if I could just talk to him, tell him how sorry I am... And tell him not to be mad at Daddy."

I hand her the phone. "Call him. Right here, in front of me. Tell him he has my permission to call you again in five years." And I'm hoping against hope she won't take the phone.

"He changed his number," she shrieks. "I tried to call him ten times today. They say it's not a working number."

I sink to the floor beside her. "Honey," I say, brushing the bangs out of her eyes. "A year from now you won't even remember this guy's name. You'll have had six boyfriends in the interim and—"

She swears she will never forget him, and the look she gives me is scary.

"Just how far did you and—" I realize I still don't know the boy's name.

She shakes her head.

"So you didn't—" This is so much harder than I thought. And I didn't think I'd be having this conversation so soon. No wonder they're putting sex ed in kindergarten. Not that I think parents shouldn't take the responsibility themselves.

"I'm still a virgin," she says, and I release the breath I didn't realize I was holding. "But—"

So much for drawing an easy breath.

"Only because he stopped us."

Whether this is true or she is saying this because she wants me not to hate the boy, I don't know.

She takes a ragged breath. "He wanted it to be special."

What am I supposed to say to that? *That's nice?*

"And Daddy…" sniff, sob, sniff "…he just wouldn't listen to Jared. He hit him and he hit him…" more sobs than sniffs here.

"Your father was only trying to protect you," I say. It isn't often I defend Rio, but I think, had I been there, I'd have kicked old Jared right in the…soprano maker.

"Jared's gonna get him for this," Dana says.

I reassure her that she doesn't have to worry about her father. That he can take care of himself.

In response she laughs a bitter laugh. "I'm not worried about him. I hope Jared hurts him really bad. Like he hurt Jared.

"And me."

I say the same thing every mother says in this situation. "You don't mean that."

I wonder if any mother really believes that. Or if we all have no choice but to go with the party line.

## CHAPTER 12

The living room is for living. Remember that when selecting fabric for your sofa, displaying your precious memorabilia, choosing a lightly colored carpet and arranging your furniture. It's fine to keep the living room free of the detritus of everyday life, but if you find yourself saving the room for formal entertaining, ask yourself if you're getting your money's worth from the real estate. You probably aren't. And in the process you're also treating your family less well than the couple you can't stand from around the corner. Are you sure that's the lesson you want your children to learn?

—TipsFromTeddi.com

**"Maybe** you could play it backward and see if it says Paul is dead," Drew says sarcastically when I make him watch the DVD of The Spare Slices he's just brought over to the house.

"Not funny," I say, serving him the brownies I promised as payment for having the tape converted to a DVD. "Don't you think he's saying *ticket* just after he waves his left arm?"

I flick the recording back a frame and yell "There!" at the appropriate moment.

Drew shrugs. I tell him about Milt Sherman's new boat. He puts his hands over his ears and tells me he doesn't want to hear it, so I skip the part about actually going on the boat. And I leave out dinner with Dave and his mother, too.

"A man who is going to buy a seventeen-thousand-dollar pool table dies a very suspicious death. The doctor who recently operated on him is murdered. The men who go in on lottery tickets with him are spending money like they've won that lottery…"

"And you make almost-good brownies," Drew says, licking off the underdone part that is sticking to his fingers. I'm about to offer to do that for him when he adds, "Really. Not half bad."

"Oh, what you just missed," I say, shaking my head.

He looks confused and I give him just a hint by brushing a crumb from his lip and then offering it up to his lips.

"Great brownies," he says, holding my hand an inch from his mouth. "Terrific. Never had better." And he licks my finger and sucks it into his mouth. Let me tell you, the brownies aren't the only thing going gooey…

"Bobbie's on her way over," I say. It comes out dreamily, and he doesn't seem to care as he pulls me gently into his lap.

He reaches for another brownie, squeezes it, and then paints my lips with the underdone chocolate.

"Love your lipstick," he says, kissing me rather passionately for ten-thirty in the morning. "You're sure you can't get the day off?"

"I'm here," Bobbie yells as she comes in the back door to my kitchen. We can hear her heels click-clack on my terra-cotta floor.

"So am I," Drew yells back, and we hear Bobbie's footsteps stop.

"Do I need to give you two a minute?" she asks, as I climb out of Drew's lap while he tries to halfheartedly hold on to me. "We're already late, you know."

I tell her to come on in while I straighten my clothes and Drew laughs at me.

"Oh, brownies!" she says with delight. "Do I have to smear them on my face, too? Or can I just eat one?"

I look at Drew. He looks like he was in a mousse-eating contest. He looks at me. I probably look like I ate the whole mousse. Bobbie hands us each napkins and says she wonders what we could have been doing.

"The rest of your pool tables are coming," she reminds me, tapping her watch. "No better way to start the day than watching men flex their muscles."

Drew's napkin is in his lap.

I couldn't agree more.


"OH, I REMEMBER FIRST LOVE," Bobbie says wistfully as we pull up to the alley. I've given her the broad outline of the Dana saga and she agreed that grounding Dana would just convince the kid that I don't get what this means to her. "The pain. The heartache. Makes me wonder if Michael Jacobs ever got over me."

I see the truck from Century Billiards parked by the doors

and two guys leaning against it drinking coffee out of foam cups. Bobbie was right about our getting here to watch the muscles work, because apparently these guys aren't flexing them without an audience.

Just as I'm about to snap off the radio and turn off the car, the news comes on. "*Coming up, police are still baffled in the murder of vascular surgeon Doris Peterson. Dr. Doris, as she was known to her patients, was brutally murdered in the early morning hours just ten days ago in the parking lot of her medical building after having completed her rounds. A vigil by former patients is scheduled for tonight outside the building. A spokesman for the group says they are 'disappointed' with the police department's efforts in the case. 'This woman saved so many lives'*" a voice says. "*'We can't save hers, but we can bring her killer to justice.'*"

"You don't see any vigils for Joey," I say. "Nobody's—"

"Give it a rest," Bobbie tells me, opening the car door. "We have to finish this place in less than two weeks. And what work have you done on the Kroll job? Shut it off and let's go." She is standing outside the car, holding the door open, waiting for me. I gather up my stuff, hoping for more news in the Dr. Doris case before I go inside, where I will simply point at the tape outline I've already put on the floor to signify where the pool tables should go. It's not like you can move those babies once they're set up.

"*In other news,*" the announcer says. "*A freak accident in the parking lot of the Walbaum's store in Plainview has left one man in critical condition. His name has not been released, pending notification of family, but he is believed to be an employee of the supermarket in its delicatessen department.*"

"Don't even think it," Bobbie says.

I spend the day thinking of little else.

At two, Drew gets around to returning my call. He tells me that since I couldn't play with him, he went in to help on the Dr. Doris case even though it's his day off. He offers me dinner but I tell him I have stuff going on with Dana and I have to be home.

He takes it like it's a brush-off.

"Really," I say. "This thing with Dana is big."

"Fine," he says, but his voice has an edge to it.

I really don't need a fourth child and I simply refuse to go there.

The billiards people are asking about which end of the table the break will be made from and other esoteric questions I assumed they'd have the answers to and I tell Drew that I have to go—that I have men waiting for me.

"Yeah, well give 'em my sympathy," he says. "I know how that can be."

This is not the time to bait me. I tell him I really do have to go.

"Yeah," he says, and I'm about to press End when I hear him say, "By the way, you hear about the Walbaum's parking lot accident?"

I point in Mark's general direction, suggesting to the guy who wants to know which end is up, that Mark will be able to tell him. I tell Drew I heard about it over the radio.

"Don't go imagining conspiracies here, Ted, but unless there's more than one Max in the deli department, this guy's your Spare Slice friend."

"Is he—" For a woman who is racking up murders faster than the guys on *Deadwood* I still seem to get creeped out by words like *dead* and *killed*.

"Nah. They think he's gonna pull through, though it's a miracle." He hesitates like he shouldn't have said that, then sighs. "Oh, what the hell. You'll find out on your own, anyway, no doubt. Car ran over him twice."

I suck in a breath. "Tell me the department isn't calling this an accident," I say.

"We're on it," Drew says. He doesn't bother with the traditional *keep out of it, Teddi* lecture.

I ask what hospital he's in and Drew reluctantly tells me he's in Plainview Hospital. The hospital is a quick five-minute drive from Syosset and I say I'll go over there after work. Then I remember I have to be home for Dana. I'm totally committed to bonding with her and the rest of my children. She needs sympathy, guidance and, frankly, a watchdog.

"Can't do dinner because you've got something with Dana, but you can get over to the hospital," he says.

I can understand his resentment. "No one's trying to kill *you,*" I say in my defense.

"*You're* killing me, Teddi," he says sadly.

And then he hangs up the phone.

The afternoon sucks. I am home when I want to be at the hospital and at the alley. Not to mention how much I'd like to be dressing for a dinner with Drew.

But Good Mom is in gear and I work on some plans for the Kroll house in the kitchen so that I'm available to my kids. Not that Dana is talking to me now that she's decided the tape from L.I. Lanes invades her right to privacy and wants to know why she isn't afforded the same constitutional rights I worry the government is taking away.

"The whole country is against me," she announced when she got home from school today. "The whole universe."

And Jesse is totally freaked about the taping business, too, which makes me wonder what I missed seeing him up to.

Only Alyssa still loves me. And I'm not sure it's me and not the refrigerator cookies that she's really fond of. I've sliced and thrown them into the toaster oven and now she's waiting expectantly.

I'd say Maggie May loves me, but this morning she dragged my best lace bra down the stairs and dropped it in her food bowl. I can't figure out what she meant by that. I'm not sure I want to, either.

Dinner is a silent affair, punctuated only by Dana's sniffing and Jesse asking how long it takes girls to grow up. Makes me glad I didn't invite Drew to join us, as I can just hear his answer to that one.

In the middle of dinner, Dana's phone plays Kelly Clarkson's "Hear Me," indicating that Rio is calling her. She ignores it. Jesse doesn't remind her that it's her father. Lys doesn't ask if she's going to get it. Maggie, sleeping by the refrigerator, doesn't even open her eyes.

Now, I have had a really hard time dealing with Dana's loyalty to her father and her hope that we would ever get back together. So I should just relish the fact that she no longer sees him as our white knight, coming back to make us whole again. Okay, maybe that's all the king's horses…and Rio is certainly a horse's—

Anyway, I am not enjoying her animosity toward her father, despite it coinciding with my own. In fact, it breaks my heart.

By the time dinner is over, we are all sullen and snippy. And I can't help but wonder whether there is any point to my staying home.

Moments after Dana's cell rings, the house phone rings as well. We all know it's Rio and everyone just lets it ring. Finally Jesse grabs the phone. He sounds truly sympathetic when he tells his dad that Dana won't talk to him. Apparently he's willing to settle for me.

"Give her time," I tell him and add that he and I need to have a very short talk, which we can have at the bowling alley tomorrow and he might want to wear shin guards.

The warning sails over his head.

"I gotta see her," he tells me. "Can I come over tonight? I won't stay long, I just gotta explain to her that I know boys like him. I *was* a boy like him. I know how they think, how they operate, how it all works.

"And I just thought I had more time before I had to warn her."

I don't say anything.

"And I thought she was smarter than that. Not that you weren't smarter, too. Don't think I don't know what you're thinking now, Teddi. Makes a helluva difference when you're on this side of the fence, don't it?"

"Yeah, it makes a difference," I agree.

"There's things I'd take back," he says.

"We got three delicious kids out of it," I tell him. There's no point now in being angry with him for not telling me about Dana. What would I have done that he didn't do better? He got rid of the kid and he's going to give Dana the talk from the male side. "Come on over. I'd like to go visit a sick friend, anyway."

He laughs. "A sick friend, huh? What's he got? Blue balls?"

You would think I'd have learned. Give Rio so much as a hair and he's wrapping it around your throat in the hope of strangling you.

I'm so ready to tell him not to come, but Dana's shut her eyes tight, as if his coming was the answer to an unspoken prayer.

"Remember it's a school night," I tell him.

He tells me he just has to bundle up Elisa and he'll be right over.

Sometimes I forget that he has another family, or the remnants of one, anyway.

What a complicated world we live in.

AT THE HOSPITAL I ask for Max Koppel's room. Drew has agreed to meet me in the restaurant cafeteria after I've seen Max.

"And I haven't sanctioned this visit. This is not police-approved and it's completely independent of the department," he warned me. "You are going to see him as a friend, a customer and not some pseudo-detective who thinks she's Miss Marple's descendant."

It's nice that he no longer thinks I'm Miss Marple herself. Ever since I made him watch *Murder Most Foul* with Margaret Rutherford, he's had a new appreciation for how obnoxious his calling me Miss Marple really is.

Which means he reserves it for when he's really ticked at me.

I am standing outside Max's room because someone else is with him. This does not qualify as eavesdropping. It's merely being polite. Is it my fault if it so happens that I can hear most of what the person is saying?

"How's it going, buddy?" a male voice asks. "They taking good care of you?"

If Max answers, I can't hear it.

"I don't get how this could happen," the voice says, and I'm pretty sure it belongs to Dave Blumstein. "I feel like I lost my best friends. Not that you're dead, or anything. But first Joey and now you. And Miles thinks he's next and won't even answer the phone. Milt says he's wearing a disguise and only answers the door to get pizza delivered. And he calls different pizza places each time, Milt says.

"He's…what's that word?" the voice asks, and now I'm sure it's Dave.

*Paranoid*, I think. Only, of course I don't think he's paranoid, since I don't think he's *imagining* he's in danger.

"You know," Dave says. "There's jokes about it. Like how do you know if you're…I can't think of the word."

*Paranoid.*

"It starts with a *P*, I think."

*Para-freakin'-noid.*

"I don't know if you can hear me," he says. "But maybe you can. So if you can and you know the word—"

I can't help myself.

"Paranoid," I say, coming into the room. I'm all set to apologize for overhearing, explain how I was just coming into the room and couldn't help but hear, blah, blah, blah.

Only he just lights up and says, "Yeah, that's it! Paranoid. Hi, Teddi! Look, Max. It's Teddi."

As you might guess, there's no reaction from Max, who is lying still in the bed, bandaged, in traction. He appears to be sleeping. I ask how he is.

Dave shrugs. "I think he's just asleep. Otherwise his family wouldn'ta gone home, right?"

I ask if the nurse has been in. Dave says she has, that she felt his pulse, so he must still be alive, right? Don't I think so?

I reassure Dave that Max is alive. I point out the monitor beside his bed, a good strong heartbeat bleeping across it. "He's probably heavily sedated," I say.

Dave says, "Yeah. And they gave him some stuff for the pain and to help him sleep, too."

A disembodied voice announces that visiting hours are now over and asks all visitors to leave patients' rooms.

I want to put my hand on Max, reassure him, but there doesn't seem to be a safe place to touch, so I lean down and whisper in his ear.

"Don't you dare give up, Max Koppel.

"And I won't either."

## CHAPTER 13

Sure bedrooms are for sleeping, but they are also for loving. If there's a man in permanent residence in the bedroom or an occasional visitor, don't make him feel he's in the wrong place by over-feminizing the room. Please, no lavenders, no pinks, no ruffles. Leave those to the seven-year-olds. But don't go to the other extreme, either. No whips, no chains, no blindfolds where the kids can see or find them. Unless there's a cop in the house, there's really no excuse for hanging the handcuffs on the headboard, is there? A good rule of thumb is to imagine breaking your leg and having your mother in and out of your bedroom to take care of you. Quick—pad the walls!

—TipsFromTeddi.com

**Drew** is waiting outside the already closed cafeteria. "You want to just go home?" he asks me.

I glance at my watch. Rio is probably still there and I'm not emotionally prepared to have our confrontation just yet. Especially not with the kids in the house. And I could do without Elisa tugging at my heartstrings, too.

"Maybe coffee and a doughnut?" he offers. "Or is that too cliché?"

*How about a roll in the hay? Or is that too cliche? A snack in the sack?*

*Another rack of billiards?*

"Coffee would be nice," I agree. The image of pudgy me on the pool table is still painful. I vow to just have coffee and skip the doughnut.

We stand in front of the counter at Dunkin' Donuts, where at least twenty dozen doughnuts know my name and are shouting it, the chorus getting louder and louder. I can barely hear Drew telling me that the sugar will give me sweet dreams.

Now how can I resist that?

In the very last booth at the back of the restaurant—can you call a doughnut place a restaurant?—Drew and I sit facing each other. If the fluorescent lights are making Drew look sallow, I don't want to know the view from his side of the table.

"You learn anything?" he asks me.

I've learned a lot. You shouldn't underestimate your ex-husband. You shouldn't assume your daughter is seeing someone age-appropriate. You shouldn't think the man across the table from you will wait forever.

"Or is Max still out of it? They told me he was under heavy sedation." He takes a sip of coffee and motions for me to take a bite of my cruller.

"Right," I say, coming back to reality. "No, he wasn't awake. But I did see one of the other Slices—Dave."

He takes a large bite of his jelly doughnut. Sugar disperses on the table and a drop of jelly clings to his pinky. "Oh," he says, licking it off. "Your new boyfriend. Not the brightest light on the runway."

"I went to dinner at his mama's, and you know why," I say with a laugh. "And no, he's not the sharpest tool in the shed."

With his mouth full, Drew tries to talk. "Not the—"

"Yeah, yeah. We're talking about the same guy. A couple of slices short of a sandwich. Anyway, he says that Miles is scared for his life."

Do you have any idea how sexy and appealing a man with powdered sugar on his upper lip is?

Where was I?

Oh, yeah, Miles. And Drew tells me that one of the guys is going around in Groucho Marx glasses, afraid that someone is after all The Slices and is going to kill him.

"Because of the lottery tickets?" I ask.

"Because—get this—they have the best chance of winning the big trophy and the $350 prize. Or they did, before Max got hit by the truck."

I ask if he's kidding, but he isn't.

"So *you're* thinking they're killing each other for the mega-million jackpot and *they're* thinking it's over a few hundred bucks." He breaks off part of my doughnut and tries to feed it to me. "What's wrong with this picture?"

Maybe it's a sugar rush. Maybe it's his finger against my lips. I'm thinking, *What picture? Where?*

"I know you think I'm crazy," I say after I've managed to swallow. "But I just know that somehow your case and mine are intertwined."

He does that one-eyebrow-up thing that cartoon characters do. I've practiced in the mirror and I can't do it. Anyway, he does it and he says, "*Your* case?"

Okay, so I don't have a case. I'm just a lowly interior designer who gets her kicks trying to solve crimes the police department doesn't seem to care about. Not that I say that, because, after being married to Rio Gallo for twelve years, I know where minefields are and I'm not about to make the same mistakes with Drew that I made with Rio. And don't think, just because of sentence structure here, that I'm implying anything about marrying Drew Scoones.

Marriage is off the table. Not in the equation. Marriage is…I get the shudders just thinking about it.

"Teddi?" Drew says. "Something wrong?"

"No," I say, and ask him, "Why?"

He says I'm not yelling at him. Hmm. Lesson learned. When I don't rise to the bait, he stops baiting me.

"As it happens," he starts. And then he leans in toward me like he's going to tell me some police secret he shouldn't. I don't lean forward because I'm convinced that he'll tell me something stupid, like he's got a detective badge for me—found it in a box of Cracker Jacks—or something.

I can see it's driving him crazy that I'm not hanging on his every word. I throw him a crumb. "As it happens, *what?*"

"Not that I'm conceding or condoning your assertion that you have *a case*, but it does seem like there may be some connection."

Man, he can work me like a light switch. Just flip me on.

"What connection?" I ask, and I'm nearly climbing over the table to hear it.

He tells me that police records show that Dr. Doris Peterson had an appointment at the sixth precinct the morning she died. In fact, she was probably on her way there when she went to her car in the medical building parking lot.

"And?" I ask.

"A check of her phone records show that before she called the police to make that appointment, she called Joey Ingraham's sister, Rita Kroll." He sits back, arms folded across his chest with a how-do-you-like-them-apples look on his face.

"Why?" I ask.

He shrugs and says the detective working the case hasn't found that out yet.

"No," I say, because he's misunderstood me. "Why did you tell me? You don't just hand over that sort of information. It's not like you."

He doesn't answer me.

And then it occurs to me. "Are you asking me to find out why Dr. Doris called Rita?"

He feigns shock. "I would never do that. It would be against department regulations. What could you find out that a detective couldn't? Especially a detective who is investigating a high-profile case and isn't really the least bit interested in another murder that's closer at hand?"

"So you think that Joey was murdered?" I ask.

He tells me, "Not officially." Pressing his fingers to my

doughnut crumbs and licking them off, he adds, "Lots of co-incidences, don't you think?"

I wonder if my mother, Rita's good friend, knows anything.

"Teddi?"

If maybe my mother and Rita and I went out for a nice little lunch, to discuss the decorating project...

"Teddi?"

Better still, if I brought Rita to my mother's for coffee and cake, so that she could point out to me what she likes in my mother's house...I could bring some vivid colors to show her how accent pieces could bring the dead back to life...

"Teddi!"

Drew, handsome, sexy Drew, is sitting across from me, playing footsies under the table. And I'm in my mother's house with a potential witness. "Hmm?"

"You know, you're a detective junkie. Give you a scrap of potential evidence and you're tripping out on me."

I fear he's right. I'm not just tripping out, I'm turning on. "Wanna go some place and neck?"

The man doesn't have to be asked twice.

"Oh, wait," I say as we begin to extricate ourselves from a booth that wasn't made to accommodate frequent doughnut eaters. "Rio is at the house. Shoot. I really better go home."

This does not make Drew happy. He makes some noises about me being a tease.

"No," I say, taking a deep breath. "I'm a mother. I've got three kids and an ex-husband and responsibilities. I have a job. And before you say it, you may have a job, too, but when you're off duty, you're *off duty*. Mom's don't go off duty."

He doesn't take this well.

I remind him that I told him stuff was going on with Dana.

"But you made it out to see Max Koppel," he says resentfully.

I explain how I didn't want to be at the house when Rio came over, how I had to let him come because Dana was mad at him for running off a boy who was too old for her, yadda, yadda, yadda.

He doesn't look appeased.

"Don't you think I'd rather be at your place screwing our brains out than going home to a sullen teenager, a secretive preteen and a whiny seven-year-old snitch?" Apparently I say this very loudly, because everyone in the doughnut shop is staring at me.

A bunch of women in hospital scrubs are sitting at the table to the side of us. "Wouldn't *you* rather be going home with him?" I ask one of them, pointing at Drew, who is trying to hustle me out of the shop.

The woman nearly drools.

At this point Drew has his arm around me and is half-carrying me out of the place.

"Wouldn't you?" I ask a woman as old as my mother as we pass her booth.

"You bet I would," she answers back, but by then we're all but out the door.

"You are off sugar," he tells me when we get outside. He puts my coat around my shoulders, but the air is still cold, and so is his body language.

"Sugar and evidence," I tell him. "And then there's the thought of sex. You can't offer me all that and not expect a reaction."

He leans me up against the window of Dunkin' Donuts. He takes my face in his hands and looks into my eyes like he's going to find evidence of crack or cocaine. "Are you all right?" he asks me.

I shut my eyes and swallow hard. And then, out it comes. "I don't want to go home. I don't want to watch Dana cry or tell her that her father was right or ask Jesse what's going on with him or find Alyssa still awake. I don't want Rio to still be there, and I don't want to hear six messages from my mother, all telling me what a mistake I made taking on L.I. Lanes and how I'll never finish it.

"I don't want to hear the other half-dozen messages from her telling me the other mistakes I've made since the last time we spoke. I don't want to try to fix the downstairs bathroom toilet because I can't afford to replace it like Mark says I have to and I don't want—"

Drew looks helpless.

*Can't fix this, can you, big guy?*

And then he leans in and kisses me. Softly at first, but then almost brutally.

"I have to—" I try to say between his lips and mine, but it only makes his mouth more urgent, more insistent.

"I guess she changed her mind," a few of the nurses, or

maybe they're doctors, say as they come out of the doughnut shop.

"Who wouldn't?" another one answers.

Drew drags me away from the harsh lights in front of the store. "I wish I could fix—" he starts to say.

I put my finger against his lips. "You just did," I tell him.

And then I head for my car and the long ride home.

## CHAPTER 14

Some great places to get ideas for redecorating are in movies and on television, in magazines, in museums that feature furniture exhibits, the furniture departments of better stores, open houses, the Net. But as beautiful as any of these may be, keep asking yourself *would this work for me?* Remember your family members, your locale, your budget and your lifestyle. Most of us don't have Marie Antoinette's space, budget, maids, etc. We don't even have Sofia Coppola's.

—TipsFromTeddi.com

**"You're** never going to get that *farkakte* alley done and you're ruining your reputation in the process," my mother says when I phone her the next morning while posting a tip. I assure her that I got all that last night from her messages. Not to mention the time I had with the kids and their visit with Rio, which apparently went about as poorly as my marriage to him did. "You should be concentrating on cultivating clients who can enhance your image, who can introduce you to a better class of people, who will then become your future clients.

"Who do you think is going to walk into a bowling alley and think 'I'd like my home to look just like this. I wonder who the designer was?'"

I hate it when she has a point.

"You need to concentrate on Rita's house." She goes on at length, telling me about how she won't be able to recommend me if I don't give her friends preferential treatment.

"We need to eat, Mom," I say, rather dramatically. "I take whatever jobs I can get and this one will pay nicely."

"Provided you get it done in time," my mother says for the millionth time, making me regret yet again having told her the conditions on this job. "Which you never will. I don't know how you could have—"

Actually, she goes on for quite a while, but since I'm not listening anymore I can't really tell you what she says. We can all guess, right?

I tell her she is absolutely right. Even that doesn't shut her up, but at least it kind of slows her down.

"Did I tell you that Rita is very fond of your house and would like to do hers in a similar palette?"

"Well, of course she does," my mother says. "I told you she had taste, didn't I?"

No, she told me Rita was cheap. But I don't correct her because that's not what I'm after. "I thought it would be nice if I brought Rita over to your house—I could pick up some pastries at that little bakery you like and she could show me what she likes about your house."

My mother hesitates. Finally: "What's not to like?" she asks.

I say how I'd just like her to point out to me what especially appeals to her, whether it's the palette or the style or the tone…

"Fine, Teddi," she says. "But what do you really want?"

"WHAT I REALLY WANT TO KNOW," I say when we've taken off our raincoats and toured my mother's taupe terrain, her ecru environs, her beige boudoir, and we're sitting down to calories with chocolate coating, "is what it is you like about this house. Does it give you a sense of calm? Monochromatic color schemes tend to do that. Spas are often shades of taupe or gray for that reason. Are you looking for a—"

My mother waves my words away with her hand. "It shouts class and Rita would like to feel she's part of a certain strata in life, a level above the hoi polloi."

I'm getting nowhere. Not in the investigation and not in the designing.

"So tell me the truth, Rita," my mother says suddenly, putting several pastries on Rita's plate and refilling her coffee cup. "You think that sweet brother of yours was murdered?"

I don't know whose jaw drops farther, mine or Rita's. "Mom!" I say sharply.

"Please," she tells me while the rain turns to sleet and pelts the window behind her. "We're all thinking about it. Unless…it didn't occur to you, Rita?"

She tells us that it did, but that Jerry said she was being ridiculous. "The police say it was an accident," she tells us.

"Did the doctor, the one who got killed after she operated on him, think it was anything other than a heart attack?" I ask.

My mother leans forward. Clearly she didn't know there was any connection. She asks for an explanation. What she really wants is not an explanation, but an apology for why I didn't tell her. Only she's not looking at me. She's looking at Rita, who says she doesn't know.

"I thought you mentioned that she called you after Joey died," I say. My mother stares at my forehead like there's a neon sign there blinking *liar, liar, liar*.

Rita denies any call from Dr. Doris.

"The day she died," I say. "Remember?"

Rita says Jerry is so right about the Alzheimer's. She doesn't remember speaking to the doctor.

"What a nice woman she was," Rita says. "Before Joey's operation he was cracking us all up, her included."

My mother and I hang on her words.

"They'd given Joey some sort of medication, to relax him for the surgery, I guess. He was really scared. So he had a reaction to the medicine and instead of getting sleepy, he was all wound up and talking a blue streak. He was like a stand-up comedian, my Joey. And the doctor was there, trying to relax him."

I ask what sort of things he was saying.

Rita says he was trying to seduce the doctor. "He told her if she wanted him to relax she should come lay down next to him. Then he said that no, that would excite him. And it actually did."

# *Play the* Lucky Hearts *Game*

### and get...

## 2 FREE BOOKS *and*
## 2 FREE MYSTERY GIFTS...
### *yes!* YOURS to KEEP!

I have scratched off the silver card. Please send me my *2 FREE BOOKS* and *2 FREE mystery GIFTS*. I understand that I am under no obligation to purchase any books as explained on the back of this card.

*Scratch Here!*
then look below to see what your cards get you...
2 Free Books & 2 Free Mystery Gifts!

**355 HDL ENS9**          **155 HDL ENZ9**

FIRST NAME

LAST NAME

ADDRESS

APT.#          CITY

STATE/ PROV.          ZIP/POSTAL CODE          (H-N-08/07)

Twenty-one gets you
**2 FREE BOOKS** and
**2 FREE MYSTERY GIFTS!**

Twenty gets you
**2 FREE BOOKS!**

Nineteen gets you
**1 FREE BOOK!**

**TRY AGAIN!**

She gestures with her napkin, putting a finger up inside it like an erection.

"It was terrible. Then he starts telling her about how one day he'll be rich."

"A man who slices meat in the deli department," my mother says, shaking her head. She immediately realizes her faux pas. "Good, honest work. You know, that's the kind of man who wins the lottery. It could happen.

"Not for Joey, but…" her voice trails off.

"No one's claimed that jackpot yet, have they?" I ask. "The thirty-seven million dollar one?" Not that I mean Joey could. Not now, anyway.

Rita shrugs. I see she's eaten all the mini-eclairs my mother put on her plate. I slide a cream puff on for her. She says, "No more," but still she pops it whole into her mouth, while my mother rolls her eyes in a gesture that all but shouts Rita will be finishing off the platter.

"So what do you like best about my humble abode?" my mother asks Rita. "Teddi needs to know so she doesn't blow your job like Deena Fishbein's."

"Mom!"

I ask you: With a mother like mine, who needs an ex? "What?" my mother asks defensively. "You didn't paint the hallway the wrong color?"

"IF I TOOK OUT A CONTRACT on my mother," my telephone conversation with Drew starts.

He interrupts me. "There's been another death," he says,

stopping me in my tracks. Well, I don't actually stop. I start pacing, but I do stop talking. "Another bowler."

"A Spare Slice?"

"Mmm-hmm." And he adds that this one is possibly suspicious.

Well, *duh*.

"And then there were three," I say. "Who?"

He tells me it was the guy with the boat. He calls him Sherman. I tell myself the roads are icy. Accidents happen. Don't get carried away.

"You talked to him about the boat, right?" Drew asks. The police don't think it was an accident. Not from Drew's tone of voice.

I assure him that I did, that it cost almost half a million dollars and that when I told Drew that, he wasn't the least bit interested. I'm snippy because I knew Milt Sherman. I didn't like him, particularly, but I knew him. He smelled my hair.

"So I want you to stay out of this, Teddi. Understand me?"

I'm not sure I do. Am I supposed to read between the lines? When he says *understand me?* does he mean this-is-the-official-line-but-you-should-know-I-don't-mean-it?

Or does *stay out of it* really mean *stay out of it*?

"It's a police matter now. And it's dangerous."

Is that supposed to warn me off? Or be an irresistible enticement?

Where's my decoder ring when I need it?

"Teddi? It was one thing when we didn't think there was any foul play involved, but this is different."

As in: we didn't mind when you were chasing your tail, but now that it's turned out that your tail is worth chasing…I mean, that it's something worth investigating, you're off and we're on.

He's digging himself a very deep hole.

"So any role you thought you had in this is over."

Right. Without implying any link at all, I casually mention that, oh, by the way, did I tell him that I had a nice coffee klatch with Rita Kroll?

"And?" he asks in his police-detective-on-the-job voice.

"Oh, my nose is out of it," I say. "Completely."

Deep sigh from the other end of the phone. Then: "I don't suppose I can ask you to give up a paying client."

"No, you can't."

"So?"

"She likes beige," I say. "Especially brocades and satin stripes. And beige on beige."

He asks, exasperated, what she said when I asked about the phone call.

I tell him she said there wasn't a phone call, or that she didn't remember getting one. Claims Alzheimer's, though my mother's assured me Rita's got a mind like a steel trap and she still blames my mother for driving over her garden hose twenty years ago.

"Wonder why she'd lie about that phone call," Drew muses. "Unless she's got something to hide."

"*If* she's lying," I say.

Drew assures me that they know the call went through. "Too long for just leaving a message. A good ten-minute call."

I remind him that two people live in that house. "*She* might not be lying at all."

THERE'S A BLACK BUNTING hanging on the glass case in the deli counter at Pathmark. I don't usually shop here, but it's not really out of our way home from the alley, where Bobbie and I just checked over the day's work. It's now going much too slowly for my comfort zone, but Bobbie says she's sure it will be a slam dunk. Of course, she doesn't play basketball and has no idea what that means.

Anyway, I figure I can pick up pickled herring here just as well as at Waldbaum's. And Bobbie would shop anywhere, anytime. She heads for the makeup aisle while I wait my turn at the deli counter.

There are only two countermen working and they appear to be on Prozac. They're pretty much operating in slow motion.

Some woman is throwing a fit about them taking people out of turn. "My number is up," she shouts.

The two men behind the counter stare at her.

"Better yours than mine," one of them says. He takes off his apron and his little hat and flings them down on the counter. "I'm outta here."

This is met with major groans from the growing crowd on our side of the glass.

"Quarter pound of Virginia ham," the remaining counter guy repeats after it's ordered. He picks the ham up out of the case and it slips out of his hands, slides down the counter in front of him and falls onto the floor. He sighs heavily.

"You got another kind of ham you like?" he asks the woman he's waiting on—who tells him to just forget it.

"I'm doing the best I can," he says.

No one on this side of the glass seems impressed.

"Who's next?" he asks. There's a ticket on the counter with the number 112 on it, left by someone who must have given up earlier. Mine says 134. The clicker indicating which customer is being waited on says 111. Bobbie, back with two lipsticks and an eyeshadow, palms the ticket and stands expectantly, waiting for him to pull the cord which changes the number.

"That's her," she says, when he calls out 112.

Two women take issue with the possibility that I could be next, since they were here before me.

Ordinarily I'd never do this. But desperate times call for desperate measures. And I'm not really here to get deli, but information—information Drew refused to give me. So, after Bobbie shoulders me front and center, I indicate the black draping on the counter and ask, "What's with the bunting?"

The counterman tells me that one of the other clerks, Milt, died in a horrible boating accident yesterday.

It occurs to me at this moment that I never asked Drew just how Milt died. "He took the boat out?" I say. "In this weather?" I gesture toward the parking lot, where we're enjoying our third straight day of sleet.

The man says the boat was brand-new. "Just bought it a week or two ago. First time out in it and he fires it up and the damn thing explodes. Can you believe that?"

I feel my knees going a little weak. I exchange a look with

Bobbie and know she's just realized the same thing I have. I was on that boat. In fact, he offered to "fire it up" for me.

Bobbie puts an arm around my shoulder as people behind us get impatient.

"You gonna order?" someone asks. "I have to get home sometime today."

"And she doesn't?" Bobbie asks. "She doesn't live here, you know."

"Could you just order?" someone else asks.

"Some pickled herring. Lots of onions and cream sauce, just a little herring. The smallest one you have," I say. I order it like a Long Islander so that he doesn't get suspicious. Then, back to the boat, I add, "Wow. He was saving for that boat forever."

"Yeah?" the guy says, holding up the runt of the litter for me to approve. "Maybe that's why he had to borrow fifty bucks from me just a couple weeks ago."

"Could you hurry it up?" someone asks, while someone else says, "This is ridiculous. I'm going to Fairway."

"I just came from there. The deli guys didn't come in today."

"This is unbelievable. The manager should get behind there."

"Do they have the turkey already sliced in the case?"

"I just want some cheese. Just one thing. For my kids. Can I go next?" someone says.

"No! You think we're standing here for our health?" someone yells back.

"You think it was murder?" Someone...oh, wait. That's me. *I* say.

The whole place goes silent.

"What was murder?" someone asks.

"Milt, the counterman," I say. "I heard it was suspicious but the police aren't looking into anything but the Dr. Doris murder."

"The bypass doctor," a woman says, nudging the man beside her.

"I don't need a bypass. I need salami," he says.

"Yeah? And if you eat enough salami, you're gonna need a bypass," she replies.

The counter guy puts the container of herring up on the counter and I reach for it. "You think it was murder?" he asks me in a whisper that implies this is just between him and me.

I shrug. "Joey at King Kullen, Max at Waldbaum's…"

"Milt here," the guy says. "That's it. I'm outta here." He, too, takes off his apron amid loud groans from the crowd.

"Good job," Bobbie says with a smile while everyone around us seethes. "Where else would you like to go spread the joy?"

## CHAPTER 15

It's hard to improve on nature's palette when choosing colors for your home. Think of a forest and you get deep green, brown and sky blue. Think of a field of wildflowers or prairie grass, or of an ice flow in Alaska. Think of the emerald-green and sea-blue of the ocean…

—TipsFromTeddi.com

**We** should go to the Krolls' place and then head on home. And we would, we really would, but a trip to the marina in Northport will take us about the same half hour we'd spend at the Krolls and the kids aren't due home for at least forty-five minutes. Okay, we're cutting it close. And Bobbie doesn't really think we should go. For some reason she thinks this is police business and has nothing to do with us.

I remind her that I knew this man, that I only narrowly escaped death and that she could be planning my funeral this very minute.

This doesn't convince her.

"Fine," I say. "I'll just drop you off and go alone."

At which point she puts on her left blinker and heads for Northport.

Hey, I learned to shovel guilt at the master's knee.

I dial up the Krolls on my cell and tell Jerry that I'm sorry I have to postpone our appointment. He is, as my mother says, a marshmallow. He all but apologizes to me for making the appointment at an inconvenient time.

"You have to get home for the children," he says. "I understand. Robby is just coming in now with a very red nose from the cold." He says this more to his son than to me. "You should bring the children. I'd love to meet them and I'm sure Robby would, too."

"Well, yes," I say. "That would be very nice. But actually, something's come up and I have to make a quick trip up to Northport. Maybe I could bring the children some other time?"

"Go pick out a packet of hot chocolate," Jerry says, presumably to Robby. "I'll be in to make it in a minute." Then in a quiet voice he asks me if I'm afraid to bring the children to his house to meet Robby.

"Of course not," I say. "But I really have to get up to the marina today. What about one day next week, perhaps? Or the week after? I'm very busy trying to get the bowling alley done in time for the grand opening."

He tells me my mother says that's a mistake and then hurries off the phone. Before he hangs up I hear him calling Rita to hurry and help Robby with the microwave and my heart breaks for him.

THERE'S POLICE TAPE EVERYWHERE at the marina but, as Bobbie points out, that's never stopped me before. See, the thing I've found about police tape is that it's rarely taken down after the fact. They mean to, but they've got more important things to do.

And they obviously don't consider it a crime scene anymore or someone would be guarding it...

Okay, okay. I'm rationalizing. I'm also ducking under the tape and heading for the slip Milt's boat was docked at. At least the rain has stopped, though the planks are wet and slippery, especially in the heels I stupidly chose to wear so that Bobbie wouldn't remind me that with wide-legged pants you can't wear flats. Especially sneakers. Who knew we'd sneak in a trip to the marina, anyway?

"Wait," Bobbie tells me, heading for the clubhouse. "I have to pee."

I tell her that I'll meet her down by the boat, because I just hate it when women go to the bathroom together. Men don't do that. Why do we need company?

So here I am, standing where I stood just a week ago, only now I'm looking at the charred skeleton of a cigarette boat. There's something ironic about a cigarette boat going up in smoke.

Everything—the sea, the sky—is gray. It's spooky, looking at where I was and realizing where, given a few days and the luck of the draw, I could have been. I mean, before they took my remains to the morgue. Creepy. I wrap my arms around myself in an effort to keep warm as I hear Bobbie's footsteps coming up behind me.

"I could be dead," I say. "I was standing right there—" I put my hand out, pointing toward the cockpit, and suddenly

I'm airborne, flying out over the remains of Milt's boat and just barely clearing the far edge before landing in the water.

Well, not exactly *landing*. My feet are in the water as well as my legs, up to about my knees, judging from the cold. Something, I suppose my coat, is hooked onto the boat and is stopping me from falling all the way in.

"Help!" I scream. "Bobbie!"

Only no one answers.

I try twisting around, but I'm terrified to cut myself loose and sink into the Long Island Sound where I'll die from the cold. Lips shivering, I mumble to myself to stay calm.

That lasts five seconds.

"HELP!" I'm shrieking now, trying to get my legs out of the water, but my nice, fresh-from-the-cleaners trousers feel like they are loaded with lead. And my feet are too numb to respond.

I think I hear high heels tip-tapping on the dock. Is that what I heard when I thought Bobbie was coming? Or did I hear very light, nearly silent, sneakery feet?

I yell again.

"Teddi?" I hear Bobbie ask, her voice vague. "If you left me here, I'll kill you."

"I'm in the freakin' water," I shout. I try to wave, but shifting sinks me a few inches deeper into the Sound.

"No you're not," Bobbie says, because denial is her favorite weapon against fear. "I don't see you."

I explain how I'm over the side of the boat, caught by my coat or something, partially submerged, freezing. And I tell her she's got to help me.

"It's Dana's purse," she says. "Oh my God—you're still carrying that thing?"

"It's carrying me," I say. "Get help. My feet are numb."

She tells me she is coming down into the boat to help me.

"No," I shout, hoping to stop her before it's too late. The boat isn't going to hold her, and we'll just both wind up in the water with no help.

She says she'll run back to the clubhouse, but I hear people's voices in the distance.

"Tell them to call the Coast Guard," I say. "Or get someone to come out and get me in another boat."

"I'll do it," Bobbie says, "I can—oh, shit. My heel's caught. Hang on."

I remind her I *am* hanging on, by a cheap purse strap, and that my clothes will weigh me down and take me to the bottom of the ocean forever if she doesn't take off her goddamn shoe and get me help.

"How did you get over there, anyway?" she asks, just as some funny-looking boat motors into the harbor.

"Over here!" I yell. "Help!"

I know the minute the man on the boat sees me. He looks like a cartoon character, his arms waving as he runs back to the steering wheel, pulls the life preserver off his wall and hoists it in my direction. It lands several feet away from me, and there is no way I'm pulling free of my noose to reach it.

"She's stuck," Bobbie yells to him. I hear lots of footsteps on the dock and suddenly hordes of people are yelling all sorts of instructions and advice.

And there's lots of "how did she get in the water in the first place?" echoing across the sound.

"DID I NOT TELL YOU to keep out of this?" Drew asks me at the hospital where everyone insisted I go to be sure I didn't get frostbite.

He can't sit still and his pacing is driving me crazy.

"Did I not say that this was dangerous? So what is the first thing you do? You go see the boat and fall into the water and nearly drown. You're lucky you're not losing your toes—you realize that?"

"*Fall* in?" I say, like he's the one with frostbite—of the brain. "*Fall* in? I'm clear on the other side of the boat, hanging by my purse strap, and you think I *slipped* off the dock?"

"It's been known to happen," he says with a smirk. Then he has the nerve to ask what shoes I was wearing. Luckily, they fell off in the water and are lost forever as evidence that I have no sense when it comes to dressing for dock work. Especially in the wet weather.

"I heard footsteps. And I felt the shove—Drew, I was definitely pushed into the water."

His head snaps around like that hadn't occurred to him before now. "Someone else was in the boat with you? And what? You just didn't notice?"

I tell him, for the third time, that I wasn't in the freakin' boat.

"That does it, Teddi," he says. "You crossed police lines. You crossed my lines. Stay the fuck out of it."

And with that, he storms out of the hospital.

Great. No shoes. No car. No ride.

That's one way to keep me out of it.

I ASK MY FATHER if he'd mind babysitting tonight. I've got to do some work on the alley and while I know I could leave the kids on their own, I've been doing it an awful lot, lately. And after Rio's visit a few nights ago, I just don't want to do it again.

Grandpa sounds thrilled. His plan is to come without Mom, bring in pizza, watch TV with Jesse, buy some love from Dana and cuddle Alyssa a bit. He warns me that he doesn't want to stay too late, so I shouldn't plan on working very long.

Naturally this plan is thwarted, as are all plans to have a good time without my mother.

"You have to go back to the alley?" my mother asks me when I open the front door and she, too, is standing there. "I told you this project was a mistake."

Before I can bend the truth just a little by letting her believe that's where I'm going, she tells the kids to get dressed up because she and Grandpa are taking them out for a real dinner.

"Not that fast-food *hazzerai* your mother lets you ruin your bodies with."

"That's how you're going to work?" my mother asks me as I shrug a jacket on over a very short skirt I bought in a weak moment at Bobbie's insistence.

"Let her be, June," my father says. It's his mantra, I think. I'm not really familiar with mantras, but aren't they words uttered over and over again which make the utterer calmer while, in reality, changing absolutely nothing?

"You really didn't have to come, Mom," I tell her, which buys me a look like I've betrayed her.

"So your father said," she snaps at me, but I really don't have time to go there. And besides, Dana comes sulking down the stairs just then.

Since Rio's visit, I've tried to find out what was said and the closest I could get was Jesse's account which included a lot of slamming of cabinets and drawers and doors, and asking his sister if everything was okay several times. She told him she hated her father with every fiber of her being. Apparently she hasn't gotten over whatever he did just yet.

I'd say she was just being a dramatic teenager, but having felt exactly the same way about the same man just a few years ago, I'm not in a position to throw stones.

She asks me if she has to go out to dinner. I tell her that no, she doesn't, but it will make her grandfather happy. It's a dirty trick, but of course it works and she agrees to go.

I blow kisses over my shoulder on my way out and hear my mother ask Dana where I'm really going dressed like I think I'm still fourteen.

You THOUGHT I WASN'T HEADED for the alley, didn't you? Well, surprise.

I go inside the alley and find that The Spare Slices have withdrawn from the league. Dave is hanging out at the bar, hoping to sub in, even though he knows it's technically against the rules.

I teeter over to him on my heels and stand next to him, doing the guy thing. You don't know what the guy thing is? They did some studies and found that women relate face to face, but guys relate shoulder to shoulder. Like how they watch sports.

So I stand beside Dave and look at the back of the bar, just like he's doing. And I say, "Hi Dave, how's it going?" without looking at him.

He tells me it's going okay, but I can tell he's as nervous as an ostrich at a Vegas showgirl convention.

"It must be pretty hard on you," I say, and I can't help looking at him out of the corner of my eye. His nose is red, his eyes are watery. "First Joey and now Milt."

"Damndest whatdayacallit…when things happen kind of at the same time but they're not connected?"

"Coincidence?" I ask him. Even Dave can't think this is simply a coincidence.

But apparently he does.

I ask after Russ and Miles. Dave's talked to them. Neither one is going to go to Milt's funeral because they think it's too dangerous.

I ask if Dave is going.

"Hell yeah, I am," he says, and he turns to me. "Milt was my buddy. Joey was my buddy. Max is my buddy. Ain't nothing gonna keep me from my buds."

I gotta admit, I like Dave. I ask him how Max is doing.

"He's going to be okay," Dave tells me. "He can't like, you know, talk or nothing yet, but they say he's got waves of brain or something."

I tell him that's very good news. "He's lucky to have a friend like you to see him through his recovery," I say.

Dave assures me Max has lots of friends, though, "like I said, they're mostly afraid to come out at the moment."

I ask him who he's seen visit Max. He names some people he tells me are from Waldbaum's, a couple of bowlers from other teams, some family. And some of the guys.

Steve, who has become significantly slimier since I showed up in Bobbie's belt-masquerading-as-a-skirt, sidles up next to me. "You know," he says, putting an arm around me, "you could get arrested for chatting up the customers in an outfit like that."

"She's probably hoping just that," Mark says, trying to wedge himself between Steve and me. "Provided it's a certain detective that arrests her."

He gives me the once-over and frowns.

"You gonna have time to check the positioning of these lamps over here?"

Happy to leave the gang at the bar, I follow Mark over to the billiards area where he warns me about Steve coming on too strong. "He's planning on screwing you both ways."

I must blush, because then Mark does.

"Not—" he can't quite find the words "—front door, back door. I mean besides wanting to jump your bones, gorgeous, he's counting on you not getting this place finished by Friday night."

"It'll be done," I say, way more breezily than the situation warrants.

Where *did* the time go?

Uh—maybe it was investigating two murders and an assault, not to mention one daughter's inappropriate liaison.

"Gorgeous, unless you got some secret weapon under that skirt—one that can get the fixtures in the bathrooms installed and the bar refinished, not just make no one care whether they are—we're in one deep doo-doo pit."

I ask him how long he thinks it'll take him to get the restrooms ready.

"With or without my elves?" he asks, like we have time for fairy tales and fun and games.

"Alone?" he asks. "And it looks like I'm gonna be alone, no way they'll be done before next week."

"And not alone?" I ask him.

"*If* I had someone helping me full-time, someone who was really here and not just saying she was here and then taking advantage of her father and going to meet some jerk who doesn't know how lucky he is—" and here he takes a breath, but not long enough for me to come up with any defense "—and *if* that person was willing to work nights along with me, I might be able to get it done by Friday."

He looks at my skimpy little skirt.

"But I don't see that happening."

I promise him that I'll be back in an hour or so and that I'll work with him all night. "I just have an appointment I can't break."

"*Appointment*, huh? With your gynecologist?"

I tug at my skirt, or what there is of it. "Huh?" I ask, wishing I could blame Bobbie, except I'm the one who forked over the cash and I'm the one who put it on tonight. Of course, tonight I have a special reason for wearing it. It's sort of undercover.

"Aren't you dressed for someone to check out your privates?" Mark asks.

I tell him I'll be back in an hour, tops, and he suggests that if I actually do come back—and he sounds really doubtful—that I might want to wear something I can bend over in. "If you want to help and not get us even farther behind."

I SHOW UP AT DREW'S PLACE and I have to say that he looks less than thrilled to see me. He takes me in from head to toe and sort of drawls, "Intent on frostbite?"

I ask if I'm invited in or if he wants me to freeze out here, where my legs are nearly as cold as they were in the Sound. He doesn't pretend not to notice how I'm dressed.

"Leave your pimp in the car?" he asks, pulling me into his condo and slamming the door shut with his foot.

I tell him I thought I'd cut out the middleman.

"Do you have any idea how good you look?" he asks me.

"If you like the ho look," I say, tugging again at my skirt.

He asks why I wore the outfit if I think I look trashy.

I don't have a good answer, but he does.

"Unless, of course, you wanted to turn me on. And you have." He sits down on his couch, leans back and locks his hands behind his head. "Wanna show me whatcha got?"

What I've got is a huge dose of embarrassment. "I'm gonna go back to the bowling alley," I say quietly, picking up my purse and heading for the door.

"Please, don't." His voice is low, earnest.

I admit I don't know what I was thinking.

He says it's probably the skirt. He can't think, either.

"You do things to me, Teddi Bayer," he says. "Scare me. I say things I'd never say, like I'm someone I don't even know, when I'm around you."

I stay facing the door, but I'm not going out. I ask what he means.

"Suddenly I'm protective, possessive. I was always the guy with the sexiest woman in the room on my arm and I wanted every guy in the place to know I was going to take her home and that piece of tail was mine. Eat your hearts out.

"Only I don't want anyone looking at you like that. I want you to wear glasses and overalls and false buck teeth. I don't want anyone seeing those legs but me. You know how many cases I've had of guys killing because someone else wanted their woman, touched their woman? Cases I never understood?"

I knew coming was a mistake. I knew that the skirt was going to turn him on and that was what I had in mind, but I didn't think he was going to go mushy on me. Scary mushy. "I'm flattered," I say. "Really. But no one else is interested. Honest."

He looks skeptically at my legs. "How about we do something with the kids this weekend?" he asks. "The Bronx Zoo? Miniature golf?"

And I thought he was scary mushy before. The only thing worse would be him asking me home to meet his mother.

"And then we could—"

I slide the zipper of my skirt down and shimmy out of it, still not facing him, still in my jacket. I've got a furry little short parka, fishnet hose and four-inch heels.

And I'm figuring he won't bring up his mother now.

His footsteps are soft as he comes up behind me and slips my jacket off my shoulders. He breathes in deeply and says I smell good as my jacket slides to the floor.

He kisses the back of my neck. As good as his kisses are in other places, my neck is still my favorite. And he knows it. He holds up my hair and rains little kisses up and down and up and down until my knees go weak. And he leads me back to the couch where he lays me down and undoes the little buttons on my sweater.

Men don't talk when they are making love. At least, in my limited experience, I don't think they do. Rio didn't. Drew doesn't. I'm relieved to lose myself in pure sensation without the complicated declarations or instructions or even murmurs of appreciation.

I don't want to think about forever, or even tomorrow. I don't want to know I'll ever leave this room, this couch, these arms. I don't want to acknowledge *after*.

I only want to be lost in right now, right here.

His skin is warm. Hot where it touches mine. And he dizzies me and thrills me and satisfies me.

"This isn't what I had in mind." I am shocked when I realize the words have come out aloud.

"Really?" Drew says drolly. He is trying to extricate his watch from my fishnet pantyhose and I'm not sure it's an accident when he rips them. "You came over in these—" He shakes my pantyhose at me. He's still fighting with them, only now they seem to be winning.

I tell him I fully intended to do what we did, I just thought that I'd be the one doing the…uh…pleasuring. "And then I thought we could talk about Miles and—"

It's a mistake. I see the wheels turning in his head and I see he doesn't like where the train is going.

"I'm not telling you anything about this case, if that's what you thought you were buying with this," he says, sitting up and pushing my legs off his lap.

"I wasn't *buying* anything," I say, reaching for something to cover myself with. Okay, maybe I was *bartering*…

He accuses me of virtually seducing him so that he'd owe me.

"I just thought—" I start, but he isn't interested in what I thought and, besides, I don't really have any good excuse. I didn't think I needed one for making love and I say so.

Only he contends I wasn't making love, I was making a trade, a bargain. *I give you my body, you give me information.* "What if I made love to you and expected something in return?" he asks me.

I think about what it is Drew wants from me. "Don't you?" I ask him.

I THINK MARK IS SURPRISED to see me back. He's down on his knees in the bathroom attaching the plumbing under the sinks. He pokes his head out and studies me from the knees down.

"Look who finally showed up," he says.

He touches the rolled-up cuffs on the jeans I borrowed from Drew, noting that they're several sizes too big.

"I don't suppose you want to do any work, do you?"

I pick up a wrench, but I just stand there with it, trying to decide what I'm supposed to do.

"You okay?" he asks, and I realize I probably look as shaky as I feel.

"Hunky-dory," I say.

He looks at me strangely.

"Peachy keen."

"That's it. I'll kill him," Mark says, uncurling himself and starting to get up.

"No need," I say. After all, I seem to have cut him to the quick myself. I sink down to the floor and hold the pipe while Mark wields the wrench. "I really screwed up."

Mark asks me if I want to talk about it—*while we work.* I think not. What happened between Drew and me seems incredibly private—and I don't mean the sex. It was that he was offering his commitment to me and I saw it as a negative, something he'd have to bribe to get out of me.

I just shake my head and Mark acknowledges that it's out of bounds with a nod.

"If it makes you feel any better—and trust me, this won't," he says. "You're not the only one who screwed up."

It's nearly midnight, and I think this is probably not something I want to hear.

"Rio—" he starts, and now I'm sure this is not something I want to hear.

In a flash I see my mother in the bridal room of the Meadowbrook Country Club as I'm getting into my wedding gown. "You will regret this for the rest of your life," she's telling me. "Every day there will be a new reason for you to regret this."

Not that she didn't like Rio, or anything. She just didn't think he was good enough for me. Or anyone else who was still breathing.

I ask what Rio did now, hoping that it (a) did not involve our children, and (b) is fixable by Friday.

"You know how the security systems were working fine," he says.

I try not to blush as I nod.

Mark avoids eye contact, busying himself with the J-trap. "There's a short in them now. We're going to have to pull up every piece of molding, check the wires and replace the molding."

"We?" I ask. "We? It's Rio's mistake. He—"

Mark cuts me off. "Your ex is some piece of work, gorgeous. He decided that it was Steve who actually cut the wire so that you wouldn't get finished in time and he wouldn't have to pay you."

It doesn't seem to me that far-fetched, but it's more the sort of thing Rio, not Steve, would do.

"And now he's not allowed within ten feet of the place or Steve's gonna call the cops."

"Why does everything always come back to the cops?" I ask.

"You and the good detective have a fight?" he asks.

I think about my answer. I cried and he was angry, so I

guess it qualified as a fight. "Yeah," I say softly, handing him the plumber's tape and a paper towel to check for leaks.

"Over…?" Mark asks.

Over my family? Over my fishnet stockings? Over what he's feeling about me versus what I'm feeling about him? About how he's free to feel whatever he wants and I'm in this box that includes three children, two parents and an ex with a new family and a dog.

Well, the dog is mine. The new baby is his.

"Over that he thinks he loves me," I say. And I put my head against Mark's big, broad shoulder and press my lips together before I say any more.

## CHAPTER 16

The most important room of your house, the one that gives others the impression of just who you are, may not be a room at all. It's your entryway, and some people will never get farther than that. Does yours say *come in*, or *beat it*? Draw the eye and the visitor into the next room with an inviting color, use a mirror with a shelf hung below it if there isn't room for a small table. Have a small rug for wiping feet both inside and outside the door so people don't hesitate to step farther in. And don't forget the door itself. Color, a door knocker, a wreath of flowers—anything that shouts, *I live here!*

—TipsFromTeddi.com

I should go directly back to the alley. Despite how much progress Mark and I made last night, and we did, it still will be down to the wire. I think that's another sports metaphor. I hate thinking that Rio rubbed off on me. Makes me want to scrub my skin with lye and a loofah.

Anyway, having collapsed on the couch after three this morning, I am stealing an hour—half of it to pay the Krolls a visit and half to check on Max at the hospital. Now, I could pretend to myself, or to Drew, that the visit to Max is just because he's a dear friend—who I hardly know—and that the visit to the Krolls is business. I just want to shore up that account. But the truth is that I can't let go of the nagging feeling in my gut that somehow the deaths of Dr. Doris and Joey Ingraham and Milt are all tied together along with Max's being in the hospital, and that somewhere in that pile lie the Krolls.

You remember the last time I ignored a gut feeling? Well, I'm not about to do it again. And if I'm right and somehow the Krolls are tied up in this—Dr. Doris did, after all, call Jerry Kroll, and he did lie about it—then they, too, could be in danger. That makes me really crazy because Rita is my mother's friend and if something were to happen to her, I just might be visiting my mother at South Winds Psychiatric Center for years to come.

If she'd let me, since she'd hold me responsible for not preventing it.

So, here I am, standing at the Krolls' front door, trying to come up with some excuse for stopping by.

Jerry Kroll answers the door in his bathrobe. He seems very surprised to see me. Maybe that's because it's early in the morning and I've arrived unexpectedly. I apologize for not calling first, but say that I was on my way out of the driveway this morning when I was struck with a brilliant idea for their house and would he mind terribly if I just came in for a few minutes?

He gestures for me to come in, one of those my-house-is-your-house sort of waves.

*Idea, idea, please have an idea.*

Nothing.

I stand in the hallway. Staring up the steps to the bedrooms.

*Please, please! An idea. Any idea.*

"Yes!" I shout brightly, I suppose because I'm so happy to have thought of anything. "It would work perfectly. Where's Rita? I'd like to present this to both of you."

He calls her and she toddles out of her bedroom in her bathrobe. I glance at my watch. Eight-thirty. I've shown up unannounced at a client's house at eight-thirty. I will never hear the end of this from my mother.

And she'll be right, unfortunately.

"Stay right there," I tell her, raising my hand to stop her at the head of the stairs. "Now. Imagine double-width stairs," I say, stretching the stairs in the air with my hands.

Jerry smiles. Rita looks like she's been anointed queen.

"It will give the entryway elegance, formality, gravitas. Instead of merely being access to the upstairs, it will be a statement."

Jerry is nodding. Rita, I think, is imagining herself coming down the staircase at Tara.

"Tiled?" Jerry asks.

I shake my head. "Too cold and austere. Either dark wood—mahogany, maybe—or sculptured carpet. Champagne beige."

Rita looks down at the steps.

"Let's talk about it," Jerry says. "Come. I've got coffee and fresh bagels."

I'm quick to agree because it gets me into their kitchen, sitting around the breakfast table with them, sort of shooting the breeze. And I'm hungry and it gets me a bagel.

"Tell us, darling, how your work is going," Rita says. "Your mother says you'll never get done in time and you won't get paid if you don't finish. I told her she had it wrong, but she insisted—"

I admit that she has it right, though it pains me.

"It's too bad Jerry can't help you," Rita says, she pats his hand affectionately. "He used to be very handy."

"What do you mean 'used to be'?" he says, puffing out his chest.

"Put himself through Brooklyn College as a handyman. When they say self-made man, they're talking about my Jerry."

Jerry says that was a long time ago, when he was young and strong, and he gets up to look out the window. He waves and I hear the toot of a bicycle horn.

"He should come in soon. It's cold out," Jerry says and looks at my coat, hanging behind me over the chair. "And you should be wearing something warmer."

"That's my Jerry. Taking care of everyone. You should have seen him with Joey. Checking with the nurses, picking up his pills. Everything, he did."

"Stop," Jerry says, waving her praise away and returning to my coat. "That jacket isn't warm enough for October, Teddi, dear."

I tell him that today it's surprisingly warm for so late in the year. "Not warm enough for a dip in the ocean, mind you..."

Jerry laughs. "Why would anyone do that?"

I tell them about Milt Sherman, who was on Joey's bowling team and who's died in a freak accident that the police are calling suspicious.

"I told you," Rita says, pointing her finger at Jerry and sputtering. "I told you it's all fishy, but no, you think it's all in my head. You think—"

"I think you keep carrying on like this you're gonna need a pill, Ritzala," Jerry says, looking at me like I should back him up.

"I do have some good news," I say, trying to lighten the mood, and I tell them how I saw Max this morning and how he's regained consciousness. I admit he isn't exactly his old self, and that he's got a lot of healing to do. "He can't remember what happened, but the doctors say that'll come back. And they feel he's definitely going to make it."

"Good," Jerry says. "That's very good."

And then the talk shifts back to decorating their house and we discuss the pros and cons of wood versus carpet. At their age I really lean toward carpeting, as a fall on wood is sure to break bones.

"We're all getting older," I say, including myself in the geriatric set. "Ailments happen."

"Like Joey," Rita says. "And he was my baby brother."

"He ate like a pig," Jerry says. "He was warned and warned, Ritzala. You know that."

"What did the doctor say?" I ask, finally getting to it. Only Jerry looks at me quizzically. "About his health. She must have thought the surgery would help him, right?"

"It was supposed to fix everything, the angioplasty," Rita says. "Put him through all that and then it didn't work, did it?"

My shrug is noncommittal, but Jerry is adamant. "She could have bought him maybe a few months more than he got, but it was a case of sooner or later with him. She should have told him to stop stuffing his face with trans-fatty acids and hydrogenated oils. We never eat that stuff."

I think about the dozen or so mini-pastries Rita wolfed down just the other day. "Good for you," I tell him. "I know everyone is talking about her like she was a saint, but it seems to me that the good doctor owed you an apology."

"That'll be the day," Jerry says. "And open herself up to a malpractice suit?"

"But I thought she did call you. Wasn't it the day she died?" I put another spoonful of sugar in my coffee so that I don't have to meet Jerry's eyes.

"What makes you think she called?" Jerry asks.

I try to look confused, because I'm not exactly going to say that the police told me, now am I? "Didn't we talk about it at my mother's?" I ask Rita. "I guess you told her."

"Rita didn't know she called," Jerry says. We both look at him. "I mean, it would have just upset her if I told her."

"Well, you must have told Marty then," Rita says, completely unperturbed. "And he told June. You know how these things get around."

"My dad," I say, my hand proudly against my chest. "Don't you adore him?"

Jerry says that actually he doesn't know him very well.

Just as a client. And he's sure he didn't tell him about the doctor's call because he can't remember the last time he spoke to him.

"Well, someone told someone," Rita says, reaching for a muffin that really doesn't look to me like it's trans-fat free.

"I guess so," I say with a laugh. "Or else how would I know?"

I LEFT DISAPPOINTED, having learned nothing about why Jerry is hiding the good doctor's call, and now I get to spend the day at the alley, tracing wires and cursing my ex-husband, who swears it was nothing he did, and my partner, who through no fault of her own is sitting in for Mike's receptionist, Marguerite, who, through no fault of *her* own had to go down to Bayside to take care of her mother. I hate it when things go wrong and you can't be mad at the people you really are mad at.

And I'm damned worried about the safety of poor old Jerry and Rita.

Just before three, when I'm ready to rush back to the house to welcome the kids home from school, by which I mean make sure they all got there and no nineteen-year-olds are rolling up my driveway, I find the problem.

"Look at this," I say to Mark, who is putting the last of the chair rails back in place. I hold up two wire ends for him to see.

"Cut," he says, looking at the placement and seeing that it would have been easy for someone to slice the wire just at the corner where the moldings meet. "Run a little blade down here at the joint and the whole system's shut down."

"Can you fix it?" I ask. "Without ripping the whole thing out?"

He tells me that there may be just enough slack to splice the wires together, but he's angry as hell. He just isn't sure who to be angry at. As I said, I know that feeling well.

"Gotta run," I tell him. "Just a quick check of the kids and I'll be back."

Mark nods grudgingly and waves me off as he kneels down to attend to the wires.

AT HOME, Maggie May and I find Dana in an uncharacteristically good mood. Either she's gotten over her lothario, or—more likely—he's not as out of the picture as I'd thought.

Maggie gets a biscuit and I even get a kiss on the cheek, something I haven't gotten since Dana's bat mitzvah, I don't think.

"What's up, sweetie?" I ask her, trying not appear accusatory or suspicious. "Good day at school?" Like I care, at this point, how school is going.

She tells me she got an A on her Spanish test and she has a paper due on Monday in social studies. "So I'm off to the library," she says, then adds, "If that's okay."

So do I say, *aha!* and tell her that no, it's not okay, and ask just how stupid she thinks I am? Or do I pretend to trust her because mistrusting her gives her license to abuse my trust?

Some days I really hate being the mom.

While Jesse wanders in and out to get a Ring Ding and milk, avoiding eye contact with me and making a production out of giving Lys a snack as well, I ask Dana what the paper is on. She's fully prepared to snow me with details.

She explains the assignment, even pulls out a photocopy and asks my opinion on which topic she should choose.

*Honesty* isn't on the list.

I tell her I have some research to do, too, and that we'll go over together.

"Okay," she says, but some of the brightness goes out of her voice.

Her cell phone rings and she turns away from me when she answers it. She tells the caller that she can't really talk because she and *her mother* are going over to the library.

Which now makes my going unnecessary.

I sit down at the kitchen table and motion for her to join me.

"You're still seeing that boy." I don't ask, I tell.

She stares at the table, picking at a spot I missed after breakfast.

"What do you think about a nineteen-year-old boy who tries to see a girl who is only thirteen?" I ask. "A girl whose father has made it abundantly clear that she isn't allowed to see him?"

"Juliet was only—" she starts.

"And look how that ended up," I say. "This isn't drama, Dana. This is real life. And in real life there's no rewind button and you can't go back and change things if they don't turn out well."

She glances up at me, but quickly looks away. "You and Daddy—"

I know I ought to hear her out, but I can't help myself. "Another example of things not ending well. Your father and I weren't right for each other and we knew it from the outset. In some ways, I was spiting your grandmother, though if you tell her that, I'll be forced to have your vocal chords removed."

A slight smile curls the edge of her lips.

"Do you think that there is even the slightest chance that this boy is trying to see you now to get back at your father for hitting him?" I ask.

She looks shocked at the suggestion. And then there is just the slightest, vaguest, littlest bit of doubt that crosses her face and I remember how she told me that Jared said he'd get even.

"It would be easy to understand that at his age he doesn't want to be told what to do by somebody's daddy. But it's not particularly admirable."

Dana looks at me like *admirable* is not the quality she's looking for in a boy at this moment. I wasn't either. Like Rio said, he understands this boy because he *was* this boy.

And then a rather nasty thought occurs to me. "By any chance, does Jared carry a little knife?" I ask, thinking about the wires at the bowling alley.

Dana is up in arms, jumping from the table, saying he would never, ever, in a million years hurt her.

*That* thought hadn't even occurred to me. Naturally, and convincingly, I sympathetically agree that of course he wouldn't—thinking to myself that he wouldn't because he will never see her again, even if that means locking her in her room until she's seventy.

And then I wonder aloud if he could possibly have sabotaged the job her father did at the alley.

I don't hear her denying it.

I remind her that if the job isn't finished by Friday, a month's worth of work goes down the drain. My work. I don't mention that so do the new Diesel jeans she wants, the movies, food.

"If he did that, he hurt *me*."

"Maybe Daddy just did it wrong," she suggests. "You know he doesn't know too much about the security business. He's just doing it to be near you, probably."

I agree that her father might have installed the system wrong. "And yet we saw it working, didn't we?"

She doesn't answer me.

Dana is a good kid. She may have more of my mother in her than I would hope, but she's smart and good and I don't see any other choice here.

I mean, sure, I could forbid her from seeing this guy, but she'd find a way. I can't watch her 24-7.

"Look," I say softly, coming up and putting an arm around her. "You have to make a choice here and it's a hard one. I know it's glamorous for an older man to be interested in you, but, as special as you are, don't you think it's a little odd? He could be dating eighteen-year-olds, women who are ready for what he is ready for."

Her back stiffens, like I've questioned her worth.

"And then there's his sense of responsibility. You and I both know it's highly unlikely that a stone from the road kicked up and broke your window. But did he own up to it? No."

It's hard for me to look at the hurt in her eyes, but no one ever said being the mother would be easy.

"And, if there is even a chance that he is the one who cut the wires at the alley, risking several thousand dollars we need to live on, Dana…"

"Maybe he didn't even do that," she says, her chin jutting out at the injustice of it all.

I point out to her that she didn't say *he didn't do it*, but that *maybe he didn't do it*.

"So?" she asks.

"So you have doubts. Weigh that against your father's love for you." I can't believe I'm saying this, pulling out Rio's love for her and holding it up like some shining beacon. But there it is. "Do you doubt that?"

Dana doesn't answer me.

I sit back down at the table. "As I said, you've got a choice."

"Can I go to the library?" she asks me.

Having painted myself into a corner, I really can't say no. I nod my head.

"Will you come with me?"

*Of course* is the only possible answer and I tell her I will, but that I've got a couple of calls to make before we go. She heads outside to wait in the car and I dial up Mark to tell him that I'm going to be a little delayed. Beyond a groan, he's understanding and accepting. Someone is going to be mighty lucky someday to snag him.

Dana's honking the horn frantically, as if one more minute will kill her, and I take my sweet time gathering up my things because sometimes I can be very childish. I mean, I can't think of any other reason, so that must be the case.

Anyway, I come outside and find Robert Kroll doing wheelies around my car, scaring the hell out of Dana. I know, I know, it's terribly un-PC, but he scares me, too. The man is big and strong and has no sense of the boundaries that he crosses. He's a lot older than he was the last time I saw him, though he was doing about the same thing then. Now his beard is going gray and his skin shows signs of every day he's spent out in the elements.

With a wave at Dana to stop honking the horn, which apparently only encourages him, I try approaching the man that scared the whole neighborhood when I was growing up. Of course, since he's riding his bike in little tight circles, that isn't easy. I remind myself that in all the years I've known about Robert, he's never hurt a soul.

"Stop, Robby," I say, trying to sound completely calm while Dana cringes in the passenger seat. "I want to see the new bike your dad got you."

Robby stops an inch from running over my foot. "You know my dad?" he asks.

"I sure do," I tell him. "And I know you. I used to live around the corner from you before I got married." I ask if he remembers the Bayers.

"The big house with the green door," he says. "I don't live there anymore."

I smile and tell him mine was the stone house with the two pillars out front and that I don't live there anymore, either.

While we have this exchange, Dana cracks open her window just a little.

"I like your new bike," I tell him. "But when you ride it so fast so close to people, I think it might scare them."

Emphatically, he nods. "I like to scare people," he tells me.

The mean, small-minded side of me thinks I really don't have time for this. But the good, responsible-mother side wins out and I think about what I'm teaching Dana—or could be.

"That's my daughter, Dana," I say, pointing at her. I tell her to open the window so that I can introduce her to an old friend.

"I don't know you," Robby says. "And I'm not supposed to talk to strangers."

"Mo-om," Dana whines at me. "He is like totally weird. We should go."

He asks me why she said he was weird. I tell him that she's thirteen, and thirteen-year-olds think everyone is weird and he shouldn't worry about it. I tell him I think he's nice. And I force Dana to say she thinks so, too. Something about the whole conversation feels like he's got a gun to our heads, that I'm diffusing some threat.

"Is he going to kill us?" Dana asks, proving my point.

"Of course not," I say at the same time as Robby says, "My dad could kill your mom."

Dana's eyes get wide and watery.

I try to laugh it off. "Your dad and I are friends," I say. "In fact, I saw him earlier today."

"We went to the ocean," he says.

"In the summer? To the beach?" I prompt.

"Then, too," he says, and he puts his foot on the pedals and rocks back and forth on his bike. "I have to go now."

"Goodbye, Robby," I say as he makes one last circle around the car and then starts down the block. "It was nice to see you again," I call after him.

After I get in the car and take a few calming breaths, Dana asks, in usual thirteen-ese, "What is wrong with that guy?"

I explain that he had some sort of illness—if memory serves, it was an infection which led to encephalitis—and his brain stopped developing.

"So he's like retarded?" Dana asks me.

"Dana!" And then I realize that I'm just looking for a nicer way to admit that yes, he is. I want to say something wise and profound and all I come up with is that he's mentally disabled, that he has the mind of an eight- or nine-year-old and he'll never really grow up. And that just as we have to look out for children, we have to look out for people like Robby.

She parrots the words, agreeing with them, processing them. "So in his head he's not much older than Lys?"

I nod.

"But he's got a beard and gray hair and all." She looks over at me behind the wheel. "I know, I know. That's outside, not inside. But he's still creepy."

I wish I could disagree with her. Instead, I just say, "Nevertheless, or maybe all the more reason, he deserves our compassion." It sounds hollow. Here was this great opportunity to teach my daughter a moral lesson and I'm blowing it.

"You were really good with him, Mom," Dana says. "It was really nice when you told him it was good to see him again."

I pat her thigh and put the car into reverse. On occasion, I do something right.

"Even," she adds, "if it was a lie."

## CHAPTER 17

Just as we tend to raise our children as we were raised, we tend to decorate our houses in the same manner as our parents did. Oh, our houses might be grander, but if the TV was in the living room in the house you grew up in, chances are it's in yours, and vice versa. It's human nature. But it may be time to cut the apron strings and take a look at what was automatic and what was purposeful. Do you really want the TV in the living room like your parents had? Do you want to sit at a desk in the basement to pay bills like your dad did? Do you want to stand at the sink to put on your makeup like mom, or sit at a dressing table in the bedroom by the window where the light is natural and divine?

—TipsFromTeddi.com

**We're** both on edge when we get to the library. I see the "boy" before Dana does. After seeing Robby, this kid doesn't look quite so old. Our eyes meet and he knows I'm aware of who he is. He does the same shoulder swag I've seen Rio do a million times. What is it that the goyim say? The sins of the father?

Very patriarchal.

I'm thinking it's more like *the sins of the mother*. Which fits, since in Jewish families matrilineality is the rule. Technically, it means that Jewish descent is passed on from the mother to the child. Apparently, in our family it also means that mistakes are passed on from mother to child. I mean, look at my mother and Carmine De'Guisseppe. Me and Rio. Dana and this tough kid in a leather jacket daring me with a look to tell him where to get off.

"He's over there," I tell Dana, jerking my head in the jerk's direction. "Do you want me to come with you?"

She gives a tiny shake of her head and then flips her hair back and walks over to him like she owns the world. She gets that from my mother, too, and maybe it's the one thing about both of them I envy. That page is missing from my *Secret Handbook*.

Oh, wait. I don't have *The Handbook* at all.

I watch the boy's face as he denies one thing after another. Dana's back is to me and her body language isn't telling me much. Not until she turns on her heel and starts to come back to me. The boy reaches out and grabs her arm and before I can do anything, she wrenches her arm away and walks slowly and deliberately toward me.

"Talk about retards," she says and I flash her a look that says even under these circumstances that's not okay.

She shrugs it off. "Come on," she says, looking over her shoulder once last time and raising her head high. "I can do the research over the Internet."

I BEGGED AND I PLEADED, but Dana insisted she was perfectly fine and could stay home instead of coming along to keep me company at the alley. I reminded her I'm only a phone call away and took off.

And now here I am, up to my elbows in plumbing fixtures with Mark and Bobbie—and wishing that I was the mother I want my children to have.

Mark has done an incredible job. I've decided that he either never sleeps or he has a crew of elves that come in after we leave. Or both. I don't know how I'll ever thank him if we actually get done in time for the grand opening— a term I've come to hate.

The theme from *NYPD Blue* gets louder and louder until Bobbie refuses to let me ignore it.

"If you don't want to talk to him, tell him," she says, pulling my phone out of my purse. "Or do you want me to?"

She opens it, expecting me to grab it from her, but I don't.

"Hello?" she says into it, her voice not as sure as it usually is. He must ask if it's me, because she says, "No. It's Bobbie. She's in the bathroom with Mark…"

She watches me hand Mark a long-handled screwdriver to tighten one of the hose clamps.

"They're screwing at the moment," she says brightly into the phone. "Can I take a message? Drew? Detective Scoones?"

She raises her shoulders at me.

"He hung up."

Mark calls her a troublemaker and offers to call Drew back, but I shrug it off.

"You gonna tell us what he did or should we just hate

him on general principles?" Bobbie asks. "Past performance and all that?"

I tell them that if they want to hate someone, they should hate me. I was the heavy this time. But I refuse to give them details.

"He said he loved her," Mark tells Bobbie.

"No he didn't," she says, fishing around in her purse for a pack of cigarettes. When she finds them, she pulls one out and stares at me. "Because I'd know. She'd tell me first. Wouldn't you?"

I remind her she can't smoke in the building and she tells me she was just going out. She slips out of her canvas slides and hikes on her suede boots with the hooker heels on them.

Fifteen minutes or so go by. "She's not coming back, is she?" I say to Mark.

"It's a girl thing, I think," Mark explains to me, like I'm not one. "Best friends, giggle, giggle, giggle, run to the ladies' room together…"

"Share Tampax…"

Mark looks stricken.

"Sorry," I say. I think best friends—not to mention partners—help when they are needed. They don't go off and sulk because they weren't the first to learn something. I mean, we are grown-ups and we should be past—

Steve bursts into the ladies' room looking frantic. "Bobbie…uh—"

I'm on my feet and out the door before he can get the rest of it out. I find Bobbie inside, on a chair by the front door, her left foot up on a second chair, her face contorted in pain.

"I was lying there for hours," she tells me. "Why didn't you come looking for me?"

I ask her what happened. She winces in agony and tells me that three hours ago, maybe four by now, maybe two weeks, she fell on the sidewalk. Steve found her and carried her in.

"It's not wet, it's not slick, it's not my fault," Steve says. "And I should get points for carrying her in."

"Points?" she shouts. "Somebody's gonna pay for my freakin' boots," she tells him, pointing at the heel-less left one.

"We should get that off before your foot gets too swollen," I say. Bobbie screams when I touch the shoe. "They'll have to cut it off."

Bobbie asks again why I didn't come looking for her, but luckily I don't have to answer her because in flies Drew—like public enemy number one is bowling on lane three and it's his big chance to make the papers.

He stares at me, stares at Bobbie and slowly his shoulders sag. "It's you," he tells Bobbie, clearly relieved.

I'd ask what he means, but I hear the wail of a siren and realize that an ambulance is coming to take Bobbie for X-rays. And you know who heard the call.

I have to admit that I'm touched.

"This was not my fault," Steve repeats. He is telling Drew this time. "Look outside. No negligence. Do you see loose gravel? Ice? Anything I could have done? I can't be responsible for stilt walkers."

Bobbie says he'll hear from her husband, who walks in the door followed by the ambulance people.

"I'm over here," she shouts to the EMS pair as they come into the alley. "I'm pretty sure I broke it."

Mike kneels by Bobbie's chair and asks what happened. I'm hoping against hope she has some excuse other than falling off her heels, since I'm sure that's what Drew is thinking.

"Some jerk on a bicycle came whizzing by," she says. "I jumped back to avoid getting run over and the next thing I knew, I was on the cement, writhing in agony." She looks at me and adds, "For hours."

"Kids," Steve says with disgust, as if they don't account for more than half his business.

"Not," Bobbie says as they transfer her to a wheelchair, her shrieking as they do. "This wasn't any kid. He was older than me."

"And he didn't stop?" Steve asks. He's so like Rio. I know he's thinking Bobbie could sue the rider and not him.

"Stop?" Bobbie asks as they are wheeling her out the door. "Son of a bitch sped up. I think he meant to hit me. "I really do."

Of course, the first thing that comes to mind is Robby Kroll and I hate myself for even thinking it. *Think eight-year-old*, I tell myself. *It's dark out, late.* There's no way...

Just because someone rides a bicycle...and is creepy... and likes to scare people...

*Stop it!* I tell myself.

Easier said than done.

IT'S LATE, everyone's gone home but Mark and me. And Drew, who called in a report for patrol cars to keep watch for a crazed cyclist.

"I don't like the idea of you working here so late," he tells me, watching Mark out of the corner of his eye.

I tell him I don't have a choice and that he doesn't have to worry about me because Mark will see me home. This doesn't seem to reassure him in the least.

I ask him if he's found out anything about Russ Oberman or Miles Weissman and he looks at me blankly. "The remaining Slices," I remind him.

Assuring me that he knows who they are, he gently reminds me that I've been told to stay out of it. Okay, he isn't gentle and it isn't a reminder. It's more like a warning. A very stern warning. In fact, it's like a threat. To lock me up. And press charges for interfering in a police investigation.

And throw away the key.

"Then you are investigating," I say. "You do think that Joey was murdered and that it's all linked—"

"What part of 'stay out of it, Teddi,' don't you understand?" he asks me.

I tell him that it's great that he's investigating, because I really don't have time to. He mumbles some sort of thank you to higher powers.

"And if you want to stay and help—" I say, even though I want him to get right to his investigating, because (a) I need the help, and (b) maybe this will somehow patch things up between us.

He laughs at the request. "Anything else you want me

to do for you, Teddi? Maybe I could drive your mother to her nail appointment in a squad car?"

Before I can tell him where to get off, he apologizes. "I'm taking a lot of heat on the Dr. Doris case," he says. Then he adds in a voice that's low and confidential, "I've checked the files on the remaining Slices already—they've all got ironclad alibis. Russ Oberman's been in the hospital under observation since Sunday with some sort of nervous condition.

"Your friend Dave's got himself barricaded in his mother's house with two neighbors vouching for him and Miles Weissman—he's a real nut job—is traveling around incognito. Only he's so obvious we know just where he's been since your friend got hit."

"So you do think they're all connected," I say.

"What's that expression you always use?" he asks me. His lips are nearly against my forehead.

"*Duh?*" I suggest.

"Yeah," he says. "Duh."

"And you are investigating?" I ask. He tells me it's not a department priority. Softly, into my hair, he says that yeah, he's looking into it.

I thank him for coming to the alley. He doesn't bother hiding the fact that when he heard the ambulance call on the scanner he thought it was me. He tells me he's sorry about Bobbie.

"I don't know how I'm going to get this place done in time," I say. "I've got a payment due on my business loan and I can't ask my father for the money because for the rest of my life I'll have to hear my mother tell me how she told me not to take this job."

He offers to help me out. "No strings," he says.

I touch his cheek, which is rough against my fingers. I imagine that someday I could tell time by that stubbly cheek. So many things he doesn't understand about me, like why I need to make this business a success on my own terms, be my own source of strength, be able to depend on me. "I can't," I say softly. "I appreciate it more than you'll ever know, but I can't go through another day depending on someone else to take care of me and mine."

His cell phone rings and he looks at me apologetically. I put my hand over his to stop him from opening his phone.

"Do you, can you understand that?" I ask him.

He flips open the phone but doesn't put it to his ear. "No," he says simply, before he lifts the phone and says, "Scoones here."

## CHAPTER 18

Working without a decorator (or at least a talented friend) is like walking the tightwire without a net. It's a long way down and while going without a decorator won't leave you with a broken neck, you might break the bank. That's why most people decorate cautiously. But you can go it alone if you bounce your ideas off someone you trust. It doesn't have to be me, though I can be reached by simply clicking on *e-mail Teddi*. It's scary out there alone. Take a buddy with you to the store.

—TipsFromTeddi.com

**After** three or four hours sleep and getting the kids off to school, I head back for the alley. Waiting there I find Carmine De'Guisseppe and a couple of his boys. Carmine's "boys" are pushing seventy, but they still swagger like they're twenty-five.

"Teddi, dear," Carmine says, taking both my hands in his and kissing first one cheek and then the other. "Just came by to check on my investment. The place secure?"

His boys laugh at the little joke.

"Rio's done here," I say. Just stick a fork in him. "I tested out the system and it's working fine."

"And you? You keeping your nose clean?" he asks me, touching his like they do in gangster movies.

I tell him that of course I am. He looks dubious. "What? What's my mother been telling you?"

Both hands go up like he's not touching that question. "Not a thing," he says. The looks that pass between his "boys" say otherwise. "I know you got a penchant for trouble, is all."

I feign disbelief. "Me?" I squeak and all his boys laugh like I'm Jon Stewart on a good night.

"So, honey—you gonna get this joint done in time?" he asks, looking around dubiously. "'Cause you know, I could have Vito here lend you a couple of hands."

Vito, Carmine's driver, offers up his hands. He's the one who's missing two fingers.

"Sorry," Carmine says, "but he already lent a few fingers to somebody else."

The boys all laugh.

"I'll be finished in time," I say with great conviction, which isn't bad, considering that I haven't a prayer of making my deadline.

"Some people don't think so," he says.

I assure him that some people are wrong. Of course, I'm talking out of my hat because, looking around, it's probably hopeless.

"No one gets where they are without a little help," Carmine says. His cronies mutter their agreement. It's like a Greek chorus—the group all speaking as one.

I tell him that I was raised to admire the man who raised himself up by his own bootstraps, whatever that expression means.

He looks me straight in the eye, like I shouldn't miss the implication when he says, "Nobody ever did that."

I know he's talking about my father. I wonder, though, if my father has any inkling of this. He's always taken great pride in being a self-made man.

"You need help, you know where to come, right?" Carmine says.

I doubt anyone understands loyalty the way the man rocking on his toes in front of me does.

"Yes," I say. "I do. I will call my father if I need a hand." There. You can't be any clearer than that, right?

"He'd be happy if you asked him," he says, like he'd know what my father wants in life. He wags a finger at me. "Fathers, they wanna be there for their kids. Doesn't matter how old those kids are."

Hey, it's not my fault my mother didn't tell him about David, is it?

"And sometimes mothers gotta let 'em. You know what I mean?" Of course I know. But he's making the point nearly fifty years too late and to the wrong woman.

"'Cause I don't think you do."

And suddenly all his cronies seem to find the wall, the floor, the ceiling interesting.

Carmine snaps his fingers and like something out of *West Side Story*, his boys fall into line behind him and they all swagger out.

SOME PEOPLE CAN SIT AROUND and watch paint dry. I leave Mark to do that (and remove all our ladders and drop cloths and clean out the brushes) while I take a quick run over to the Krolls, ostensibly to go over some more decorating ideas. I stop at Waldbaum's to get some rugelach because you can't just drop by empty-handed, and find the deli department in shambles, people screaming at each other and the store manager giving out pagers to call the next customer while he or she continues to shop in the store.

And if I thought tensions were running high at the supermarket, the atmosphere in the Kroll house when I arrive is so thick you could spread it on a scooped-out sesame bagel and still not be able to get your mouth around it.

Jerry and I sit down at the kitchen table while Rita fusses with a new coffee machine. "You just put this little plastic pot in here," she says as though it couldn't be simpler, yet she's having a good deal of difficulty doing it.

"Robby out riding?" I ask.

Jerry says he is, at the same time Rita says he isn't. Then they try to cover for each other. Jerry gives me *the look*, the one that says that Rita's gone over the edge and there'll be no pulling her back.

"She thinks he's sweet on a girl," Jerry says. "Pure fantasy. He doesn't know from girls."

"He's got a man's body," Rita reminds him. "I know. Believe me."

"Don't go there," he warns her.

"Physical needs," she says. "The doctor said—"

"Doctors are idiots," Jerry says, getting up from the table

and taking his cup to the sink. "They think they know everything. They think they know better than you, doesn't matter about what. About everything. They're in their sterilized, hermetically-sealed towers doing whatever they want and they think they know all about what you should do. What you shouldn't do. How the world works.

"How the heart works." I can see his shoulders shaking and I watch Rita get up and go to him, take him around and soothe him.

"He's mad about Joey," she tells me.

"She cries for him every morning," he says.

They plead their case in front of me. And she says Joey was murdered and he says that if it was murder it was the doctor who killed him by not fixing his heart and now she's dead, so Rita should let it rest.

"And his friends? Milt and Max? That was coincidence?" she says.

And then they turn to me. "What does your friend the police detective say?" Jerry asks me.

"That it's suspicious," I say. But I admit they seem to be getting nowhere. "I keep trying to come up with how Dr. Doris's death could be related, but I can't figure out how."

Jerry asks if Milt or Max had surgery, suggesting that could be a link. I tell him that the police have checked that out already.

"So they have no theories?" Jerry asks. "They got *bubkes?*"

"Seems like. At least that's what they tell me."

"It's the bowling team," Rita says. "Grown men going out

and playing every week like boys. Arguing over whether they stepped over the line..."

"I never trusted that one...what's his name, Ritzala? The one who took Robby to the arcade?"

She tells him it was Dave and that he's wrong about that one. I'm still back on *stepping over the line*. What if Joey wasn't talking about bowling?

"The important thing," Jerry says, more to Rita than to me, "is that Teddi should stay out of it. It could be dangerous, putting her sweet nose in there."

Rita agrees, reluctantly, that he is right.

"If only I could figure out that connection," I say. "Who did Joey argue with about stepping over the line?"

"Dave," Rita tells me. "Dave was always telling Joey what was fair and what wasn't. Like he was the referee or the umpire or something and my Joey was the big cheat. Can you imagine?"

"Russell—now he was the one who'd put his finger on the scale every now and then," Jerry says. "But not Joey. Never Joey. Straight as an arrow."

I glance at my watch and Jerry urges me to go, saying I shouldn't miss my deadline.

"I'm going," I say, giving each of them a quick hug before slipping into my peacoat. "But I promise you that I will keep my ear to the ground and try to figure out who killed Joey."

"See if you can get trans fat arrested," Jerry says, and I can hear Rita arguing with him as I shut the door behind me and head for L.I. Lanes.

I STOP HOME and find a bouquet of flowers waiting on the front steps. Now Drew's never sent me flowers before, and try as I might, I can't come up with any anniversary or any other reason he might have sent these.

Which doesn't make me any less disappointed when I open the little envelope and find that they are from Rio, apologizing for being unable to help and thanking me for not ratting on him to Carmine. At least I assume that's what "Sorry and Thanks, Rio," means.

Jesse comes up the walk, surprised to see me. Nervous, maybe. He asks if anything is wrong. Until that moment, I'd have to say no.

"So how come you're home?" he asks. "Isn't Alyssa going home with that new girl? Olivia?"

He's a good big brother, keeping track of Lys for me the way he has while I get this job done.

"So are you going back to the Lanes?" He seems in an inordinate hurry to get rid of me and he hasn't even asked about the flowers I'm holding. When I ask him about both, he's quick to deny the former and inquire about the latter.

"They're from your father," I say, expecting him to direct me to throw them out.

Instead, he tells me that was a nice thing for Rio to do. What exactly did Carmine tell me earlier? A father wants to be there for his kids?

And a mother's got to let him.

"Something you want to tell me, Jess?" I ask, opening the door and holding it for him.

He shakes his head and offers to walk Maggie. "I know you're busy," he says.

Jesse is a good kid, but no kid is this good. Do I ask what he's hiding? I weigh my options while I study his sweet face. I suggest we walk her together, but again he tells me how busy I am and says he can do it himself.

And with a peck on the cheek, he and Maggie are out the door and I have a moment of peace I can't help but relish.

It doesn't last long.

"What are you doing tonight?" my father asks when I pick up the ringing phone.

"I have to work," I tell him. He asks me until when.

My answer, "Until I drop," doesn't please him.

"I'll come watch the kids," he says. "Your mother's got her mah-jongg game here and five women clacking tiles and tongues is more than a man should have to take."

I tell him I'd appreciate it. I almost tell him that I'm worried about Jesse, but my father isn't exactly subtle and I don't want Jess to think I'm spying on him.

"Or I could come to the alley and lend a hand," he adds, and I can hear the hope in his voice.

Once upon a time, in his prime, I thought my father could do anything. Then I learned about his affair with our housekeeper and thought he was "capable of anything" in a wholly different way. Now that he's well past seventy, I can't imagine asking him to reach, to bend, to carry or tighten or screw.

According to my mother, he isn't doing that last one all

that well anymore. Just the kind of information every daughter wants to know.

So I thank him kindly but tell him that Mark and I have it all under control. Twice he asks me if I'm sure and twice I tell him that being here with the kids is more help to me than he could possibly be at the alley.

And then I leave a quick note for Dana, who I pray is really at a drama club rehearsal, and head out to the car. I figure I'll do a quick turn around the block to say bye to Jess and then meet Bobbie and Mark at L.I. Lanes.

It's a good plan, unless I find Jesse around the corner standing next to the Rio Grande Security van talking to his dad. Which is what happens, of course. It's not him talking to Rio that bothers me—I mean, the man is his father. It's the guilty look that comes over his face when he sees me, the sudden change in demeanor, pulling back from the van, calling Maggie back from the street, the shrug he gives his father instead of a wave goodbye.

Rio pulls away and Jesse saunters over to the car.

"What's up?" I ask, as casually as I can. Jesse tells me his father is a jerk. "What did he want?" I ask, and I'm actually getting ready to defend him when Jesse just shakes his head.

I want so much to let the whole thing just drop. Face it and fix it after that damn bowling alley grand opening is over and I've gotten paid. Only Jesse's eyes are just a little too bright for me to pretend everything is fine.

*Being the mother so sucks sometimes*, I think as I put the car into neutral and tell him to grab Maggie and get in the car.

I drive, because Jesse talks better when I'm not reading

his face. It's a handicap for me that puts us on more equal footing, since my face-reading skills are better than his. I ask him if he wants to tell me what's going on.

And we do the nothing/something's bothering you/no, nothing/you can tell me/no I can't/of course you can/nothing's bothering me thing for two trips around the block during which I resist checking my watch, though I do throw a quick glance at the car clock every now and then.

I do not tell him I don't have time for this part of the game, despite the fact that those exact words are batting around in my brain plotting their escape route.

"Something up with your Dad?" I throw out there, hoping it'll stick.

My nerves are fraying after another circumnavigation of the neighborhood narrated by nothing's up/something's wrong, honey/nothing's wrong/silence/I love you, Mom.

"I love you, too." I reach back in my arsenal of young Jesse stories. "Remember when you borrowed Aunt Bobbie's tennis racket and her balls and you lost one down the sewer? And you thought it was such a big deal that you kept it a secret for two days, thinking that when we discovered what had happened we'd be mad? And remember how it made you so miserable that you finally broke down and cried because you felt like you didn't deserve our love and praise…all over a stupid ball no one cared about? Remember?"

"It's not like that," he says.

So finally we have an *it's*. At this rate I can kiss my check goodbye. "Isn't it?"

I pull over and turn off the engine, in part to signal that it's time to fess up and in part because I'm in danger of Maggie driving the car, as she keeps trying to reach the gas pedal with her head.

"Dad and I have been shooting pool," he says flatly.

So my heart is racing and I'm thinking that Rio's been putting money on him and God knows, they are going to Vegas for a tournament and he's taken up smoking because everyone knows that pool halls are full of smoke and maybe he likes the nicotine rush. Maybe he's addicted to second-hand smoke. "And?" I say, and I pull it off perfectly. I sound like a calm, rational woman who hasn't thought of any of the possibilities that have flown through my brain at break-neck speed.

"You're not mad?" he asks, genuine amazement tinging his voice.

I look at this sweet, sweet child, who has stood by me and bolstered me and told me a hundred times I could make it on my own and there are tears in the big blue eyes he got from his father.

And it's hard not to break down and bawl.

"He's your dad," I say, opening my arms and trying to hug him across the gear shift and the console.

"But he hurt you and he did really bad stuff to you, Mom," he says. "And I really didn't want to like…betray you, but he's lonely and he's not so good at much, and…"

"He needs you," I say, and Jesse nods silently. How ever did a messed-up woman and a cheat ever produce and raise such a *mensch?* "I guess I'd better learn to share."

## CHAPTER 19

Decorating can be an exciting adventure. Don't rush it. Remember that "haste makes waste." Taste all the possibilities. Let them roll around on your tongue, savor them like good dark chocolate—but without the calories. Let yourself imagine your room in a hundred different incarnations. Enjoy the process. When you're sure, don't stop at just a lick—plunge in all the way. Think of it like love or sex—how wonderful is it when you know it's right.

—TipsFromTeddi.com

I relate to Bobbie, who arrived just moments before me, and Mark how Jesse felt guilty for seeing his dad—proof that I am a rotten, no good, lousy mother.

They are quick to agree.

"You should turn in your mother card," Bobbie says, hobbling over to the computer where she is printing up menu cards for the bar.

"They should make you hold down a job, raise three kids and hire a mother to tell you twice a day that you don't do either well. Oh, wait," Mark says. "That's your life."

"If only you tried harder," Bobbie says. "Instead of just breezing along, eating bonbons and watching soap operas while your kids get stoned and shoplift."

"And you neglect your clients," Mark adds. "Which reminds me—some weird guy stopped by singing your praises and left you some cookies. He said to call his dad."

"Robby Kroll," I say, pulling out my phone and punching in his number. While I wait for him to answer I tell Mark what amazing progress he's made. For the first time I really think I might be telling the truth when I say we'll make the deadline. Maybe.

Jerry tells me Rita put him up to the call. "She wants to know if you've found out anything," he says. I hear Robby in the background telling his father to hurry up. "In a minute," he says.

"It's the doctor thing," I tell him. "I can't shake it. Does Rita have any ideas? Did Dr. Doris and Joey maybe have a thing…you know, something going?"

Talk about groping for straws. Joey was probably twenty years her senior and, as my mother would say, worked in a deli slicing meat while Dr. Doris, a well-respected surgeon, was slicing open chests for a lot more money.

Jerry says he certainly doesn't think so, but how would he know? Maybe he should check it out. He'll go to the hospital tonight and check it out, he says.

"No, I'll go," I say. "My father is watching the kids and I'll need a break here anyway, come midnight or so." I tell him that I'll go find the closest Dunkin' Donuts to Plainview Hospital and catch some of the nurses after their shift.

"Ritzala would so appreciate that," he says. "She just won't let go of this murder idea."

"Me, either," I admit sheepishly. Somehow, it seems ridiculous when it's somebody else, you know?

"But don't eat any doughnuts," he warns me.

"I know," I say. "Trans fats."

AFTER FIRST TELLING MY DAD I was staying past midnight at the alley and getting an earful, I lied and told him that I was meeting Drew. I told him it was perfectly fine to go ahead home. Dana is a fully qualified babysitter. She actually took the Red Cross course and he needn't worry.

Just to be on the safe side, Bobbie calls Mike and tells him to keep an ear open for my kids along with theirs. He asks when the hell she's coming home. She looks at me and seems to make up her mind to irritate him, telling him that she and I are going out for drinks. She doesn't reveal that those drinks are coffee.

Mark shoos us out and locks the door behind us with orders that we go straight home after our little doughnut run. "Do not come back here," he warns. "Or you'll learn my elfin secret and be cast forever in a pit of remorse."

"Whatever," Bobbie says as she scoops up a few of Jerry's cookies and we head to my car.

"She's one," Bobbie says as we sit at a table at the back of the Dunkin' Donuts on Jericho Turnpike having a cup of the best coffee known to man. She nods toward a woman in her early forties wearing pink polyester pants that stick out from under her black ski jacket. "Bet you a doughnut her shirt has little teddy bears on it."

She's wrong.

They're lambs. But I don't make her buy, because both of us are too tired to drag ourselves to the counter.

"Pediatrics," we both say in unison. Then we watch several other women come in, all too wide awake to be housewives finishing up a night on the town. Or even housewives who have been working all day, like us. They are all in polyester pants in varying pastel shades. It's sort of an Easter egg convention without the bonnets. Bobbie, with only one eye open, is still nearly gagging at the lack of panache.

"They could wear scarves," she whispers to me. "Or at least something in their hair and a little makeup, for God's sake."

I'm still trying to figure out how to approach any of them when she shifts around in her seat and asks the women in the booth behind her if they have any Sweet'n Low on their table.

A somewhat frazzled blonde in green scrubs hands her a yellow packet, at which Bobbie shakes her head. Gotta be pink, she tells them. One of the women agrees with her while another says they're all the same. They all do the same thing.

"No," Bobbie says, shaking her head for emphasis until I'm dizzy from watching. "That's like saying all surgeons are the same. Maybe they all cut you open, but there are the good ones, the bad ones, the loose ones, the tight ones…"

"Dreamy ones," I add, following her lead now that I've finally gotten the drift of where this conversation is going.

One of the women laughs at that one and someone adds a "Mc" to it, along with an "I wish!"

Bobbie continues her lecture. "There are snobs that fool around with only other surgeons, slummers that hit on the nurses, fishermen that do the patients…"

"Fishermen?" the blond nurse asks.

Bobbie explains her theory about women surgeons, how they're looking for a great catch and hoping some patient will be Mr. Right.

"Like Dr. Doris?" I ask. "Was she fishing?" Not that I think Joey would have made a particularly good catch…

The women take great offense at the implication. "That woman was a doll," one of them says and all the others agree.

"And she treated us like equals." It's the blonde again. "Some doctors seem to think we're part of the maintenance crew—change the bedpans and dole out the meds. But she'd come in late at night and sit with us and shoot the breeze for hours."

"She'd tell us about her patients," a pretty young woman with short brown hair from another table says, joining the conversation.

"She never used names, but she'd tell us about the things they'd say after some Versed or midazolam. Like they cheated on their wife or they were stealing from their boss. All sorts of stuff."

I kick Bobbie under the table to be sure she's heard and not fallen asleep. "Did she ever mention anybody saying something about winning the lottery?" I ask.

"They all say that," one of the women says. "And when they do, they're gonna buy all of us new cars and—"

"Diamonds. Don't forget diamonds. If they live."

"—and win the lottery."

"Actually," a nurse at another table says, getting pensive. "Remember that guy with the tricky procedure who told her that he had a winning ticket but he wasn't going to split it with his partners?"

"He had some kind of plan worked out," another one says.

"Yeah. He'd split it with her, instead."

I'm lucky I don't break my jaw when it hits the table. Oh…my…God.

"And no one else?" I ask, but the conversation has moved on to, "the woman who wanted to have a sex-change operation but hadn't told her husband yet. And he was standing right there!"

Gales of laughter. Ha. Ha. Ha.

I knew he won the lottery. I knew it.

OKAY, I ADMIT IT. After the rush I get from sugar—and I probably shouldn't have had the doughnut, not to mention the three cookies—I totally get wiped out. I thought the coffee would perk me up, but I'm blinking hard to stay alert behind the wheel. Beside me, Bobbie is slumped against the window as I frantically try to find my way home after turning the wrong way on Jericho Turnpike and winding up somewhere in Old Brookville. I turn onto the shortcut up CR 106, a narrow road right through the horsey set's backyards.

"Objects in the mirror," Bobbie says, checking the one on her side, "better be farther away than they appear."

There's no question the guy behind us is quickly closing the gap, now on my tail and probably drunk, considering the way he's weaving.

I try to find my cell phone without taking my left hand off the wheel. Staying awake, controlling the car and dialing involves one task too many.

"Maybe you should pull over," Bobbie says, a quiver in her voice.

"He'll hit us if we slow down," I tell her. "Call Drew."

"Oh, like he can help us now," she says. "Turn into a driveway, for Pete's sake."

"Do you see a driveway?" I yell back at her. "It's pitch freakin' black. Why don't these people need lights?"

"They've got money," she says just as I feel a tap against my bumper and realize the car behind me has made contact. Made contact and is staying there, pushing me forward.

"Shit! Shit! Call Drew. Tell him we're being forced off the road. Call 9-1-1."

The speedometer is speeding past eighty-five and I try hitting the brake, but I can feel the tires skidding when I do. I graze a tree on Bobbie's side and cut the wheel carefully so that we don't go careening off the road.

"Are you calling?" I scream at her.

"We're gonna die," Bobbie shouts at me. "I told Mike he could go screw himself and anyone else he was already screwing and now we're gonna die and he'll think he has my permission."

"Are you calling the police for God's sake?" I ask again.

"Mike first," she tells me, and it's almost enough to make me take my eyes off the road.

"Reach over and honk the horn," I tell her, not daring to take my hands off the wheel.

The car behind us backs off slightly and I try to navigate the curve. Just as I think I've mastered it, he speeds up and smacks into my left rear. And we are aloft. It feels like slow motion and all in just a heartbeat at the same time.

The car comes down on its right wheels, travels I don't know how far up someone's horse meadow and finally lands on its side a few yards from a house.

"Bobbie?" Please, let her be all right. "Are you okay?"

"Let's just say my foot doesn't hurt anymore," she says. "Not compared to my shoulder."

I lean on the horn because I don't know what else to do.

THE EMERGENCY ROOM PERSONNEL are getting as familiar with me as they used to be with my mother, who would attempt suicide—feebly—on a rather regular schedule.

Bobbie's got a cut above her eye, which the plastic surgeon assures her will not leave a scar, and a bruised but not dislocated shoulder. Not only will she not be able to help me meet my deadline, I'm not sure she will ever speak to me again.

I've got bruises and contusions, but no permanent damage. The doctor tells me I just need to take it easy for a few days. "Bed rest and time is about all you can do for this sort of thing," he tells me, after telling me how lucky

I am no matter how many times I tell him that I need to finish my job or I won't get paid. "And some ibuprofen wouldn't hurt."

If that's true, it's the only thing that won't. Hurt, that is. I think even my eyelashes are paining me.

Mike comes to retrieve us. If I thought that Bobbie was mad at me, it was only because I had nothing to compare her anger with.

"He ran me off the road," I say for the millionth time tonight, first to the couple whose probably-beautiful-in-the-daylight meadow I destroyed, then to the police, the EMS workers, the people at the hospital and to Bobbie and Mike.

No one cared.

In fact, I'm not sure anyone believed me. Not even Bobbie, who was there and is now pretending I forced her to go to Dunkin' Donuts with me.

DREW AND HAL show up at my door at an ungodly hour, looking very somber.

"Teddi Bayer, you—" Hal starts, but Drew stops him.

"I'll take care of this," he tells his partner. He looks at the bump on my head which has turned an ugly shade of purple and winces. "Hurt bad?"

"Not good," I say, showing him the bandage on my wrist. "And I've got to get to work."

Drew shakes his head. Hal says he doesn't think so, before Drew shoots him a look.

"You nervous yesterday, Ted?" he asks me.

Aren't I always? I ask. He smiles, but the smile doesn't reach his eyes.

He shoves his hands in his pockets, a sure sign that he's nervous, too. "So what'd you do about it?"

He's lost me. I ask him what he's getting at and Hal seems to lose patience. He pulls out his cuffs and says that I was driving under the influence.

"Of what?" I ask, like he's crazy. "Coffee?"

But no, it's not coffee and it's not sugar, both of which I consumed. He says it's narcotics.

"Impossible."

Only they don't appear to be kidding.

"What are you going to come up with next? That I was hallucinating about someone chasing me up Route 106? That I set out to maim a horse?"

Drew is quick to assure me that someone definitely chased me up Route 106, and that he hit the back of my fairly-totaled RAV4. Just when I'm feeling vindicated, he adds that the tests they ran at the hospital revealed a considerable amount of diazepam, better known as Valium, a medication my mother is always pushing at me, in my system.

I tell him that's ridiculous. "I'm not about to take something that is going to relax me at this point in the game," I say. "I need all my wits and energy to get the damn bowling alley done."

"It is possible, though unlikely, that there could have been a mistake," Drew says.

"Yeah," Hal agrees. "Hers."

Drew argues that hospitals screw up all the time. Tests

results get switched, reports get mislaid. "Come on," he says. "You know she's got a point. How likely is it she'd take downers rather than uppers with what she's got on her plate?"

"Wait a minute," I say, not any more thrilled that they'd believe I'm on uppers rather than downers.

"Look, you don't like her," Drew says to Hal matter-of-factly. "She doesn't like you. Is that a crime?"

"No," Hal answers. He pauses for effect and then adds, slowly and deliberately, "DUI is a crime. And that's what she did."

"Didn't," I insist.

"Did," Hal repeats.

"Didn't," I say again, more adamantly.

Hal says, "This is ridiculous," and reaches for his handcuffs.

"No, *that* is ridiculous," I say, pointing at them. "*This* is harassment, you realize."

"Let me handle it," Drew says, this time to me and not Hal, who I think he's told that to several times already.

I sense that Drew is going to call in a favor and I really don't want him doing that on my behalf, especially since this is totally bogus.

"Where were you coming from at one-thirty in the morning, anyway?" Drew asks.

I tell him I'd just left a john at a swinger party where we all did meth. He tells me I'm not really helping myself.

"Fine. I was at the Dunkin' Donuts on Jericho Turnpike." I don't think breaking my diet is a crime in their book, though it's possible that in my mother's *Handbook* it's punishable by a colonic.

Hal wants to know why I had to get a doughnut at 1:00 a.m. From the look on Drew's face, I think he's figured it out.

I don't think telling the police you were investigating a murder cuts much ice with them. They seem to think that's their job.

"So you go to Dunkin' Donuts and you go inside? Or you stay in the car?" Drew asks me.

This gives me the opportunity to avoid why I was there, so I go into a whole song and dance about how we went in, how we couldn't decide between crullers and doughnuts and which have more calories, how we sat at a booth at the back and had several cups of coffee and how yes, lots of people saw us.

"Lots of people? At one o'clock in the morning?" Hal says.

"Half-a-dozen women, I'd guess," I say. "A few men, but I'm not sure they noticed me."

This, of course, earns Hal's usual smirk.

I tell Drew I really have to talk to him, in private. By now Hal seems to be losing interest and agrees to go out to the car.

"It's the lottery," I tell Drew, who looks thoroughly disgusted at my inability to let this thing go. "I know, I know," I admit, but then I tell him what the nurses told me and his ears perk up.

Could any one of them have possibly put something into my coffee? And then followed me out of the shop and up 106?

Before I can answer, there's a commotion outside my front door. I turn to see two of Carmine's men following Hal into my house.

"Friends of yours?" Hal asks me, but he's looking at Drew like *See? I told you she was trouble*.

"Actually, yes," I say. I look at Vito and the other one, whose name I can never remember. "Coffee?" I offer, gesturing to the pot on the counter.

They're quick to tell me they've got their own, like they've been warned about mine.

"You okay?" they ask me. "We heard about your accident and the boss is not too pleased."

What do you say to that? Especially in front of two cops? Sorry?

"We shoulda been there," Vito says.

"*She* shouldn't have been there, is more like it," Drew says. And then he seems to brighten. "I take it you guys want to look after Ms. Bayer. Am I right?"

Vito and his pal don't answer, looking for the trick to the question.

"Hey, it's all right with me," Drew says. "Better than all right. Because if anything happens to her, I'm gonna hold you two responsible. So what I suggest is this…"

And he huddles with Vito and friend, who keeps looking over his shoulder at me while they talk.

"Come on," Drew says to Hal. He gives me a wave and heads for the door.

"Just a sec—" I say, going after him. Vito and friend block my path.

"Kinda like house arrest," Vito says. "Ya got anything to eat?"

## CHAPTER 20

Don't underestimate the effect of just one thing on everything else. The wrong color, the wrong scale, the wrong style. The right rug, the right window treatment, the perfect room divider. Just one piece of the puzzle can make or break the picture.

—TipsFromTeddi.com

**Turns** out one mafia boss trumps two cops. It takes a simple phone call to Carmine to get his goons to back off and agree to watch me from a distance so that I can meet my deadline.

This is good.

Carmine tells my mother what's going on.

This is bad.

"You're out of your mind," my mother says when I answer my cell in the back of Vito's car. "The whole world has gone nuts."

She's telling me? I'm being chauffeured in a black sedan by Carmine De'Guisseppe's driver and she's telling me the world is outta whack? Still, I resist asking if the pot isn't calling the kettle black.

"First your father and now you," she says. "I'd swear it's a plot to make me *meshuggener*."

"Honestly, Mom," I say, and I mean this from the bottom of my heart. "It's not about you."

Dead silence.

"Can we talk about all of this after Friday?" I ask. "I'm at the alley and—"

I stop because I see a man, a very familiar man, carrying the end of a long length of molding, the end of which is being held up by Mark. The man is wearing overalls, a ratty jacket I remember from a hundred years ago, and a smile so bright you need sunglasses to focus on his face.

"Mom?" I say. "What's Dad been doing to drive you nuts?"

The tirade starts with how he isn't going to the doctor despite the fact that all he does is sleep all day. Of course, this is because he gallivants all night long, going she doesn't know where. He's full of aches and pains and she'd swear he was having an affair, but she knows Carmine would be the first to tell her if he was.

Vito opens the door for me and I can hear my father whistling. It stops the moment he sees me.

I tell my mother not to worry about my father. I have a feeling he's better than he's been in years. I hang up on her stammering.

"You look awful," he says to me when I come up to him. I tell him I'm great, but that I'm going to get better. "I just stopped by for a minute," he says, glancing at Mark.

"Elves?" I ask my carpenter.

He shrugs. "What are you gonna do? If we make it, it's your dad that did it."

"A couple of nights," my father says. "That's all. Nothing much. I thought you wouldn't mind."

"Mind?" I say. "Mind? Why didn't you tell me you were helping? I would never have let you…I mean, you could have gotten hurt. You didn't let him—" I start, turning to Mark.

"That, *mammela*, is why I didn't tell you. You'd have treated me like a fragile old man." He hefts the molding onto his shoulder and starts off toward the saw Mark has set up in the lot.

"He's done almost as much work as I have," Mark tells me, watching him walk away. "I nearly had to carry him to his car the first night. Now he all but carries me."

I remind him that the man is nearly seventy-five years old.

"Dad!" I yell, signaling for him to cut the power to the saw.

"Look at him, gorgeous," Mark tells me. It's true. There's spring in his step, he's kibitzing with some kid in the lot, he's grinning from ear to ear. "Don't make him go home. Don't make him useless."

My father cups his ear, waiting for me to tell him what I want. His eyes are sparkling in the cold air and his cheeks are rosy.

"Hurry up!" I yell. I hold up my bandaged wrist. "I need help inside when you're done here."

He salutes me and blows me a kiss before turning back to his saw.

"You think he could maybe work for us part-time?" I ask Mark. "Kind of be your helper? That way we could at least keep an eye on him. No doubt he'll try to join the steelworkers' union if we don't."

Mark tells me that Bobbie called and told him about the accident. "Of course she tends to be a bit melodramatic. Someone didn't really run you off the road, did they?"

I tell him I must be close to figuring out this case. "So close that someone wants me dead," I say.

"Jeez, Teddi," he says, pushing back the hair I've tried to cover my bruises with. "You've got to give it up. You know that, don't you?"

"I do," I say. And I mean it.

Really.

Only…

"Let's say that one of The Slices has the winning lottery ticket all The Slices were supposed to split. Only he had a deal with Joey that they'd knock off the other Slices and then split the money. Joey tells the doc this before his surgery—"

Mark grabs me by the arm and I shout from the pain. "What is it going to take to stop you?" he asks as Vito and friend come running at my cry. "Did your brains get scrambled in that accident? Someone tried to kill you, Goddammit."

"Back off, buster," Vito says, and his hand is in his pocket pointing something at Mark.

"Friend," I say. "Pal. He's just doing the same thing you're doing. Trying to protect me from myself."

Vito warns Mark to keep his hands off me and then takes his hand out of his pocket. In it is a banana, which he proceeds to peel and eat with a grin.

Mark points out how I'm not going to be able to touch up the trim around the light switches with my wrist wrapped up. Vito says he can do it and takes off toward the alley.

"You ought to feed this crew," my dad says as he walks past me with several pieces of molding which I know he measured twice so that he would have to cut only once. He manages to reach into his pocket and hand me a twenty. "Go get some pizza," he says, pointing with his chin toward Pastaeria.

"Dad, you know you're not supposed to have—" I start.

Mark nudges me toward the restaurant. "He likes it with hot peppers," he says.

I can just hear my mother complaining tomorrow.

I ORDER THE PIZZA and sit on a stool to wait for it, resting my arm on the counter because it feels like there's a lead weight attached to it.

"Yeah," I hear Raymond, one of the counter guys, say into the phone. "Where in Hicksville? Yeah, we deliver there." I listen with half an ear while he repeats the address, which sounds familiar. "Yeah, Blumstein. Got it."

"I'll give you twenty bucks to let me deliver that pizza," I hear myself say. Raymond can't believe it any more than I can.

"Why?" he asks.

"Dave's a friend from the alley," I say. True, no? "I want to surprise him." Again, true.

Raymond knows me. Hell, I've been in nearly every day since I started the alley job, and loads before that with the kids.

"I'll need to use your car," I say. "With the Pizza Delivery sign on the side. So he doesn't guess before I get to the door."

He pulls the keys off the pegboard and tosses them to me. "Knock yourself out," he says, putting the pizza in a box and sliding it across the counter to me. "Car's out back. We'll keep your order warm."

I SEE THE CURTAINS MOVE as I pull up to the house Dave shares with his mother. I wait until they stop moving to get out of the car. That way he'll be on his way to the door and unable to see me. I struggle with the box, my hand almost as useless as my wrist. It looks more swollen than it did this morning. Which isn't a surprise since the doctor told me to keep it elevated.

I ring the bell. "Pizza delivery," I shout when he asks who's there.

Dave opens the door and I quickly stick my foot in, realizing as I do that it's about the only thing that doesn't hurt and that could change in an instant.

"Teddi?" He seems surprised, but not threatened. He opens the door wider to let me in. "I didn't know you worked two jobs," he says. "What happened to you? Did you walk into a door?"

Mrs. Blumstein comes out from the kitchen with an apron on as if she's been cooking, though clearly I'm the one who is supplying lunch. She hears the tail end of my cock-and-bull story about how I hit a tree avoiding a squirrel. I watch for a reaction from either of them.

They both want to know if the squirrel survived.

Dave seems relieved when I say it got away and wants to know if I was delivering pizzas when it happened.

Mama B's gaze goes from me to the box in my hands and back to my face again. Her eyes narrow. Like a mother tiger, she suddenly senses danger to her six-foot, one-hundred-and-eighty-pound cub. But does she think that I'm the murderer or that I know her son is?

Not, of course, that I *know* that. I'm not even sure I suspect that.

I explain how I was in the shop, yadda, yadda, yadda, and hope they enjoyed the joke and the pizza.

His mother opens the door to usher me out.

"Oh," I say, very Columbo-like as I'm about to walk out the door. "Dave, about the lottery tickets The Slices went in on…?"

"Dave doesn't gamble on the lottery," Mrs. B says, which I think reminds Dave that I didn't give him away before and that he owes me.

He repays me by inviting me to join them for lunch.

"I am starving," I say, shrugging out of my jacket and heading for the kitchen.

Mama B is not thrilled to have me join them. Since I know I'm not the killer, I'm the one with my life on the line, so tough on her. In fact, I decide to add her to my list of suspects.

Except I think she really, truly believes he doesn't play the lottery.

Oh, my head aches and it's not from the bruise alone.

"So, Dave," I say after I've polished off a slice because I wasn't kidding about being starving. "Do you know if The Slices still go in on lottery tickets? I mean, other than you, of course?"

He tells me that the gang has pretty much split up since they don't have enough bowlers to field a team. Besides, with Miles afraid to go out and Russ in the hospital…

"So then, no," I say. "How did that work, anyway?"

Mama B doesn't want to hear about gambling, even when it doesn't involve her son, and she excuses herself to go iron—a lame excuse if ever I heard one, since I've never seen Dave in anything but polyester wash-and-wear.

Dave wants to know how come I care so much about the lottery tickets. I tell him the truth, because nothing else comes to mind and I just don't think he's smart enough to pull off a scheme as complicated as this one is turning out to be.

He says it's impossible. For one thing, they all are good guys and they trust each other. I'm treated to a recitation of every nicety each of them ever performed before I remind him that he probably had a second thing in mind.

He does. Every week the person who bought tickets would show the losing tickets to everyone else.

"And you all took turns buying the tickets," I say, like that's a fact. "Except you," I amend when I sense Mama B standing in the doorway behind me.

Dave scrunches up his face in deep thought. "Not Russ," he says, "'cause the stationery store near him had a winner two years ago and everyone figured they wouldn't get another one for a long time."

"But everyone else?" I ask.

He thinks hard again. You can actually see it happening. And while he thinks, so do I. Like, although he was putting in his share, it isn't likely he was buying the tickets because he'd be more certain about who else was in the schedule, wouldn't he?

"What about Max?" I ask. "Did he ever buy?"

Dave is pretty sure he did. Along with Joey and with Milt. "Just about everyone," he says.

"Except you," his mother reminds him.

"Yeah," he agrees.

"Miles?" I ask.

He worries the corner of his mouth with his tongue. Six-foot tall, not bad looking, tongue on the edge of lips and I'm not the least bit turned on.

"Nope, not Miles," he says.

And now I'm turned on, but good.

When I go to leave, both mother and son make a production out of my going out the door, like we're living in a war zone. Mama tells me that even though they've pulled out of the league, all The Slices are potentially in danger.

Dave says he'll walk me to my car, but Mama isn't happy with the idea.

Turns out we all go, they push me into the driver's seat and scurry back into the house before I've got the key in the ignition.

Which is very different from the reception I get when I return to the alley. I don't know who is more furious—Vito and company, Mark, or my dad. Seems Raymond brought the pizza over himself and spilled the tomato sauce, so to speak.

I am reminded by each of them of what my investigating led to last night. My father reminds me I have an ex-husband who'd get custody of my children if something should happen to me. A very sobering thought.

Vito reminds me I'm under house arrest and adds, "Sort of." I notice that his jogging suit has green paint on it and that his pal's hair is full of dust.

"Put 'em to work," Mark says. "Looks like we're gonna make it, thanks to your dad."

I can't quite believe it.

"I think you can go home and get a little rest," he says. "Or I'm gonna have to start calling you something other than *gorgeous*."

"Like what?" I ask him.

He steps back and looks me over, tilting his head one way and then the other. "How about *shit on a stick?*" he says.

"Nice, and not only does it describe how I look, but also how I feel."

He says he much prefers *gorgeous*, but at the moment I'm teetering on the edge. If I don't go home and lie down, he might have to go with door number two.

Vito appears and offers to drive me home. I tell him I'd like to just sit in the car for a few minutes before I decide if I've really got to go home or not, and I climb into the back seat and dial up Drew.

"Not all The Slices bought the tickets," I tell him when he answers.

"How's your head?" he asks.

I tell him it stings when I touch it, which I only do accidentally, that it itches a little where it's cut and that the three men who are still alive didn't buy tickets, but the two who are dead, and Max, did.

"And you know this how?" he asks me.

Before I answer that, I ask just how serious he was about that house-arrest business.

"Where are you now?" he wants to know.

"At the alley," I say honestly. When he says it's too quiet for that I add, "in the parking lot. In Carmine's car."

He urges me to go home.

"So the way I figure it," I say, "is that four of them were in cahoots to cut out the other two. Dave's not all that bright, but I don't think he'd have told me who bought tickets for the group and who didn't if that pointed to him as the killer, right?"

"I'll look into all of this if you promise to go home," he says.

"Which means that it's got to be either Miles or Russ, right?"

"And I'll let Hal bring you in on the DUI charge if you don't."

"Are you really going to check out the rest of The Slices?" I ask.

He swears he'll check out the whole damn sandwich if I will go home. And I want to believe him, I really, really do.

"Today?" I press.

"Tonight." There's a funny tone in his voice. Something he's not telling me.

"Why not today?" I ask.

"I'm on something else today," he says. He doesn't elaborate.

"Is she blond?" I ask.

"Yeah," he says. "Blond, blue-eyed and built. Just my type."

"Dead?"

He doesn't answer me. I decide that it's best to drop it and I ask him again if he'll look into Miles and Russ tonight.

"I said I would," he says, then hedges. "If I can."

## CHAPTER 21

There is an order to the way you make decisions when redecorating and it's based on availability. Because there is no limit to the variety of paint colors, the walls come last. Because sofas come in more fabric and pattern choices than area rugs, the rugs must be selected first. Unless you are doing carpeting or hardwood floors. Then the order is reversed, since, like paint, the choices are nearly infinite for carpet and wood. That said, the decision to go with carpet or wood has to be made before a single stick of furniture is chosen. Remember the rule: order is based on availability.

—TipsFromTeddi.com

**I'm** sitting in the car, stewing, contemplating my next move when my cell phone rings. It's Jerry Kroll and I wish I had more news for him than I do. And that what I do know didn't implicate his brother-in-law. And that I didn't suspect his poor son.

"Hi Mr. Kroll," I say. "How are you?"

"How are *you, maydela?*" he asks me. "We heard about

your terrible accident. They aren't going to charge you, are they? I know a very good lawyer if you need."

I tell him I think everything will be fine.

"You're hurt, sweetheart?" he asks me and I assure him that it's nothing that won't mend. "And you'll give up this wild goose chase and let poor Joey rest in peace? And let my Ritzala live in peace?"

I tell him that I know she'll feel better once she can put his death and her suspicions behind her. But that, between him and me, I can't help wondering, since two other Slices have had attempts made on their lives, if one of the remaining Slices isn't somehow involved.

Jerry assures me that The Slices were all Joey's friends. They'd never hurt him. "Besides. Joey had a heart attack. How could they make that happen?"

He's got a point. Everyone has a point. That's what makes this case so prickly.

"Still," I say, as much to myself as to Jerry. "I'd like to check out Miles and Russ."

"What would you ask them?" Jerry says. "If they killed anybody lately?"

I say that I'd mention lottery tickets and see if that raised any eyebrows. He wants to know why it would. Instead of saying that I think Joey was trying to cheat his teammates out of their share of the money, which, for all I know, doesn't even exist, I just say I think they're involved, somehow.

Jerry offers to talk to them both. He implies it will be exciting for him, but I think it's more likely he's trying to protect me. When I refuse, he offers to interrogate one while I "put the screws" to the other.

Still I refuse. He tells me he doesn't want to be a nag, but maybe could I possibly drop by and show Rita some sketches, anything to take her mind off Joey?

I tell him that of course I can and offer to come straight away.

But right now Rita, despite her grief, is at the beauty parlor. "And I have to go out in a little while and do the food shopping before I pick her up."

An empty house. Can I resist nosing around in it? Of course not, so I offer to come anyway, do some preliminary measuring and figuring and lay out some sketches to go over with Rita when he gets back with her.

"Such a good idea," he says. "I love it."

I tell myself how this proves that Robby has nothing to do with any of these murders—would they let me in their house if they had anything to hide?

I think not.

You know, when my mother first suggested I work with one of her friends I thought I'd be better off slitting my own throat rather than having someone else do it for me. But working with Jerry and Rita has turned into an oasis of sweetness in a world where people aren't very nice, where they don't praise your ideas or effort, because they're too busy making sure you aren't taking advantage of them.

I ASK VITO to take me to the Krolls' instead of home. He doesn't like the idea much and has to clear it first with

Carmine. He's a little hard of hearing, so he has the volume turned way up on the phone and I can clearly hear Carmine ask my mother if these Krolls' are "on the level."

He should ask my mother if she is. While my father has been busting his butt to help me, she's been seeing an awful lot of him. Maybe too much. Which is one more thing I'll deal with after Friday.

I've been putting off my whole life until Friday, and now it's less than twenty-four hours away.

I tell Vito he can take me to the Krolls and wait outside, or I can give him the slip and let him explain that to Carmine. When he tells me he ain't that easy, I cross my hands over my chest and say, "Pizza, pizza," like I'm a commercial on TV.

"And remind me to charge my cell phone," I tell him, because, like me, it's running on empty.

And ten minutes later I'm at the foot of the Krolls' driveway and Jerry is getting into his car. "Door's open," he yells to me before he takes off, giving me a "you must be doing quite well" look at me and the limo I arrive in.

As an interior designer I spend a good deal of time in other people's houses. It's something I should be used to, but I always feel suspect in them.

I sit in the living room for a few minutes, trying to get the feel, the vibe of the house. Maybe it's because of the shrine to Joey in the corner, but the house feels incredibly sad.

I wander the rooms. Jerry and Rita's, their nightstands covered with pill bottles and liniment, tissues and glasses of both the drinking and seeing variety, magazines, a bottle of antacid. I make a mental note to replace their nightstands with a headboard that incorporates shelves and cabinets. I think Rita would like that.

I pass Robby's room. Posters of ninjas cover the walls. Little warriors line the shelves.

"Why are you in my room?" a husky voice asks and I jump high enough to nearly bang my head on the ceiling.

Robby is probably close to six feet tall. I'm guessing he weighs around two hundred pounds. He fills the doorway, not menacingly, just physically.

"Hi, Robby," I say, and I can hear the fear in my voice. Can he?

He repeats his question with no emotion.

I explain that I'm helping his mom and dad redecorate their house. I babble a little, but he seems oblivious.

"They aren't here," he tells me.

Calmly, which is a joke considering what's going on inside me, I ask if he'd like to help me come up with some ideas for how to redecorate? What kind of furniture should we use in his room? What color does he like? Where the hell are his parents?

He says his favorite color is black. He would like black on the walls, black on the ceiling, black sheets and black carpet. "Do they make black carpet?" He is blocking the doorway, but he seems content to talk about decorating his room, which takes a good deal of the menace out of his presence.

I assure him that they do, but that an all black room might be depressing. It might make him sad.

Feeling cornered, I tell him I have some sample carpet in the living room, but he doesn't move. "Would you like to see it?" I ask him.

"Is there black?" he wants to know.

I lie and tell him I'm not sure and suggest we go and check. I don't breathe until he heads down the hall and gallops down the steps to the living room.

I open my satchel and tell him I'm sorry that I don't have black and that I'll go get some.

"Don't go," he tells me. I'm not sure if it's a request or an order.

"Your mom and dad will be home soon," I respond. I don't know if I mean that as reassurance or a threat, either. Depends on what he meant, I guess.

"Can you wait for them?" he asks me. He's pretzeled on the floor like a child, the ends of his shirt not meeting his pants and revealing the hairy lower back of a middle-aged man. And he is intent on rearranging the squares of carpet on the floor into a giant checkerboard.

My heart breaks and I feel all the worse for suspecting him. And even *worse*, for *still* suspecting him.

But because he's close to Alyssa in mental age, I tell him that of course, I can. "Wanna help me do my work?" I offer chipperly.

He ignores me as he exchanges small carpet squares, sits back, looks at them, arranges them differently and repeats the process again.

"Do you mind if I work?" I ask.

I think there is a slight shake of his head. Gingerly, because my hand still hurts, I reach into my bag and dig around for a measuring tape, some graph paper, a pen and my Mace, because a girl can't be too careful. And then I head off for the kitchen and Jerry's office beyond it to put some space between Robby and me.

In the stillness of Jerry's office I pull myself together and corral my imagination, which tends to get the best of me.

So, unless Jerry and Rita have left Robby home to finish me off and he's forgotten that's what he's supposed to do…*stop, imagination, stop*… I think I'd better come up with some suggestions for the house so that when they do get home—and find me alive and standing in Jerry's office—I'll have something to offer.

My first suggestion is easy. We should move the office into the basement now that Jerry no longer sees clients. I mean, why take up prime real estate that could be put to better use? I can feel myself relax as I start envisioning the changes. How great would it be to put in a pass-through or knock down the wall between the kitchen and office entirely?

The space would make a lovely reading room and if their nightstands are any indication, Jerry and Rita like to read. I decide to do what I always advise my clients to do. Clear the room of as much furniture as possible and then just sit in the room and get the feel for it. See which way your body naturally orients itself. Facing the doorway? The window? Kitty-corner to the closet? I nudge the couch away from the wall. No dead bodies. No rat poison. No photocopied death threats…

I look through the desk drawers. Accounting is terribly boring, I think, though Jerry has lots of nifty little notepads and a million different colored pens.

There's no way I'm moving all the stuff out of Jerry's office. The furniture is heavy. I'm injured. I decide to settle for just taking a thing or two down from the walls, which will make it look like I've at least been considering what I'm supposed to be here for.

I start with the big painting behind Jerry's desk, which would actually be exquisite in the upper hallway after we expand the stairs.

Using my right hand to bear the weight and my left hand to simply steady the painting, I remove it from the wall and stand it on the couch. Something falls from behind it and I pick it up, assuming it's the bill of sale or certificate of authenticity or some such thing, even while a piece of me expects some sort of crayoned confession.

"Whadja find?" Robby asks me as I look down at the paper and see the work schedules for Joey, Milt and Max graphed out on From The Desk of Jerry Kroll paper. He comes closer and looms over me. "Whaddya got?"

"Nothing," I say when I've collected my thoughts. "I…"

I don't know what I'm going to say after that. Luckily the phone rings and Robby gets distracted.

"That could be my mom," he says.

I suggest he answer it. He tells me he isn't supposed to. While I tell him that I'm sure it'll be all right, we hear the answering machine pick up and Jerry's message going out.

"Are you there, Jerry?" I hear Rita ask. "Pick up if you're there."

"He's not here," Robby tells the machine without picking up. "He went to the hospital."

## CHAPTER 22

Sometimes the problem with a room is staring you in the face and you just can't see it. I had a client call to have all the moldings in her living room replaced. She hated the finish, yet loved the same moldings upstairs. Never occurred to her that what she hated was the way the moldings clashed with her paint downstairs. We darkened the walls a shade and she's a happy camper. Sometimes our emotions cloud our vision. Just take a step or two back and really look.

—TipsFromTeddi.com

**Can't** be.

That's what I keep thinking as I stare at the schedule in my hands. And then pieces begin to fall into place. Did I tell Jerry I was going down to the marina the day I was pushed into the water? Surely no one else knew.

I pick up the phone to call Drew. And then I think: Jerry is a sweet old man. Like my dad. My dad who I didn't know was still strong enough to do physical labor with Mark, toting and carrying and swinging a hammer.

My mother was right. Jerry is nothing like my dad. Besides old, that is.

I start to dial, my eyes on Robby. Can I tell Drew without Robby hearing? I end the call, tell Robby I've got to get something from the car and head for the door, thinking: who did Dr. Doris call before she was murdered? Jerry. And did he ever explain why?

But kill Rita's brother? For money?

Robby starts to cry.

"When do you think my mom will get home?" he asks. "She's gonna be mad that my dad left me alone."

"And your dad's at the hospital?" I ask, thinking of poor vulnerable Max, lying in that bed without the memory of who hit him, not knowing who to be wary of…

Robby sniffs and nods.

And I remember Vito in the limo. "I'm going to send my friend in to play with you," I say. "He's a very nice man and—"

Robby's sniffs turn to sobs. I'm headed for the front door, grabbing my handbag as I go, wracking my brain for the right thing to tell Robby, who follows me pathetically like a puppy—a mastiff puppy.

"He's very special. Do you know *Lord of the Rings?*" Robby nods and says he saw the movie. "Well, you remember Frodo with the nine fingers? Vito has just eight. That makes him even more special than Frodo!"

And then I'm out the door. I argue, stomp and finally convince Vito to watch Robbie, borrow the car and race to the hospital with my cell phone speaker on, dialing Drew as I go.

But does he answer his phone? Of course not.

I'm not panicking. Really I'm not. I always run the stop sign at the end of the Krolls' block.

Okay, maybe I'm worried enough to call Drew's partner, Hal. I won't even gloat about how right I was about a plot to kill off The Spare Slices.

He doesn't respond well to the bare outline I give him.

"I have the work schedules of all The Slices in my hand, Hal," I say. "And it's in Jerry's handwriting. And the nurses told me that Joey promised Dr. Doris a cut of his lottery winnings."

There's a moment of silence in which I imagine Hal getting up, grabbing his badge out of his desk drawer (like on television, though I think in real life they always carry them) and signaling to the troops that they should follow him.

Only after the pause he just sighs and asks, "What nurses? And what exactly did they tell you that somehow they didn't tell the police?"

I'd have to stretch the truth pretty taut to say that they told me it was actually Joey who'd promised to split his winnings. On the other hand, how many tricky surgeries do you think Dr. Doris has done?

Don't answer that.

And the nurses' names? Did I even think to get them? Hal hums while I explain how I managed to find all this out. And then he starts to tell me the story of the boy who cried wolf.

"Listen to me," I shout toward the phone, which I am no longer holding because I've got both hands on the wheel and am driving a good fifteen miles over the speed limit. I'm actually hoping a cop will stop me so that I can get him to come to the hospital with me. I mean, where's a cop when you need one? Oh, right. On the other end of the phone. "Jerry Kroll is on his way to the hospital to finish off Max Koppel. I made the mistake of telling him that Max is conscious but he doesn't remember the accident. So, you see, Jerry has to kill him before he remembers and tells the police."

"Sure," Hal says, but I'm not convinced he'll send the police. In fact, I'm pretty sure he's clipping his fingernails as we speak.

I tell him that I'm on my way to the hospital and he should get a hold of Drew and send him.

"Yeah, what a surprise," is his response. "And who would you like for backup? George Clooney?"

When I tell him to send the whole freaking department if he has to, the answer I get rivals the adults in a Charlie Brown cartoon. Yawn, yawn. *Whaa, whaa, whaa.*

"I'm begging you," I say, and I hope he hears the desperation in my voice and takes me seriously. "Send somebody. Come yourself. A man is going to die if you don't. Do you want that on your conscience?"

Nothing. No response.

"Hal?"

I glance at the seat beside me. The lights have gone out on my phone just as I turn into the hospital parking lot. I turn off the car and look at my dead phone.

*Hal will call Drew*, I tell myself.

*God, I hope so*, myself says back as I open the car door, summon all the courage I have, and head for the emergency room door, because if ever there was an emergency, this is it.

I race to Max's room like someone's life depended on it since I firmly believe it does, only to find him gone. Even his bed is gone. I lean against the wall and feel that awful itch in the back of my throat and top of my nose that means I'm going to cry, and cry hard.

I'm sliding down the wall when a nurse comes in. She's got that efficient, nurse walk that seems to mean business. I guess she deals with death all the time.

"Oh!" she says when she sees me headed for the floor. Her perkiness doesn't seem diminished by my impending collapse. "I didn't realize anyone was in here. Are you here to visit Mr. Koppel?"

I nod silently. Sadly.

"They took him down to X-ray a couple of minutes ago," she says. "Do you want to wait for him here or go down there?"

"He's not dead?" I ask. Of course he's not dead. They don't X-ray dead people. Not unless they've got something hidden in their bodies... Jeesh, I am developing a really sick mind.

She tells me that all I have to do is follow the red lines on the hallway floor until they intersect the green lines and then take the third door after the second left.

I think there is more, but I figure if there aren't signs, I'll just ask as I go frantically running down the hall toward— I hope—Max in the X-ray area.

Amazingly, I find the X-ray department. Now, even if I had my cell phone it wouldn't work, according to the signs.

"I'm looking for Max Koppel," I tell a person in hospital garb. He has a tag hanging from his neck like he is on sale. Better than a tag on his toe in this place. He responds with a shrug, but a woman wearing Pepto-Bismol pink overhears and tells me that Max is waiting on a gurney in one of the rooms while they develop his pictures. She gestures toward a door marked 2.

"Should be just another few minutes and then we'll take him back to his room."

I do my best to sneak in unnoticed, but since I lack the Bayer grace, I trip over something and lurch into the room like a comedian doing a pratfall. Like everyone who trips, I look back to see what it was that got me and it looks like a bag of sand. The technician looks up from the portable computer cart, surprised, and tells me that's exactly what it is—for traction on Max's broken leg. "They took it off for the X-rays. Lab's backed up," she tells me. "The X-rays'll take about twenty minutes to develop. You can stay with him while he waits. It'll be nice for him to have his daughter help him pass the time."

I don't bother to correct her. I just move toward Max and grasp his hand.

He opens his eyes and it takes him a minute to remember who I am. I'm hoping he doesn't give me away to the technician, but before he can find his words she says she'll go check on things since Max isn't alone now.

I paste a smile on my face—I'm so relieved to find Max

alive that it isn't hard—and wait for her to leave before I tell him that I'm sure that what happened to him was no accident. He seems reluctant to believe me.

"What if I told you that Milt has had an accident, too?"

He closes his eyes. I think he's processing this news, so I give him a minute.

"He bought a new boat. When he started it up, the engine exploded."

Max's eyes snap open and they are full of questions.

I nod. "Dead. First Joey, then the attempt on your life and now Milt is dead. I'm here to help you. I know Joey's brother-in-law, Jerry, is involved—"

Just as I say that, I follow Max's line of vision and hear the door slam shut. There, in the flesh, is not-so-sweet-anymore Jerry Kroll. There's a bulge in his jacket pocket.

"You know," I say, moving closer to Max's head and trying to put some distance between myself and Jerry, "with all the talk about security, there doesn't seem to be much of it, does there?" I know that I couldn't find a security guard on my way to Max's room.

"Of course, you realize that the police are on their way. I called my friend Drew and he's meeting me here. I must have just beat him by a couple of minutes."

"I don't think so, *maydela*," he says.

What is it about me that no one believes what I say? It must be that neon sign on my head that flashes *liar, liar* when I stray an iota from the truth.

"Anyone ever tell you that you're too smart for your own good?"

Honestly? No.

"My friend is at your house with Robby," I start to say because even if Jerry turns out to be a killer, I know he is a good father to Robby and I want to reassure him that Robby's not alone.

Only he takes that as some sort of threat and pulls out his gun. "Anything happens to Robby," he says, leaving the end of the sentence to my imagination. Of course, he's going to shoot me anyway, if Drew doesn't get the hell over here in time.

If I die, I am never, ever going to forgive him.

"I didn't want to leave him alone," I say. "I have children too, Jerry. I know how a parent—a good parent—worries. I was surprised you left him alone." I figure it's as good a time as any to play the guilt card.

"I don't have to worry about Robby anymore," Jerry tells me. "He'll be provided for. He'll be taken care of now. I have it all arranged."

Plunk. That piece of the puzzle falls into place and now I see the whole picture. He had to have the lottery winnings to make sure that after he and Rita are gone someone will take care of Robby.

That doesn't mean that the gun he's holding won't go off and leave *my* children destitute.

Well, there's no place for me to hide, my phone is useless, and even if I could distract Jerry, I can't just run out and leave Max to him, can I?

Which means I've only got one choice. Do what I do best, especially when I'm scared.

I babble. I banter. And I stall.

"So then, you have the lottery ticket, right?" I ask Jerry. Hell, if I'm going to die, I at least want to know the whole story.

Jerry shrugs, which is as good as an admission in my book.

"Did you steal it from Joey?" I ask.

While Jerry laughs, I quickly glance at Max to make sure he's all right. He is slowly shaking his head, looking guilty as sin in that bed, like maybe he thinks he deserves to be broken and crumpled and maybe a cripple for life.

"Why don't you tell her?" Jerry asks him. "It was your idea, wasn't it?"

Max doesn't answer.

"Wasn't it you who figured out that you'd only have to split the pot three ways if you and Joey and Milt always bought an extra ticket in case one was a winner? Buy one to show that there were twenty losers and up your chances for a winner by twenty tickets every week?"

"I don't understand," I say, thoroughly lost. "And I don't get where you fit in."

"*Maydela*, you're a sweet woman without a devious thought in her head. What would you know about connivers? Joey, Max and Milt rotated buying the tickets each week. Since they used the 'easy pick' and didn't choose the numbers themselves, no one knew what the numbers were. If they bought twenty-one tickets each week, paying for the extra themselves, they had twenty-one chances to win and they'd have twenty losing tickets to show the other Slices that they'd lost."

"But I don't get how you fit in," I say, catching on to the scheme.

"When they actually won, they knew that they couldn't cash the ticket in or the others would find out."

"So they gave it to you," I say, wondering if the nurse will ever come into the room, if Drew will show up, if there is some way out of this mess.

Jerry nods. He seems completely unconcerned about anyone possibly coming in on us. I can't understand why.

"But why didn't you come forward when Joey died?" I ask Max.

"Fraud," Max squeaks out. It's clear he hasn't used his voice in a long time.

"What could they say?" Jerry asks. "That they were perpetrating a fraud? And who would benefit from Joey's death? Max and Milt."

"You killed Rita's brother?" I say, just to be clear. I mean, he loves her.

"The man was going to die anyway. I told you that. If he didn't have respect for his life, why should I?"

"But with the money, he'd have taken care of Robby—"

Jerry shakes his head. "Robby gave him the creeps. You don't think I know how people feel about my son? How they look at him?"

"He can be a little reckless with that bicycle," I say, thinking about how he scared Dana. "He nearly ran down my friend, Bobbie."

"You don't take warnings easily do you?" Jerry asks. "It was me on the bike. I did everything I could to avoid this moment with you. I pushed you in the Sound. I even drugged the cookies with Rita's medicine so you'd be too sleepy to run around looking for evidence, but no, you just wouldn't be stopped."

"You drugged the cookies?" I squeak. "I could have gotten killed—" I start to say. Considering he is holding a gun on me, this doesn't seem like something that would bother him.

"Hell-bent on getting yourself killed," he says. He is aiming his gun at Max while picking at something between his teeth with his free hand. "Damn dentures. Gonna have them replaced right away."

I get the feeling he means on his way home and he seems ready to get going.

"Aren't you worried that someone is going to come in here and find you?" I ask. I don't mean to say it aloud, but it pops out.

"Sign on the door says Test In Progress," he says with a sly smile. "You don't get to be as old as I am without learning a few tricks," he adds, and begins to elaborate.

While he talks, I move around just a little, creeping slowly—and hopefully, imperceptibly—until I am behind the computer cart which is on wheels. I look over at the clock, hoping he will, too, and as soon as he does, with all the strength I have, I send the cart flying as fast as I can, straight at him.

It catches him off balance and knocks him into the wall. The gun flies from his grasp and scuttles across the linoleum floor. We both watch it slide under a cabinet.

Dazed, frantic, he lunges for me and I grab the nearest

thing—Max's IV stand—and strike him with it. As Max shrieks, Jerry, like the last bowling pin standing, teeters back and forth. Finally he falls down not far from the cabinets where the gun handle might still be within his reach.

Lying between us on the floor is the sandbag I tripped over. I snatch it up, raise it over my head and—well, I *sandbag* him.

I run to the door and yank it open to yell for help, when who do I see running down the hall? My personal cavalry, also known as Drew Scoones. Late, as usual.

"Where the hell were you?" I shout at him as he rushes past me into the X-ray room, gun drawn.

Medical personnel follow him in, some gathering around Max, others rushing to the old man lying crumpled by the cabinet.

Drew kneels beside him and catches sight of the gun. He pulls it toward him with a pen and lifts it by the barrel.

"Same old, same old, I take it?" he asks me while a doctor pushes him out of the way to get to Jerry. "Do something idiotic and see if you can get killed?"

"I *told* you," I say as he comes to his feet and walks over to me, cornering me as he reaches for his cell. "And I told Hal, too," I say. "I wasn't being brave or acting on my own. I called him and told him to tell you and to send a whole platoon."

This seems to come as some surprise to Drew.

"But if he didn't tell you, how did you know to come?" I ask him.

He lifts one finger, putting me on pause while he calls in

the report and directs them to send officers immediately. It takes him a while and I have to remind him of the question when he's done.

"How did you know to come here?" I ask again.

"Your bodyguard," he says. When I look at him blankly, he elaborates. "Vito called. I'm not sure if he wanted me to rescue you or him, but I figured you were in more imminent danger."

"He was going to kill us," I say, pointing with my thumb back at the X-ray room behind me. Drew's eyes have been glued there while we talk. "Max and me. God, is Max all right?"

Drew tilts his head a little and assures me that he appears to be. "Not sure I can say the same for Jerry Kroll."

I whirl around. "I didn't kill him, did I?" I ask, but I can see him moving and hear him moaning as the doctor ministers to him.

"You know the whole story?" I ask Drew. "All about the lottery tickets and—"

He tells me he knows enough for now and asks one of the officers who shows up to take me home.

OF COURSE, I can't go home. I have a grand opening in just a few hours and my chances of getting paid are still in the uncertain column, so I ask the officer to drop me at L.I. Lanes. He asks if I didn't just almost get killed.

Not for the first time I think of Scarlett's famous words. *I'll think about that tomorrow*, when I'll either be swilling cappuccino and celebrating or trying to figure out how to make two boxes of spaghetti feed five people indefinitely.

Carmine and my father are waiting for me at the entrance to the alley. They are like two elephant seals on an ice flow that won't accommodate both of them.

"It's done," my dad says proudly. "Mark and I loaded his truck with the crap from the job and all the place needed was a good vacuuming." He looks at Carmine with disgust.

"Someone owed me a favor," Carmine says with a shrug as I open the doors and see a cleaning crew of at least six scurrying around the alley with sprays and rags and an industrial vacuum the size of a Volkswagen Beetle.

Steve is behind the counter. When he sees me, he reaches into the register and then thinks better of it.

"Tonight," he says. "At the opening."

## CHAPTER 23

A room is never really finished. And for me, that's intentional. I never want to stop collecting, changing, adding and subtracting, and I wouldn't want my clients to. Who knows what they'll want to bring back from their next adventure? Life, as they say, is cumulative.
—TipsFromTeddi.com

**The** Grand Opening Celebration is amazing. Everyone is walking around the alley like they've never seen the place before. The pool tables are all in use and people are jostling for position around them. The cappuccino maker is whooshing and whistling and they're two deep at the bar where my mother is ordering precise proportions in her latte and demanding Sweet'n Low. My eye is on Steve, who is in his glory.

The minute he goes near the register, I'm there, flanked by Mark, my dad and Carmine.

"Pleased?" I ask.

Without answering he pops open the drawer of the register, reaches in and then stops, the hand with the check in midair. He seems to reconsider and then he whistles to get everyone's attention.

"Folks? Folks! Hate to interrupt your good time, but it's time to do a little business here." He grabs a chair and stands on it so everyone can see him. "Nice place, huh?" he asks, and everyone cheers.

"Bring over another chair," he tells Mark, who indicates he doesn't need one and lifts me up until I'm perched on his shoulder like a five-year-old. Had I known they were going to do this I wouldn't have let Bobbie and Dana dress me in a skirt so short that I have to use my hands to cover my thighs instead of holding on for dear life.

A glance at my mother says I will never, ever hear the end of this.

"Everyone," he says, and there isn't a man in the joint who isn't enjoying the view while I argue with Mark to put me down. "Teddi! Pay attention! I hereby turn this check over to Ms. Teddi Bayer for services well rendered."

I blush. I know because I can feel my cheeks get very, very hot. Mark has put his arm across my thighs to both balance me and give me a modicum of dignity to match my modicum of skirt.

"Think she's a great decorator?" Steve shouts and everyone claps. "Think she's earned her check?" he shouts, and again people clap. He looks directly at me and says sincerely, "Well, me, too."

I'm flabbergasted as Mark twirls me around to applause. It's great. That is, until I'm turned around and I can see that behind me, near the door, just coming in, is Drew Scoones.

And he has a blonde on his arm. Mark slides me down his

body and sets me on the floor. I tug at my skirt while people lose interest and turn back to whatever they were doing.

"I told you I prefer my blondes live," Drew says when I make my way over to him through hordes of—okay, a *few*—people who waylay me to congratulate me on a great job and ask if I do entertainment rooms, home theaters, media centers. I don't know the difference, but I tell them I surely do.

"I'll take a beer," Drew tells Steve, who is doubling as the bartender tonight. I think the man was afraid that someone else would be too generous. "You want?" I don't know if Drew's asking the blonde or me.

She assumes it's her, gives a little shake of her bleached head and gives him a peck on the cheek as she waves an emaciated arm (no Hadassah arms for her) at some guy across the alley. She scurries away on her four-inch mules while all the men watch, tongues hanging out. When she reaches someone I'm pretty sure is another officer, she drapes herself over him like a silk drop cloth.

And Drew stares at me. His eyes take in every inch of leg that's showing, the camisole under my black see-through blouse with the ruffles. "Nice outfit," he drawls.

"My daughter," I say by way of explanation.

"Alyssa? Should have figured," he says. I don't correct him. "You look like Hooker Barbie."

"Thanks," I say sarcastically and turn to walk away.

He catches my arm and pulls me back toward him. I have to admit it feels good, feels right, when I am snug up against his body. Of course, the place is crowded and I'm snug up against the guy on my right, too.

"Just stopped by to tell you that your friend gave a full confession," he says.

"Is that all?" I ask. I am so bad at coy, but I can't help trying.

"I didn't know about the fashion show," he says.

I tug at my skirt and he stops my hand.

"You look good," he says.

"She looks like a ho," my mother says. And loudly, too. I think she watches too much TV. That's what I'd say if one of my kids talked like that. And I'd wash their mouths out, but I don't think that's an option here.

"Nice to see you, Mrs. Bayer," Drew says to her, throwing her a look that says *drop dead*.

"Not much skirt to sniff," my mother says.

"Sometimes less is more," Drew answers her.

In an effort to end the torture, I ask what Jerry told him that I might not already know.

You like how I got in that little dig about how I knew before the police?

"Well, you were right about Joey spilling the beans to the good doctor," Drew says.

"Of course she was right," my mother says in a rare display of maternal pride. "She's my daughter. What did you expect?"

I warn him not to answer that.

"When she heard about Joey dying the way he did, she got suspicious and called Jerry for details. Seems Joey was supposed to be taking some kind of medication and they found none in his system when they did the autopsy and the doctor wanted to know who the other men who went in on the lottery tickets were because she was going to the police with her concerns."

"Jerry picked up Joey's medicine for him. I remember Rita telling me that," I say.

My mother tells me not to interrupt. "And then?" she asks Drew, who tries to move us away from her but has to settle for lowering his voice.

"Apparently he said he'd go with her and arranged to meet her at her office parking lot—"

"Where that SOB took a hammer to that poor woman's head," my mother finishes for him.

"I thought you said he was a marshmallow?" I tell my mother.

"I thought you said you were going to wear something appropriate," my mother says in return and Drew laughs. "You look like one of those housewife hookers," Mom says as Drew reaches for his pocket, a sure sign that his phone is vibrating.

"Scoones here," he says, putting a finger in his other ear and heading for the door with me on his heels. Hey, this could be about my case. And I bet he won't say I don't have a case now!

"Calm down," I hear him say as we stand outside in the cold night air. "Who's dead?"

I snuggle up against him, pretending it's just the cold and not the fact that I want to hear who's on the phone and what they're saying.

Drew looks disgusted. "Well, what the hell were you meeting Peaches Lipschitz for, anyway?"

"Who?" I whisper to Drew.

Dumb move. Until then he'd only been aware of me on an unconscious level. Now he gently pushes me away.

"Who's Peaches?" I press.

He waves me away. "Okay, don't touch anything, don't move anything, and for God's sake, Hal, put little Hal away and zip your pants."

My jaw falls open.

"I gotta go," he tells me. "Police emergency."

"But who's Peaches Lipschitz? And is she dead?" I ask as he puts up his collar and heads for his car, me a half-step behind him.

"I don't know how you Bayers do it," he says, talking over his shoulder as he opens his car door. "A housewife hooker. Isn't that what your mother just said?"

I shrug. She might have said I looked like one, not that one was dead.

But now it seems like maybe one is.

"I'm coming with you," I say, running around to the other side of the car. The door is locked. "Open it, Drew," I say.

"Step away from the car, Teddi," he says in his policeman's voice. "Now. Step away from the car."

I take one step back and he opens the window enough for me to hear him clearly.

"And go put on some damn clothes for Christ's sake." He puts the car in gear and then adds softly, "I don't want you to be next."

* * * * *

*Be sure to watch for the*
*further adventures of Teddi Bayer*
*in the coming months from Harlequin NEXT.*

*Be sure to return to NEXT in September for
more entertaining women's fiction about
the next passion in a woman's life.
For a sneak preview of Marie Ferrarella's
DOCTOR IN THE HOUSE,
coming to NEXT in September,
please turn the page.*

**He** didn't look like an unholy terror.

But maybe that reputation was exaggerated, Bailey Del-Monico thought as she turned in her chair to look toward the doorway.

The man didn't seem scary at all.

Dr. Munro, or Ivan the Terrible, was tall, with an athletic build and wide shoulders. The cheekbones beneath what she estimated to be day-old stubble were prominent. His hair was light brown and just this side of unruly. Munro's hair looked as if he used his fingers for a comb and didn't care who knew it.

The eyes were brown, almost black as they were aimed at her. There was no other word for it. Aimed. As if he was debating whether or not to fire at point-blank range.

Somewhere in the back of her mind, a line from a B movie, "Be afraid—be very afraid…" whispered along the perimeter of her brain. Warning her. Almost against her will, it caused her to brace her shoulders. Bailey had to remind herself to breathe in and out like a normal person.

The chief of staff, Dr. Bennett, had tried his level best to put her at ease and had almost succeeded. But an air of tension had entered with Munro. She wondered if Dr. Bennett was bracing himself as well, bracing for some kind of disaster or explosion.

"Ah, here he is now," Harold Bennett announced needlessly. The smile on his lips was slightly forced, and the look in his gray, kindly eyes held a warning as he looked at his chief neurosurgeon. "We were just talking about you, Dr. Munro."

"Can't imagine why," Ivan replied dryly.

Harold cleared his throat, as if that would cover the less than friendly tone of voice Ivan had just displayed. "Dr. Munro, this is the young woman I was telling you about yesterday."

Now his eyes dissected her. Bailey felt as if she was undergoing a scalpel-less autopsy right then and there. "Ah yes, the Stanford Special."

He made her sound like something that was listed at the top of a third-rate diner menu. There was enough contempt in his voice to offend an entire delegation from the UN.

Summoning the bravado that her parents always claimed had been infused in her since the moment she first drew breath, Bailey put out her hand. "Hello. I'm Dr. Bailey DelMonico."

Ivan made no effort to take the hand offered to him. Instead, he slid his long, lanky form bonelessly into the chair beside her. He proceeded to move the chair ever so slightly so that there was even more space between them. Ivan faced the chief of staff, but the words he spoke were addressed to her.

"You're a doctor, DelMonico, when I say you're a doctor," he informed her coldly, sparing her only one frosty glance to punctuate the end of his statement.

Harold stifled a sigh. "Dr. Munro is going to take over your education. Dr. Munro—" he fixed Ivan with a steely gaze that had been known to send lesser doctors running for their antacids, but, as always, seemed to have no effect on the chief neurosurgeon "—I want you to award her every consideration. From now on, Dr. DelMonico is to be your shadow, your sponge and your assistant." He emphasized the last word as his eyes locked with Ivan's. "Do I make myself clear?"

For his part, Ivan seemed completely unfazed. He merely nodded, his eyes and expression unreadable. "Perfectly."

His hand was on the doorknob. Bailey sprang to her feet. Her chair made a scraping noise as she moved it back and then quickly joined the neurosurgeon before he could leave the office.

Closing the door behind him, Ivan leaned over and whispered into her ear, "Just so you know, I'm going to be your worst nightmare."

◆ HARLEQUIN®

# *Mediterranean* NIGHTS™

*Experience glamour, elegance, mystery and revenge aboard the high seas....*

**Coming in September 2007...**

# BREAKING ALL THE RULES

*by*

## Marisa Carroll

Aboard the cruise ship *Alexandra's Dream* for some R & R, sports journalist Lola Sandler is surprised to spot pro-golfer Eric Lashman. Years after walking away from the pro circuit with no explanation to the public, Eric now finds himself teaching aboard a cruise ship.

Lola smells a career-making exposé... but their developing relationship may force her to make a difficult choice.

# REQUEST YOUR FREE BOOKS!

## 2 FREE NOVELS PLUS 2 FREE GIFTS!

There's the life you planned. And there's what comes next.

NEXT07R

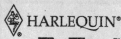

# HARLEQUIN®

## Next™

## GET $1.00 OFF
### your purchase of any
### Harlequin NEXT novel.

---

## Receive $1.00 off
### any Harlequin NEXT novel.

*Available wherever books are sold, including
most bookstores, supermarkets, drugstores
and discount stores.*

Coupon expires January 31, 2008.
Redeemable at participating retail outlets
in the U.S. only. Limit one coupon per customer.

5 65373 00076 2    (8100)0 11435

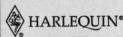

# HARLEQUIN®

# NEXT™

## GET $1.^{00} OFF

### your purchase of any Harlequin NEXT novel.

---

## Receive $1.^{00} off

### any Harlequin NEXT novel.

*Available wherever books are sold, including most bookstores, supermarkets, drugstores and discount stores.*

Coupon expires January 31, 2008.
Redeemable at participating retail outlets
in Canada only. Limit one coupon per customer.

52608038

Always passionate, always proud.

**The richest royal family in the world—
a family united by blood and passion,
torn apart by deceit and desire.**

By royal decree, Harlequin Presents is delighted to bring
you The Royal House of Niroli. Step into the glamorous,
enticing world of the Nirolian Royal Family. As the king
ails he must find an heir. Each month an exciting new
installment follows the epic search for the true Nirolian
king. Eight heirs, eight romances, eight fantastic stories!

**Coming in September:**

# BOUGHT BY THE
# BILLIONAIRE PRINCE
## by Carol Marinelli

Luca Fierezza is ruthless, a rogue and a rebel....
Megan Donavan's stunned when she's thrown into
jail and her unlikely rescuer is her new boss, Luca!
But now she's also entirely at his mercy...in his bed!

**Be sure not to miss any of the passion!
Coming in October:**

### THE TYCOON'S PRINCESS BRIDE
by Natasha Oakley

**www.eHarlequin.com**                    HP12659

# HARLEQUIN®

## COMING NEXT MONTH

**#91 DOCTOR IN THE HOUSE • Marie Ferrarella**
Having taken several wrong turns in her own life,
Bailey DelMonico is passionate about her new career as a
doctor. And she has resolved not to let other "passions"
interfere. That is until she is paired with the sharp-tongued
Dr. Ivan Munro. Skilled at saving patients' lives, this
arrogant doctor doesn't know how to save himself from the
isolated existence he's created. In reaching out to Ivan,
Bailey is about to discover that there are many ways to save
a life...and it's never too late for love.

**#92 BEAUTY SHOP TALES •**
**Nancy Robards Thompson**
Washed-up "beauty operator to the stars" Avril Carson
left L.A. for a fresh start in her Florida hometown—only
to discover an explosive secret between her deceased
husband and her best friend. Suddenly Avril's new life had
scandal, betrayal, even a handsome hunk waiting in the
wings, whom she'd met on the plane ride home. And she'd
thought her days of Hollywood-style drama were over!